Voyager

ARTHUR C. CLARKE

The Sentinel

HarperCollins*Publishers*

Voyager
An Imprint of HarperCollins*Publishers*
77–85 Fulham Palace Road,
Hammersmith, London W6 8JB

www.voyager-books.com

This paperback edition 2000
2

Previously published in paperback by
HarperCollins Science Fiction & Fantasy 1993,
and by Grafton 1991, reprinted once

First published in Great Britain by
Panther Books 1985

The Sentinel Copyright © Byron Preiss
Visual Publications, Inc. 1983
All story introductions
Copyright © Arthur C. Clarke 1983
For further copyright details see page vi

ISBN 0 583 21204 3

Set in Times

Printed in Great Britain by
Clays Ltd, St Ives plc

Special thanks to Russ Galen, Roger Cooper, Rena Wolner, Susan Allison, Victoria Schochet, Melissa Ann Singer, Joan Brandt, Ony Ryzuk, Olive Bridget Brown and Arthur Byron Cover.

Contents

Introduction: Of Sand and Stars

Forty miles to the east, the sun has just climbed above the Sacred Mountain, which for so long has haunted my imagination. Another quarter turn of the planet, and it will bring a cold winter dawn to the English seaside town where I was born sixty-five years ago this morning.

So it is already a little late in the day to consider *why* I became an author, or to wonder if there was ever any real alternative; that may have been as genetically determined as the color of my eyes or the shape of my head. But the *kind* of author I became is another matter: here, I suspect, both chance and environment played decisive roles.

The fact that I was born half a mile from the sea – or at least an arm of the Bristol Channel, which to a child seemed positively oceanic – has certainly colored all my life. As usual, A. E. Housman expressed it perfectly, in the poem from which I took the title of my first novel:

> Smooth between sea and land
> Is laid the yellow sand,
> And here through summer days
> The seed of Adam plays.

Much of my youth was spent on the Minehead beach, exploring rock-pools and building wave-defying battlements. Even now, I feel completely relaxed only by the edge of the sea – or, better still, hovering weightless beneath it, over the populous and polychromatic landscape of my favorite reef.

So in an earlier age, I would probably have written stories about the sea. However, I was born at the time when men were first thinking seriously of escaping from their planetary cradle, and so my imagination was deflected into space.

Yet first I made a curious detour, which is obviously of great importance because it involves virtually the only memory I have of my father – a shadowy figure who has left no other mark, even though I was over thirteen when he died.

The date would have been around 1925; we were riding together in a small pony-cart near the Somerset farm into which First Lieutenant Charles Wright Clarke had sunk what was left of his army gratuity, after an earlier and still more disastrous adventure as a gentleman farmer. As he opened a pack of cigarettes, he handed me the card inside; it was one of a series illustrating prehistoric animals. From that moment, I became hooked on dinosaurs, collected all the cards I could on the subject, and used them in class to illustrate little adventure stories I told the other children in the village school. These must have been my first ventures into fiction – and the schoolmistress who encouraged them celebrated *her* birthday a week ago. Sorry I forgot to send a card, Maud Hanks – I'll make a special point of it for your 95th . . .

There is a certain irony in the fact that the tobacco trade (one of the few professions where I consider the mandatory death penalty is justified) had such a decisive and indeed beneficial impact on my career. To this day I retain my fascination with dinosaurs, and eagerly look forward to the time when the genetic engineers will re-create *Tyrannosaurus rex*.

For a couple of years I collected fossils, and at one time even acquired a mammoth's tooth, until the main focus of my interest shifted rather abruptly from the past to the future. Once again – significantly – I can recall exactly how this happened, though almost all the other events of my childhood seem irretrievably lost.

There were three separate crucial incidents, all of equal importance, and I can even date them with some precision. The earliest must have been in 1929, when at the age of twelve I saw my first science fiction magazine, the November 1928 *Amazing Stories*.

The cover is in front of me at the moment – and it really *is* amazing, for a reason which neither editor Hugo Gernsback nor artist Frank Paul could ever have guessed.

A spaceship looking like a farm silo with picture windows is disgorging its exuberant passengers onto a tropical beach, above which floats the orange ball of Jupiter, filling half the sky. The foreground is, alas, improbable, because the temperature of the Jovian satellites is around minus a hundred and fifty degrees centigrade. But the giant planet is painted with such stunning accuracy that one could use this cover to make a very good case for precognition; Paul has shown turbulent cloud formations, cyclonic patterns and enigmatic white structures like earth-sized amoebae which were not revealed until the Voyager missions over fifty years later. *How did he know?*

Young readers of today, born into a world when science fiction magazines, books and movies are part of everyday life, cannot possibly imagine the impact of such garish pulps as that old *Amazing* and its colleagues *Astounding* and *Wonder*. Of course, the literary standards were usually abysmal – but the stories brimmed with ideas, and amply evoked that 'sense of wonder' which is (or should be) one of the goals of the best fiction. No less a critic than C. S. Lewis has described the ravenous addiction that these magazines inspired; the same phenomenon has led

11

me to call science fiction the only genuine consciousness-expanding drug.

During my lunch hour from school I used to haunt the local Woolworth's in search of my fix, which cost threepence a shot – roughly a quarter, at today's prices. Much of the hard-earned money my widowed mother had saved for my food went on these magazines, and I set myself the goal of acquiring complete runs. By 1940 I had almost succeeded – but, alas, all my beloved pulps disappeared during the war years. That collection would now be worth thousands of dollars.

In 1930 I came under the spell of a considerably more literate influence, when I discovered W. Olaf Stapledon's just-published *Last and First Men* in the Minehead Public Library. No book before or since ever had such an impact on my imagination; the Stapledonian vistas of millions and hundreds of millions of years, the rise and fall of civilizations and entire races of men, changed my whole outlook on the universe and has influenced much of my writing ever since. Twenty years later, as Chairman of the British Interplanetary Society, I persuaded Stapledon to give us an address on the social and biological aspects of space exploration, which he entitled 'Interplanetary Man.' His was the noblest and most civilized mind I have ever encountered; I am delighted to see a revival of interest in his work, and have just contributed a preface to a new collection of his writings.

By the time I encountered Stapledon I had begun my secondary (US: high school) education in the nearby town of Taunton, making the ten-mile round trip by bicycle every day *after* sorting the local mail in the small hours of the morning and then delivering it (another five or so miles). It was at Huish's Grammar School – now Richard

12

Huish College – that I began to write sketches and short stories for the school magazine.

I can still recall those editorial sessions, fifty years ago. About once a week, after class, our English master, Captain E. B. Mitford (who was actually a fiery Welshman), would gather his schoolboy staff together, and we would all sit around a table on which there was a large bag of assorted toffees. Bright ideas were rewarded instantly; 'Mitty' invented positive reinforcement years before B. F. Skinner. He also employed a heavy meter rule for *negative* reinforcement, but this was used only in class – never, so far as I recall, at editorial conferences.

My very first printed words thus appeared in the *Huish Magazine* and from the beginning my science-fictional tendencies were obvious. Although this Christmas 1933 message purports to come from 'Ex-Sixth Former' stationed at a torrid and high-altitude Outpost of Empire (Vrying Pan, British Malaria) its true locale is at least a quarter of a million miles further away:

The precautions we have to take to preserve our lives are extraordinary. Our houses are built on the principle of the Dewar vacuum flask, to keep out the heat, and the outsides are silvered to reflect the sunlight . . . We have to take great care to avoid cutting ourselves in any way, for if this happens our blood soon boils and evaporates.

Such attention to technical detail shows that even at sixteen I was already a hard-core science fiction (as opposed to fantasy) writer. Credit for this must go to the book which had almost as great an impact on me as Stapledon's epic – and which illustrates rather well the fundamental distinction between art and science. No one else could ever have created *Last and First Men* – but if David Lasser had not written *The Conquest of Space* in

13

1931, someone similar would certainly have appeared in a very few years. The time was ripe.

Although there was already considerable German and Russian literature on the subject, *The Conquest of Space* was the very first book in the English language to discuss the possibility of flight to the Moon and planets, and to describe the experiments and dreams (mostly the latter) of the early rocket pioneers. Only a few hundred copies of the British edition were sold, but chance brought one of them to a bookstore a few yards from my birthplace. I saw it in the window, knew instinctively that I *had* to read it, and persuaded my good-natured Aunt Nellie – who was looking after me while Mother struggled to run the farm and raise my three siblings – to buy it on the spot. And so I learned, for the first time, that space travel was not merely delightful fiction. *One day it could really happen.* Soon afterwards I discovered the existence of the British Interplanetary Society, and my fate was sealed.

When he wrote *The Conquest of Space*, the twenty-eight-year-old David Lasser was editor of a whole group of Gernsback magazines, including *Wonder Stories*. Later he became a labor organizer and was denounced in Congress – not only as a dangerous radical but also as a madman, because he believed that we would one day fly to the Moon . . . When I met him in Los Angeles just a couple of weeks ago, he told me he was working on a new book; a good title might be *Lasser's Last Laugh*.

Despite all these influences, I was well over thirty before writing graduated from a pleasant and occasionally profitable hobby to a profession. The Civil Service, the Royal Air Force and editorship of a scientific abstracting journal provided my bread-and-butter until 1950. By that time I had published numerous stories and articles, and a slim technical book, *Interplanetary Flight*. The modest success

14

of this volume led me to seek a wider public with *The Exploration of Space*, which the Book of the Month Club, in a moment of wild abandon, made a dual selection in 1952. To allay the alarm of its anxious readership, Clifton Fadiman explained in the BoM newsletter that *The Exploration of Space* was no crazy fantasy but a serious and level-headed work because 'Mr Clarke does not appear to be a very imaginative man.' I've never quite forgiven him, and my agent, Scott Meredith, has never forgotten my plaintive query: 'What *is* the Book-of-the-Month Club?'

This stroke of luck – repeated exactly thirty years later with *2010: Odyssey Two*, so I can claim it wasn't a fluke – encouraged me to give up my editorial job and become a full-time writer. It was not a very daring or heroic decision: if all else failed, I could always go back to the farm.

I was lucky; unlike most of the writers I know, I had very few setbacks or disappointments, and my rare rejection slips were doubtless thoroughly justified. And because every author is unique, the only advice I have ever been able to pass on to would-be writers is incorporated in a few lines on the notorious form letter which Archie, my word-processor, spits out at all hopeful correspondents at the drop of a floppy disk: 'Read at least one book a day, and write as much as you can. Study the memoirs of authors who interest you. (Somerset Maugham's *A Writer's Notebooks* is a good example.) Correspondence courses, writer's schools, etc., are probably useful – but all the authors I know were self-taught. There is no substitute for living; as Hemingway wisely remarked, "Writing is not a full-time occupation."'

Nor is reading – though it would have to be, if I tried to keep up with the avalanche of science fiction now being published. I estimate that almost as much is printed each day as appeared every year when I was a boy.

Today's readers are indeed fortunate; this really is the Golden Age of science fiction. There are dozens of authors at work today who can match all but the giants of the past. (And probably one who can do even that, despite the handicap of being translated from Polish . . .) Yet I do not really envy the young men and women who first encounter science fiction as the days shorten towards 1984, for we old-timers were able to accomplish something that was unique.

Ours was the last generation that was able to read *everything*. No one will ever do that again.

Of course, it may well be argued that no one should want to do so, in deference to Theodore Sturgeon's much-quoted Law: 'Ninety percent of everything is crud.' It is – to say the least – a sobering thought that this might apply even to *my* writing.

I can only hope that everything that follows comes from the other ten percent.

Colombo, Sri Lanka
16 December 1982

Rescue Party

'Rescue Party,' written in March 1945, while I was still in the Royal Air Force, was the first story I sold to the legendary John W. Campbell, Jr., editor of Astounding Science-Fiction. It was not, however, the first of my stories he published; 'Loophole' (April 1946) beat it by a month.

I don't believe I've reread it since its original appearance, and I refuse to do so now – for fear of discovering how little I have improved in almost four decades. Those who claim that it's their favorite story get a cooler and cooler reception over the passing years.

However, I cannot resist tantalizing any readers who may be new to this tale with a quotation from a recent paper by Gregory Benford, 'Aliens and Knowability: A Scientist's Perspective':

'Aliens as a mirror for our own experiences abound in sf. Arthur Clarke's "Rescue Party" has humans as the true focus, though the action follows aliens who are a dumber version of ourselves. The final lines give us a human-chauvinist thrill, telling us more about ourselves than we may nowadays wish to know.'

I must admit that I'd never thought of it that way; but Dr Benford may be right. You have been warned.

Who was to blame? For three days Alveron's thoughts had come back to that question, and still he had found no answer. A creature of a less civilized or a less sensitive race would never have let it torture his mind, and would have satisfied himself with the assurance that no one could be responsible for the working of fate. But Alveron and his kind had been lords of the Universe since the dawn of history, since that far distant age when the Time Barrier had been folded round the cosmos by the unknown powers that lay beyond the Beginning. To them had been given all knowledge – and with infinite knowledge went infinite responsibility. If there were mistakes and errors in the administration of the galaxy, the fault lay on the heads of Alveron and his people. And this was no mere mistake: it was one of the greatest tragedies in history.

The crew still knew nothing. Even Rugon, his closest friend and the ship's deputy captain, had been told only part of the truth. But now the doomed worlds lay less than a billion miles ahead. In a few hours, they would be landing on the third planet.

Once again Alveron read the message from Base; then, with a flick of a tentacle that no human eye could have followed, he pressed the 'General Attention' button. Throughout the mile-long cylinder that was the Galactic Survey Ship S9000, creatures of many races laid down their work to listen to the words of their captain.

'I know you have all been wondering,' began Alveron, 'why we were ordered to abandon our survey and to proceed at such an acceleration to this region of space. Some of you may realize what this acceleration means. Our ship is on its last voyage: the generators have already been running for sixty hours at Ultimate Overload. We will be very lucky if we return to Base under our own power.

'We are approaching a sun which is about to become a Nova. Detonation will occur in seven hours, with an uncertainty of one hour, leaving us a maximum of only four hours for exploration. There are ten planets in the system about to be destroyed – and there is a civilization on the third. That fact was discovered only a few days ago. It is our tragic mission to contact that doomed race and if possible to save some of its members. I know that there is little we can do in so short a time with this single ship. No other machine can possibly reach the system before detonation occurs.'

There was a long pause during which there could have been no sound or movement in the whole of the mighty ship as it sped silently toward the worlds ahead. Alveron knew what his companions were thinking and he tried to answer their unspoken question.

'You will wonder how such a disaster, the greatest of which we have any record, has been allowed to occur. On one point I can reassure you. The fault does not lie with the Survey.

'As you know, with our present fleet of under twelve thousand ships, it is possible to reexamine each of the eight thousand million solar systems in the Galaxy at intervals of about a million years. Most worlds change very little in so short a time as that.

'Less than four hundred thousand years ago, the survey ship S5060 examined the planets of the system we are approaching. It found intelligence on none of them,

20

though the third planet was teeming with animal life and two other worlds had once been inhabited. The usual report was submitted and the system is due for its next examination in six hundred thousand years.

'It now appears that in the incredibly short period since the last survey, intelligent life has appeared in the system. The first intimation of this occurred when unknown radio signals were detected on the planet Kulath in the system X29.35, Y34.76, Z27.93. Bearings were taken on them; they were coming from the system ahead.

'Kulath is two hundred light-years from here, so those radio waves had been on their way for two centuries. Thus for at least that period of time a civilization has existed on one of these worlds – a civilization that can generate electromagnetic waves and all that that implies.

'An immediate telescopic examination of the system was made and it was then found that the sun was in the unstable pre-nova stage. Detonation might occur at any moment, and indeed might have done so while the light waves were on their way to Kulath.

'There was a slight delay while the supervelocity scanners on Kulath II were focused on to the system. They showed that the explosion had not yet occurred but was only a few hours away. If Kulath had been a fraction of a light-year further from this sun, we should never have known of its civilization until it had ceased to exist.

'The Administrator of Kulath contacted Sector Base immediately, and I was ordered to proceed to the system at once. Our object is to save what members we can of the doomed race, if indeed there are any left. But we have assumed that a civilization possessing radio could have protected itself against any rise of temperature that may have already occurred.

'This ship and the two tenders will each explore a

21

section of the planet. Commander Torkalee will take Number One, Commander Orostron Number Two. They will have just under four hours in which to explore this world. At the end of that time, they must be back in the ship. It will be leaving then, with or without them. I will give the two commanders detailed instructions in the control room immediately.

'That is all. We enter atmosphere in two hours.'

On the world once known as Earth the fires were dying out: There was nothing left to burn. The great forests that had swept across the planet like a tidal wave with the passing of the cities were now no more than glowing charcoal and the smoke of their funeral pyres still stained the sky. But the last hours were still to come, for the surface rocks had not yet begun to flow. The continents were dimly visible through the haze, but their outlines meant nothing to the watchers in the approaching ship. The charts they possessed were out of date by a dozen Ice Ages and more deluges than one.

The S9000 had driven past Jupiter and seen at once that no life could exist in those half-gaseous oceans of compressed hydrocarbons, now erupting furiously under the sun's abnormal heat. Mars and the outer planets they had missed, and Alveron realized that the worlds nearer the sun than Earth would be already melting. It was more than likely, he thought sadly, that the tragedy of this unknown race was already finished. Deep in his heart, he thought it might be better so. The ship could only have carried a few hundred survivors, and the problem of selection had been haunting his mind.

Rugon, Chief of Communications and Deputy Captain, came into the control room. For the last hour he had been striving to detect radiation from Earth, but in vain.

'We're too late,' he announced gloomily. 'I've monitored the whole spectrum and the ether's dead except for our own stations and some two-hundred-year-old programs from Kulath. Nothing in this system is radiating any more.'

He moved toward the giant vision screen with a graceful flowing motion that no mere biped could ever hope to imitate. Alveron said nothing; he had been expecting this news.

One entire wall of the control room was taken up by the screen, a great black rectangle that gave an impression of almost infinite depth. Three of Rugon's slender control tentacles, useless for heavy work but incredibly swift at all manipulation, flickered over the selector dials and the screen lit up with a thousand points of light. The star field flowed swiftly past as Rugon adjusted the controls, bringing the projector to bear upon the sun itself.

No man of Earth would have recognized the monstrous shape that filled the screen. The sun's light was white no longer: great violet-blue clouds covered half its surface and from them long streamers of flame were erupting into space. At one point an enormous prominence had reared itself out of the photosphere, far out even into the flickering veils of the corona. It was as though a tree of fire had taken root in the surface of the sun – a tree that stood half a million miles high and whose branches were rivers of flame sweeping through space at hundreds of miles a second.

'I suppose,' said Rugon presently, 'that you are quite satisfied about the astronomers' calculations. After all – '

'Oh, we're perfectly safe,' said Alveron confidently. 'I've spoken to Kulath Observatory and they have been making some additional checks through our own instruments. That uncertainty of an hour includes a private

23

safety margin which they won't tell me in case I feel tempted to stay any longer.'

He glanced at the instrument board.

'The pilot should have brought us to the atmosphere now. Switch the screen back to the planet, please. Ah, there they go!'

There was a sudden tremor underfoot and a raucous clanging of alarms, instantly stilled. Across the vision screen two slim projectiles dived toward the looming mass of Earth. For a few miles they traveled together, then they separated, one vanishing abruptly as it entered the shadow of the planet.

Slowly the huge mother ship, with its thousand times greater mass, descended after them into the raging storms that already were tearing down the deserted cities of Man.

It was night in the hemisphere over which Orostron drove his tiny command. Like Torkalee, his mission was to photograph and record, and to report progress to the mother ship. The little scout had no room for specimens or passengers. If contact was made with the inhabitants of this world, the S9000 would come at once. There would be no time for parleying. If there was any trouble the rescue would be by force and the explanations could come later.

The ruined land beneath was bathed with an eerie, flickering light, for a great auroral display was raging over half the world. But the image on the vision screen was independent of external light, and it showed clearly a waste of barren rock that seemed never to have known any form of life. Presumably this desert land must come to an end somewhere. Orostron increased his speed to the highest value he dared risk in so dense an atmosphere.

The machine fled on through the storm, and presently

the desert of rock began to climb toward the sky. A great mountain range lay ahead, its peaks lost in the smoke-laden clouds. Orostron directed the scanners toward the horizon, and on the vision screen the line of mountains seemed suddenly very close and menacing. He started to climb rapidly. It was difficult to imagine a more unprom-ising land in which to find civilization and he wondered if it would be wise to change course. He decided against it. Five minutes later, he had his reward.

Miles below lay a decapitated mountain, the whole of its summit sheared away by some tremendous feat of engineering. Rising out of the rock and straddling the artificial plateau was an intricate structure of metal girders, supporting masses of machinery. Orostron brought his ship to a halt and spiraled down toward the mountain.

The slight Doppler blur had now vanished, and the picture on the screen was clear-cut. The latticework was supporting some scores of great metal mirrors, pointing skyward at an angle of forty-five degrees to the horizontal. They were slightly concave, and each had some compli-cated mechanism at its focus. There seemed something impressive and purposeful about the great array; every mirror was aimed at precisely the same spot in the sky – or beyond.

Orostron turned to his colleagues.

'It looks like some kind of observatory to me,' he said. 'Have you ever seen anything like it before?'

Klarten, a multitentacled, tripedal creature from a glob-ular cluster at the edge of the Milky Way, had a different theory.

'That's communication equipment. Those reflectors are for focusing electromagnetic beams. I've seen the same kind of installation on a hundred worlds before. It may even be the station that Kulath picked up – though that's rather unlikely, for the beams would be very narrow from mirrors that size.'

'That would explain why Rugon could detect no radiation before we landed,' added Hansur II, one of the twin beings from the planet Thargon.

Orostron did not agree at all.

'If that is a radio station, it must be built for interplanetary communication. Look at the way the mirrors are pointed. I don't believe that a race which has only had radio for two centuries can have crossed space. It took my people six thousand years to do it.'

'We managed it in three,' said Hansur II mildly, speaking a few seconds ahead of his twin. Before the inevitable argument could develop, Klarten began to wave his tentacles with excitement. While the others had been talking, he had started the automatic monitor.

'Here it is! Listen!'

He threw a switch, and the little room was filled with a raucous whining sound, continually changing in pitch but nevertheless retaining certain characteristics that were difficult to define.

The four explorers listened intently for a minute; then Orostron said, 'Surely that can't be any form of speech! No creature could produce sounds as quickly as that!'

Hansur I had come to the same conclusion. 'That's a television program. Don't you think so, Klarten?'

The other agreed.

'Yes, and each of those mirrors seems to be radiating a different program. I wonder where they're going? If I'm correct, one of the other planets in the system must lie along those beams. We can soon check that.'

Orostron called the S9000 and reported the discovery. Both Rugon and Alveron were greatly excited, and made a quick check of the astronomical records.

The result was surprising – and disappointing. None of the other nine planets lay anywhere near the line of transmission. The great mirrors appeared to be pointing blindly into space.

There seemed only one conclusion to be drawn, and Klarten was the first to voice it.

'They had interplanetary communication,' he said. 'But the station must be deserted now, and the transmitters no longer controlled. They haven't been switched off, and are just pointing where they were left.'

'Well, we'll soon find out,' said Orostron. 'I'm going to land.'

He brought the machine slowly down to the level of the great metal mirrors, and past them until it came to rest on the mountain rock. A hundred yards away, a white stone building crouched beneath the maze of steel girders. It was windowless, but there were several doors in the wall facing them.

Orostron watched his companions climb into their protective suits and wished he could follow. But someone had to stay in the machine to keep in touch with the mother ship. Those were Alveron's instructions, and they were very wise. One never knew what would happen on a world that was being explored for the first time, especially under conditions such as these.

Very cautiously, the three explorers stepped out of the airlock and adjusted the antigravity field of their suits. Then, each with the mode of locomotion peculiar to his race, the little party went toward the building, the Hansur twins leading and Klarten following close behind. His gravity control was apparently giving trouble, for he suddenly fell to the ground, rather to the amusement of his colleagues. Orostron saw them pause for a moment at the nearest door – then it opened slowly and they disappeared from sight.

So Orostron waited, with what patience he could, while the storm rose around him and the light of the aurora grew even brighter in the sky. At the agreed times he called the mother ship and received brief acknowledgments from Rugon. He wondered how Torkalee was faring, halfway round the planet, but he could not contact him through the crash and thunder of solar interference.

It did not take Klarten and the Hansur long to discover that their theories were largely correct. The building was a radio station, and it was utterly deserted. It consisted of one tremendous room with a few small offices leading from it. In the main chamber, row after row of electrical equipment stretched into the distance; lights flickered and winked on hundreds of control panels, and a dull glow came from the elements in a great avenue of vacuum tubes.

But Klarten was not impressed. The first radio set his race had built was fossilized in strata a thousand million years old. Man, who had possessed electrical machines for only a few centuries, could not compete with those who had known them for half the lifetime of the Earth.

Nevertheless, the party kept their recorders running as they explored the building. There was still one problem to be solved. The deserted station was broadcasting programs, but where were they coming from? The central switchboard had been quickly located. It was designed to handle scores of programs simultaneously, but the source of those programs was lost in a maze of cables that vanished underground. Back in the S9000, Rugon was trying to analyze the broadcasts and perhaps his researches would reveal their origin. It was impossible to trace cables that might lead across continents.

The party wasted little time at the deserted station. There was nothing they could learn from it, and they were seeking life rather than scientific information. A few minutes later the little ship rose swiftly from the plateau and headed toward the plains that must lie beyond the mountains. Less than three hours were still left to them.

As the array of enigmatic mirrors dropped out of sight, Orostron was struck by a sudden thought. Was it imagination, or had they all moved through a small angle while he had been waiting, as if they were still compensating for the rotation of the Earth? He could not be sure, and he dismissed the matter as unimportant. It would only mean that the directing mechanism was still working, after a fashion.

They discovered the city fifteen minutes later. It was a great, sprawling metropolis, built around a river that had disappeared leaving an ugly scar winding its way among the great buildings and beneath bridges that looked very incongruous now.

Even from the air, the city looked deserted. But only two and a half hours were left – there was no time for further exploration. Orostron made his decision, and landed near the largest structure he could see. It seemed reasonable to suppose that some creatures would have sought shelter in the strongest buildings, where they would be safe until the very end.

The deepest caves – the heart of the planet itself – would give no protection when the final cataclysm came. Even if this race had reached the outer planets, its doom would only be delayed by the few hours it would take for the ravening wavefronts to cross the Solar System.

Orostron could not know that the city had been deserted not for a few days or weeks, but for over a century. For

29

the culture of cities, which had outlasted so many civilizations, had been doomed at last when the helicopter brought universal transportation. Within a few generations the great masses of mankind, knowing that they could reach any part of the globe in a matter of hours, had gone back to the fields and forests for which they had always longed. The new civilization had machines and resources of which earlier ages had never dreamed, but it was essentially rural and no longer bound to the steel and concrete warrens that had dominated the centuries before. Such cities as still remained were specialized centers of research, administration or entertainment; the others had been allowed to decay, where it was too much trouble to destroy them. The dozen or so greatest of all cities, and the ancient university towns, had scarcely changed and would have lasted for many generations to come. But the cities that had been founded on steam and iron and surface transportation had passed with the industries that had nourished them.

And so while Orostron waited in the tender, his colleagues raced through endless empty corridors and deserted halls, taking innumerable photographs but learning nothing of the creatures who had used these buildings. There were libraries, meeting places, council rooms, thousands of offices – all were empty and deep with dust. If they had not seen the radio station on its mountain eyrie, the explorers could well have believed that this world had known no life for centuries.

Through the long minutes of waiting, Orostron tried to imagine where this race could have vanished. Perhaps they had killed themselves knowing that escape was impossible; perhaps they had built great shelters in the bowels of the planet, and even now were cowering in their millions beneath his feet, waiting for the end. He began to fear that he would never know.

It was almost a relief when at last he had to give the order for the return. Soon he would know if Torkalee's party had been more fortunate. And he was anxious to get back to the mother ship, for as the minutes passed the suspense had become more and more acute. There had always been the thought in his mind: What if the astronomers of Kulath have made a mistake? He would begin to feel happy when the walls of the S9000 were around him. He would be happier still when they were out in space and this ominous sun was shrinking far astern.

As soon as his colleagues had entered the airlock, Orostron hurled his tiny machine into the sky and set the controls to home on the S9000. Then he turned to his friends.

'Well, what have you found?' he asked.

Klarten produced a large roll of canvas and spread it out on the floor.

'This is what they were like,' he said quietly. 'Bipeds, with only two arms. They seem to have managed well, in spite of that handicap. Only two eyes as well, unless there are others in the back. We were lucky to find this; it's about the only thing they left behind.'

The ancient oil painting stared stonily back at the three creatures regarding it so intently. By the irony of fate, its complete worthlessness had saved it from oblivion. When the city had been evacuated, no one had bothered to move Alderman John Richards, 1909–1974 . For a century and a half he had been gathering dust while far away from the old cities the new civilization had been rising to heights no earlier culture had ever known.

'That was almost all we found,' said Klarten. 'The city must have been deserted for years. I'm afraid our

31

expedition has been a failure. If there are any living beings on this world, they've hidden themselves too well for us to find them.'

His commander was forced to agree.

'It was an almost impossible task,' he said. 'If we'd had weeks instead of hours we might have succeeded. For all we know, they may even have built shelters under the sea. No one seems to have thought of that.'

He glanced quickly at the indicators and corrected the course.

'We'll be there in five minutes. Alveron seems to be moving rather quickly. I wonder if Torkalee has found anything.'

The S9000 was hanging a few miles above the seaboard of a blazing continent when Orostron homed upon it. The danger line was thirty minutes away and there was no time to lose. Skillfully, he maneuvered the little ship into its launching tube and the party stepped out of the airlock.

There was a small crowd waiting for them. That was to be expected, but Orostron could see at once that something more than curiosity had brought his friends here. Even before a word was spoken, he knew that something was wrong.

'Torkalee hasn't returned. He's lost his party and we're going to the rescue. Come along to the control room at once.'

From the beginning, Torkalee had been luckier than Orostron. He had followed the zone of twilight, keeping away from the intolerable glare of the sun, until he came to the shores of an inland sea. It was a very recent sea, one of the latest of Man's works, for the land it covered had been desert less than a century before. In a few hours it would be desert again, for the water was boiling and clouds of steam were rising to the skies. But they could not veil the loveliness of the great white city that overlooked the tideless sea.

Flying machines were still parked neatly round the square in which Torkalee landed. They were disappointingly primitive, though beautifully finished, and depended on rotating airfoils for support. Nowhere was there any sign of life, but the place gave the impression that its inhabitants were not very far away. Lights were still shining from some of the windows.

Torkalee's three companions lost no time in leaving the machine. Leader of the party, by seniority of rank and race, was T'sinadree, who like Alveron himself had been born on one of the ancient planets of the Central Suns. Next came Alarkane, from a race which was one of the youngest in the Universe and took a perverse pride in the fact. Last came one of the strange beings from the system of Palador. It was nameless, like all its kind, for it possessed no identity of its own, being merely a mobile but still dependent cell in the consciousness of its race. Though it and its fellows had long been scattered over the galaxy in the exploration of countless worlds, some unknown link still bound them together as inexorably as the living cells in a human body.

When a creature of Palador spoke, the pronoun it used was always 'We.' There was not, nor could there ever be, any first person singular in the language of Palador.

The great doors of the splendid building baffled the explorers, though any human child would have known their secret. T'sinadree wasted no time on them but called Torkalee on his personal transmitter. Then the three hurried aside while their commander maneuvered his machine into the best position. There was a brief burst of intolerable flame; the massive steelwork flickered once at the edge of the visible spectrum and was gone. The stones were still glowing when the eager party hurried into the building, the beams of their light projectors fanning before them.

The torches were not needed. Before them lay a great hall, glowing with light from lines of tubes along the ceiling. On either side, the hall opened out into long corridors, while straight ahead a massive stairway swept majestically toward the upper floors.

For a moment T'sinadree hesitated. Then, since one way was as good as another, he led his companions down the first corridor.

The feeling that life was near had now become very strong. At any moment, it seemed, they might be confronted by the creatures of this world. If they showed hostility – and they could scarcely be blamed if they did – the paralyzers would be used at once.

The tension was very great as the party entered the first room, and only relaxed when they saw that it held nothing but machines – row after row of them, now stilled and silent. Lining the enormous room were thousands of metal filing cabinets, forming a continuous wall as far as the eye could reach. And that was all; there was no furniture, nothing but the cabinets and the mysterious machines.

Alarkane, always the quickest of the three, was already examining the cabinets. Each held many thousand sheets of tough, thin material, perforated with innumerable holes and slots. The Paladorian appropriated one of the cards and Alarkane recorded the scene together with some close-ups of the machines. Then they left. The great room, which had been one of the marvels of the world, meant nothing to them. No living eye would ever again see that wonderful battery of almost human Hollerith analyzers and the five thousand million punched cards holding all

34

that could be recorded of each man, woman and child on the planet.

It was clear that this building had been used very recently. With growing excitement, the explorers hurried on to the next room. This they found to be an enormous library, for millions of books lay all around them on miles and miles of shelving. Here, though the explorers could not know it, were the records of all the laws that Man had ever passed, and all the speeches that had ever been made in his council chambers.

T'sinadree was deciding his plan of action, when Alarkane drew his attention to one of the racks a hundred yards away. It was half empty, unlike all the others. Around it books lay in a tumbled heap on the floor, as if knocked down by someone in frantic haste. The signs were unmistakable. Not long ago, other creatures had been this way. Faint wheel marks were clearly visible on the floor to the acute sense of Alarkane, though the others could see nothing. Alarkane could even detect footprints, but knowing nothing of the creatures that had formed them he could not say which way they led.

The sense of nearness was stronger than ever now, but it was nearness in time, not in space. Alarkane voiced the thoughts of the party.

'Those books must have been valuable, and someone has come to rescue them – rather as an afterthought, I should say. That means there must be a place of refuge, possibly not very far away. Perhaps we may be able to find some other clues that will lead us to it.'

T'sinadree agreed; the Paladorian wasn't enthusiastic.

'That may be so,' it said, 'but the refuge may be anywhere on the planet, and we have just two hours left. Let us waste no more time if we hope to rescue these people.'

35

The party hurried forward once more, pausing only to collect a few books that might be useful to the scientists at Base – though it was doubtful if they could ever be translated. They soon found that the great building was composed largely of small rooms, all showing signs of recent occupation. Most of them were in a neat and tidy condition, but one or two were very much the reverse. The explorers were particularly puzzled by one room – clearly an office of some kind – that appeared to have been completely wrecked. The floor was littered with papers, the furniture had been smashed, and smoke was pouring through the broken windows from the fires outside.

T'sinadree was rather alarmed.

'Surely no dangerous animal could have got into a place like this!' he exclaimed, fingering his paralyzer nervously.

Alarkane did not answer. He began to make that annoying sound which his race called 'laughter.' It was several minutes before he would explain what had amused him.

'I don't think any animal has done it,' he said. 'In fact, the explanation is very simple. Suppose *you* had been working all your life in this room, dealing with endless papers, year after year. And suddenly, you are told that you will never see it again, that your work is finished, and that you can leave it forever. More than that – no one will come after you. Everything is finished. How would you make your exit, T'sinadree?'

The other thought for a moment.

'Well, I suppose I'd just tidy things up and leave. That's what seems to have happened in all the other rooms.'

Alarkane laughed again.

'I'm quite sure you would. But some individuals have a

different psychology. I think I should have liked the creature that used this room.'

He did not explain himself further, and his two colleagues puzzled over his words for quite a while before they gave it up.

It came as something of a shock when Torkalee gave the order to return. They had gathered a great deal of information, but had found no clue that might lead them to the missing inhabitants of this world. That problem was as baffling as ever, and now it seemed that it would never be solved. There were only forty minutes left before the S9000 would be departing.

They were halfway back to the tender when they saw the semicircular passage leading down into the depths of the building. Its architectural style was quite different from that used elsewhere, and the gently sloping floor was an irresistible attraction to creatures whose many legs had grown weary of the marble staircases which only bipeds could have built in such profusion. T'sinadree had been the worst sufferer, for he normally employed twelve legs and could use twenty when he was in a hurry, though no one had ever seen him perform this feat.

The party stopped dead and looked down the passageway with a single thought. A tunnel, leading down into the depths of Earth! At its end, they might yet find the people of this world and rescue some of them from their fate. For there was still time to call the mother ship if the need arose.

T'sinadree signaled to his commander and Torkalee brought the little machine immediately overhead. There might not be time for the party to retrace its footsteps through the maze of passages, so meticulously recorded in the Paladorian mind that there was no possibility of going astray. If speed was necessary, Torkalee could blast his way through the dozen floors above their head. In any case, it should not take long to find what lay at the end of the passage.

It took only thirty seconds. The tunnel ended quite abruptly in a very curious cylindrical room with magnificently padded seats along the walls. There was no way out save that by which they had come and it was several seconds before the purpose of the chamber dawned on Alarkane's mind. It was a pity, he thought, that they would never have time to use this. The thought was suddenly interrupted by a cry from T'sinadree. Alarkane wheeled around, and saw that the entrance had closed silently behind them.

Even in that first moment of panic, Alarkane found himself thinking with some admiration: Whoever they were, they knew how to build automatic machinery!

The Paladorian was the first to speak. It waved one of its tentacles toward the seats.

'We think it would be best to be seated,' it said. The multiplex mind of Palador had already analyzed the situation and knew what was coming.

They did not have long to wait before a low-pitched hum came from a grill overhead, and for the very last time in history a human, even if lifeless, voice was heard on Earth. The words were meaningless, though the trapped explorers could guess their message clearly enough.

'Choose your stations, please, and be seated.'

Simultaneously, a wall panel at one end of the compartment glowed with light. On it was a simple map, consisting of a series of a dozen circles connected by a line. Each of the circles had writing alongside it, and beside the writing were two buttons of different colors.

Alarkane looked questioningly at his leader.

'Don't touch them,' said T'sinadree. 'If we leave the controls alone, the doors may open again.'

He was wrong. The engineers who had designed the automatic subway had assumed that anyone who entered it would naturally wish to go somewhere. If they selected no intermediate station, their destination could only be the end of the line.

There was another pause while the relays and thyratrons waited for their orders. In those thirty seconds, if they had known what to do, the party could have opened the doors and left the subway. But they did not know, and the machines geared to a human psychology acted for them.

The surge of acceleration was not very great; the lavish upholstery was a luxury, not a necessity. Only an almost imperceptible vibration told of the speed at which they were traveling through the bowels of the earth, on a journey the duration of which they could not even guess. And in thirty minutes, the S9000 would be leaving the Solar System.

There was a long silence in the speeding machine. T'sinadree and Alarkane were thinking rapidly. So was the Paladorian, though in a different fashion. The conception of personal death was meaningless to it, for the destruction of a single unit meant no more to the group mind than the loss of a nail-paring to a man. But it could, though with great difficulty, appreciate the plight of individual intelligences such as Alarkane and T'sinadree, and it was anxious to help them if it could.

Alarkane had managed to contact Torkalee with his personal transmitter, though the signal was very weak and seemed to be fading quickly. Rapidly he explained the situation, and almost at once the signals became clearer. Torkalee was following the path of the machine, flying above the ground under which they were speeding to their unknown destination. That was the first indication they had of the fact that they were traveling at nearly a thousand miles an hour, and very soon after that Torkalee was able to give the still more disturbing news that they were rapidly approaching the sea. While they were beneath the land, there was a hope, though a slender one, that they might stop the machine and escape. But under the ocean – not all the brains and the machinery in the great mother ship could save them. No one could have devised a more perfect trap.

T'sinadree had been examining the wall map with great attention. Its meaning was obvious, and along the line connecting the circles a tiny spot of light was crawling. It was already halfway to the first of the stations marked.

'I'm going to press one of those buttons,' said T'sinadree at last. 'It won't do any harm, and we may learn something.'

'I agree. Which will you try first?'

'There are only two kinds, and it won't matter if we try the wrong one first. I suppose one is to start the machine and the other is to stop it.'

Alarkane was not very hopeful.

'It started without any button pressing,' he said. 'I think it's completely automatic and we can't control it from here at all.'

T'sinadree could not agree.

'These buttons are clearly associated with the stations, and there's no point in having them unless you can use them to stop yourself. The only question is, which is the right one?'

His analysis was perfectly correct. The machine could be stopped at any intermediate station. They had only been on their way ten minutes, and if they could leave now, no harm would have been done. It was just bad luck that T'sinadree's first choice was the wrong button.

The little light on the map crawled slowly through the illuminated circle without checking its speed. And at the same time Torkalee called from the ship overhead.

'You have just passed underneath a city and are heading out to sea. There cannot be another stop for nearly a thousand miles.'

Alveron had given up all hope of finding life on this world. The S9000 had roamed over half the planet, never staying long in one place, descending ever and again in an effort to attract attention. There had been no response; Earth seemed utterly dead. If any of its inhabitants were still alive, thought Alveron, they must have hidden themselves in its depths where no help could reach them, though their doom would be nonetheless certain.

Rugon brought news of the disaster. The great ship ceased its fruitless searching and fled back through the storm to the ocean above which Torkalee's little tender was still following the track of the buried machine.

The scene was truly terrifying. Not since the days when Earth was born had there been such seas as this. Mountains of water were racing before the storm which had now reached velocities of many hundred miles an hour. Even at this distance from the mainland the air was full of flying debris – trees, fragments of houses, sheets of metal, anything that had not been anchored to the ground. No airborne machine could have lived for a moment in such a gale. And ever and again even the roar of the wind was drowned as the vast water-mountains met head-on with a crash that seemed to shake the sky.

Fortunately, there had been no serious earthquakes yet. Far beneath the bed of the ocean, the wonderful piece of

41

engineering which had been the World President's private vacuum-subway was still working perfectly, unaffected by the tumult and destruction above. It would continue to work until the last minute of the Earth's existence, which, if the astronomers were right, was not much more than fifteen minutes away – though precisely how much more Alveron would have given a great deal to know. It would be nearly an hour before the trapped party could reach land and even the slightest hope of rescue.

Alveron's instructions had been precise, though even without them he would never have dreamed of taking any risks with the great machine that had been entrusted to his care. Had he been human, the decision to abandon the trapped members of his crew would have been desperately hard to make. But he came of a race far more sensitive than Man, a race that so loved the things of the spirit that long ago, and with infinite reluctance, it had taken over control of the Universe since only thus could it be sure that justice was being done. Alveron would need all his superhuman gifts to carry him through the next few hours.

Meanwhile, a mile below the bed of the ocean Alarkane and T'sinadree were very busy indeed with their private communicators. Fifteen minutes is not a long time in which to wind up the affairs of a lifetime. It is indeed, scarcely long enough to dictate more than a few of those farewell messages which at such moments are so much more important than all other matters.

All the while the Paladorian had remained silent and motionless, saying not a word. The other two, resigned to their fate and engrossed in their personal affairs, had given it no thought. They were startled when suddenly it began to address them in its peculiarly passionless voice.

'We perceive that you are making certain arrangements

concerning your anticipated destruction. That will probably be unnecessary. Captain Alveron hopes to rescue us if we can stop this machine when we reach land again.'

Both T'sinadree and Alarkane were too surprised to say anything for a moment. Then the latter gasped, 'How do you know?'

It was a foolish question, for he remembered at once that there were several Paladorians – if one could use the phrase – in the S9000, and consequently their companion knew everything that was happening in the mother ship. So he did not wait for an answer but continued, 'Alveron can't do that! He daren't take such a risk!'

'There will be no risk,' said the Paladorian. 'We have told him what to do. It is really very simple.'

Alarkane and T'sinadree looked at their companion with something approaching awe, realizing now what must have happened. In moments of crisis, the single units comprising the Paladorian mind could link together in an organization no less close than that of any physical brain. At such moments they formed an intellect more powerful than any other in the Universe. All ordinary problems could be solved by a few hundred or thousand units. Very rarely, millions would be needed, and on two historic occasions the billions of cells of the entire Paladorian consciousness had been welded together to deal with emergencies that threatened the race. The mind of Palador was one of the greatest mental resources of the Universe; its full force was seldom required, but the knowledge that it was available was supremely comforting to other races. Alarkane wondered how many cells had coordinated to deal with this particular emergency. He also wondered how so trivial an incident had ever come to its attention.

To that question he was never to know the answer, though he might have guessed it had he known that the chillingly remote Paladorian mind possessed an almost human streak of vanity. Long ago, Alarkane had written a book trying to prove that eventually all intelligent races would sacrifice individual consciousness and that one day only group-minds would remain in the Universe. Palador, he had said, was the first of those ultimate intellects, and the vast, dispersed mind had not been displeased.

They had no time to ask any further questions before Alveron himself began to speak through their communicators.

'Alveron calling! We're staying on this planet until the detonation waves reach it, so we may be able to rescue you. You're heading toward a city on the coast which you'll reach in forty minutes at your present speed. If you cannot stop yourselves then, we're going to blast the tunnel behind and ahead of you to cut off your power. Then we'll sink a shaft to get you out – the chief engineer says he can do it in five minutes with the main projectors. So you should be safe within an hour, unless the sun blows up before.'

'And if that happens, you'll be destroyed as well! You mustn't take such a risk!'

'Don't let that worry you; we're perfectly safe. When the sun detonates, the explosion wave will take several minutes to rise to its maximum. But apart from that, we're on the night side of the planet, behind an eight-thousand-mile screen of rock. When the first warning of the explosion comes, we will accelerate out of the Solar System, keeping in the shadow of the planet. Under our maximum drive, we will reach the velocity of light before leaving the cone of shadow, and the sun cannot harm us then.'

T'sinadree was still afraid to hope. Another objection came at once into his mind.

44

'Yes, but how will you get any warning, here on the night side of the planet?'

'Very easily,' replied Alveron. 'This world has a moon which is now visible from this hemisphere. We have telescopes trained on it. If it shows any sudden increase in brilliance, our main drive goes on automatically and we'll be thrown out of the system.'

The logic was flawless. Alveron, cautious as ever, was taking no chances. It would be many minutes before the eight-thousand-mile shield of rock and metal could be destroyed by the fires of the exploding sun. In that time, the S9000 could have reached the safety of the velocity of light.

Alarkane pressed the second button when they were still several miles from the coast. He did not expect anything to happen then, assuming that the machine could not stop between stations. It seemed too good to be true when, a few minutes later, the machine's slight vibration died away and they came to a halt.

The doors slid silently apart. Even before they were fully open, the three had left the compartment. They were taking no more chances. Before them a long tunnel stretched into the distance, rising slowly out of sight. They were starting along it when suddenly Alveron's voice called from the communicators.

'Stay where you are! We're going to blast!'

The ground shuddered once, and far ahead there came the rumble of falling rock. Again the earth shook – and a hundred yards ahead the passageway vanished abruptly. A tremendous vertical shaft had been cut clean through it.

The party hurried forward again until they came to the end of the corridor and stood waiting on its lip. The shaft in which it ended was a full thousand feet across and descended into the earth as far as the torches could throw their beams. Overhead, the storm clouds fled beneath a moon that no man would have recognized, so luridly brilliant was its disk. And, most glorious of all sights, the S9000 floated high above, the great projectors that had drilled this enormous pit still glowing cherry red.

A dark shape detached itself from the mother ship and dropped swiftly toward the ground. Torkalee was returning to collect his friends. A little later, Alveron greeted them in the control room. He waved to the great vision screen and said quietly, 'See, we were barely in time.'

The continent below them was slowly settling beneath the mile-high waves that were attacking its coasts. The last that anyone was ever to see of Earth was a great plain, bathed with the silver light of the abnormally brilliant moon. Across its face the waters were pouring in a glittering flood toward a distant range of mountains. The sea had won its final victory, but its triumph would be short-lived for soon sea and land would be no more. Even as the silent party in the control room watched the destruction below, the infinitely greater catastrophe to which this was only the prelude came swiftly upon them.

It was as though dawn had broken suddenly over this moonlit landscape. But it was not dawn: it was only the moon, shining with the brilliance of a second sun. For perhaps thirty seconds that awesome, unnatural light burnt fiercely on the doomed land beneath. Then there came a sudden flashing of indicator lights across the control board. The main drive was on. For a second Alveron glanced at the indicators and checked their information. When he looked again at the screen, Earth was gone.

The magnificent, desperately overstrained generators quietly died when the S9000 was passing the orbit of Persephone. It did not matter, the sun could never harm them now, and although the ship was speeding helplessly out into the lonely night of interstellar space, it would only be a matter of days before rescue came.

There was irony in that. A day ago, they had been the rescuers, going to the aid of a race that now no longer existed. Not for the first time Alveron wondered about the world that had just perished. He tried, in vain, to picture it as it had been in its glory, the streets of its cities thronged with life. Primitive though its people had been, they might have offered much to the Universe. If only they could have made contact! Regret was useless; long before their coming, the people of this world must have buried themselves in its iron heart. And now they and their civilization would remain a mystery for the rest of time.

Alveron was glad when his thoughts were interrupted by Rugon's entrance. The chief of communications had been very busy ever since the take-off, trying to analyze the programs radiated by the transmitter Orostron had discovered. The problem was not a difficult one, but it demanded the construction of special equipment, and that had taken time.

'Well, what have you found?' asked Alveron.

'Quite a lot,' replied his friend. 'There's something mysterious here, and I don't understand it.

'It didn't take long to find how the vision transmissions were built up, and we've been able to convert them to suit our own equipment. It seems that there were cameras all over the planet, surveying points of interest. Some of them were apparently in cities, on the tops of very high buildings. The cameras were rotating continuously to give panoramic views. In the programs we've recorded there are about twenty different scenes.

'In addition, there are a number of transmissions of a different kind, neither sound nor vision. They seem to be

47

purely scientific – possibly instrument readings or something of that sort. All these programs were going out simultaneously on different frequency bands.

'Now there must be a reason for all this. Orostron still thinks that the station simply wasn't switched off when it was deserted. But these aren't the sort of programs such a station would normally radiate at all. It was certainly used for interplanetary relaying – Klarten was quite right there. So these people must have crossed space, since none of the other planets had any life at the time of the last survey. Don't you agree?'

Alveron was following intently.

'Yes, that seems reasonable enough. But it's also certain that the beam was pointing to none of the other planets. I checked that myself.'

'I know,' said Rugon. 'What I want to discover is why a giant interplanetary relay station is busily transmitting pictures of a world about to be destroyed – pictures that would be of immense interest to scientists and astronomers. Someone had gone to a lot of trouble to arrange all those panoramic cameras. I am convinced that those beams were going somewhere.'

Alveron started up.

'Do you imagine that there might be an outer planet that hasn't been reported?' he asked. 'If so, your theory's certainly wrong. The beam wasn't even pointing in the plane of the Solar System. And even if it were – just look at this.'

He switched on the vision screen and adjusted the controls. Against the velvet curtain of space was hanging a blue-white sphere, apparently composed of many concentric shells of incandescent gas. Even though its immense distance made all movement invisible, it was clearly expanding at an enormous rate. At its center was a blinding point of light – the white dwarf star that the sun had now become.

'You probably don't realize just how big that sphere is,' said Alveron. 'Look at this.'

He increased the magnification until only the center portion of the nova was visible. Close to its heart were two minute condensations, one on either side of the nucleus.

'Those are the two giant planets of the system. They have still managed to retain their existence – after a fashion. And they were several hundred million miles from the sun. The nova is still expanding – but it's already twice the size of the Solar System.'

Rugon was silent for a moment.

'Perhaps you're right,' he said, rather grudgingly. 'You've disposed of my first theory. But you still haven't satisfied me.'

He made several swift circuits of the room before speaking again. Alveron waited patiently. He knew the almost intuitive powers of his friend, who could often solve a problem when mere logic seemed insufficient.

Then, rather slowly, Rugon began to speak again.

'What do you think of this?' he said. 'Suppose we've completely underestimated this people? Orostron did it once – he thought they could never have crossed space, since they'd only known radio for two centuries. Hansur II told me that. Well, Orostron was quite wrong. Perhaps we're all wrong. I've had a look at the material that Klarten brought back from the transmitter. He wasn't impressed by what he found, but it's a marvelous achievement for so short a time. There were devices in that station that belonged to civilizations thousands of years older. Alveron, can we follow that beam to see where it leads?'

Alveron said nothing for a full minute. He had been

more than half expecting the question, but it was not an easy one to answer. The main generators had gone completely. There was no point in trying to repair them. But there was still power available, and while there was power, anything could be done in time. It would mean a lot of improvisation, and some difficult maneuvers, for the ship still had its enormous initial velocity. Yes, it could be done, and the activity would keep the crew from becoming further depressed, now that the reaction caused by the mission's failure had started to set in. The news that the nearest heavy repair ship could not reach them for three weeks had also caused a slump in morale.

The engineers, as usual, made a tremendous fuss. Again as usual, they did the job in half the time they had dismissed as being absolutely impossible. Very slowly, over many hours, the great ship began to discard the speed its main drive had given it in as many minutes. In a tremendous curve, millions of miles in radius, the S9000 changed its course and the star fields shifted round it.

The maneuver took three days, but at the end of that time the ship was limping along a course parallel to the beam that had once come from Earth. They were heading out into emptiness, the blazing sphere that had been the sun dwindling slowly behind them. By the standards of interstellar flight, they were almost stationary.

For hours Rugon strained over his instruments, driving his detector beams far ahead into space. There were certainly no planets within many light-years; there was no doubt of that. From time to time Alveron came to see him and always he had to give the same reply: 'Nothing to report.' About a fifth of the time Rugon's intuition let him down badly; he began to wonder if this was such an occasion.

Not until a week later did the needles of the mass-detectors quiver feebly at the ends of their scales. But Rugon said nothing, not even to his captain. He waited until he was sure, and he went on waiting until even the short-range scanners began to react, and to build up the first faint pictures on the vision screen. Still he waited patiently until he could interpret the images. Then, when he knew that his wildest fancy was even less than the truth, he called his colleagues into the control room.

The picture on the vision screen was the familiar one of endless star fields, sun beyond sun to the very limits of the Universe. Near the center of the screen a distant nebula made a patch of haze that was difficult for the eye to grasp.

Rugon increased the magnification. The stars flowed out of the field; the little nebula expanded until it filled the screen and then – it was a nebula no longer. A simultaneous gasp of amazement came from all the company at the sight that lay before them.

Lying across league after league of space, ranged in a vast three-dimensional array of rows and columns with the precision of a marching army, were thousands of tiny pencils of light. They were moving swiftly; the whole immense lattice holding its shape as a single unit. Even as Alveron and his comrades watched, the formation began to drift off the screen and Rugon had to recenter the controls.

After a long pause, Rugon started to speak.

'This is the race,' he said softly, 'that has known radio for only two centuries – the race that we believed had crept to die in the heart of its planet. I have examined those images under the highest possible magnification.

'That is the greatest fleet of which there has ever been a record. Each of those points of light represents a ship larger than our own. Of course, they are very primitive – what you see on the screen are the jets of their rockets. Yes, they dared to use rockets to bridge interstellar space! You realize what that means. It would take them centuries to reach the nearest star. The whole race must have embarked on this journey in the hope that its descendants would complete it, generations later.

'To measure the extent of their accomplishment, think of the ages it took us to conquer space, and the longer ages still before we attempted to reach the stars. Even if we were threatened with annihilation, could we have done so much in so short a time? Remember, this is the youngest civilization in the Universe. Four hundred thousand years ago it did not even exist. What will it be a million years from now?'

An hour later, Orostron left the crippled mother ship to make contact with the great fleet ahead. As the little torpedo disappeared among the stars, Alveron turned to his friend and made a remark that Rugon was often to remember in the years ahead.

'I wonder what they'll be like?' he mused. 'Will they be nothing but wonderful engineers, with no art or philosophy? They're going to have such a surprise when Orostron reaches them – I expect it will be rather a blow to their pride. It's funny how all isolated races think they're the only people in the Universe. But they should be grateful to us; we're going to save them a good many hundred years of travel.'

Alveron glanced at the Milky Way, lying like a veil of silver mist across the vision screen. He waved toward it with a sweep of a tentacle that embraced the whole circle of the galaxy, from the Central Planets to the lonely suns of the Rim.

'You know,' he said to Rugon, 'I feel rather afraid of

these people. Suppose they don't like our little Federation?' He waved once more toward the star-clouds that lay massed across the screen, glowing with the light of their countless suns.

'Something tells me they'll be very determined people,' he added. 'We had better be polite to them. After all, we only outnumber them about a thousand million to one.'

Rugon laughed at his captain's little joke.

Twenty years afterward, the remark didn't seem funny.

Guardian Angel

'Guardian Angel' was written in July 1946, and when I submitted it to Astounding it was promptly rejected by John W. Campbell, Jr. – with, I am sure, a fascinating and sympathetic letter, which I hope may one day be located in the lower Cambrian strata of my correspondence files. (All previous searches have failed, so it's a race against petrification.) I would like to find that letter, because I wonder if John asked whether I had borrowed my aliens from his own story, 'The Mightiest Machine.' (In a word, Yes . . .)

The next year I rewrote it, and submitted it to my new agent – Scott Meredith, then at the beginning of his career. At that time, James Blish was working with Scott – and he did a major rewrite, tacking on a new ending. That version duly appeared in Famous Fantastic Mysteries for April 1950, where it might have remained to this day had I not decided to develop it further.

'Guardian Angel,' a couple of years later, began to metamorphose into Childhood's End, and became the first part of that novel ('Earth and the Overlords'). But that, to coin a phrase, is another story . . .

I

Pieter van Ryberg shivered, as he always did, when he came into Stormgren's room. He looked at the thermostat and shrugged his shoulders in mock resignation. 'You know, Chief,' he said, 'although we'll be sorry to lose you, it's nice to feel that the pneumonia death-rate will soon be falling.'

'How do you know?' smiled Stormgren. 'The next Secretary-General may be an Eskimo. The fuss some people make over a few degrees centigrade!'

Van Ryberg laughed and walked over to the curving double window. He stood in silence for a moment, staring along the avenue of great white buildings, still only partly finished.

'Well,' he said, with a sudden change of tone. 'Are you going to see them?'

Behind him he heard Stormgren fidgeting nervously with his famous uranium paperweight.

'Yes I think so. It usually saves trouble in the long run.'

Van Ryberg suddenly stiffened and pressed his face against the glass.

'Here they are!' he said. 'They're coming up Wilson Avenue. Not as many as I expected, though – about two thousand, I'd say.'

Stormgren walked over to the Assistant-Secretary's side. Half a mile away, a small but determined crowd was moving along the avenue towards Headquarters Building.

It carried banners which Stormgren could not read at this distance, but he knew their message well enough. Presently he could hear, even through the insulation, the ominous sound of chanting voices. He felt a sudden wave of disgust sweep over him. Surely the world had had enough of marching mobs and angry slogans!

The crowd had now come abreast of the building: it must know that he was watching, for here and there fists were being shaken in the air. They were not defying him, though the gesture was meant for him to see. As pygmies may threaten a giant, those angry fists were directed against the sky fifty miles above his head.

And as likely as not, thought Stormgren, Karellen was watching the whole thing and enjoying himself hugely.

This was the first time that Stormgren had ever met the head of the Freedom League. He still wondered if the action was wise: in the final analysis he had only taken it because the League would employ any refusal as ammunition against him. He knew that the gulf was far too wide for any agreement to come from this meeting.

Alexander Wainwright was a tall but slightly stooping man in the late fifties. He seemed inclined to apologize for his more boisterous followers, and Stormgren was rather taken aback by his obvious sincerity and considerable personal charm. It would be rather hard to dislike him, whatever one's views of the cause for which he stood.

Stormgren wasted no time after van Ryberg's brief and somewhat strained introductions.

'I suppose,' he began, 'the chief object of your visit is to register a formal protest against the Federation Scheme. Am I correct?'

Wainwright nodded.

'That is my main purpose, Mr Secretary. As you know, for the last five years we have tried to awaken the human race to the danger that confronts it. I must admit that, from our point of view, the response has been disappointing. The great majority of people seem content to let the Overlords run the world as they please. But this European Federation is as intolerable as it will be unworkable. Even Karellen can't wipe out two thousand years of history at the stroke of a pen.'

'Then do you consider,' interjected Stormgren, 'that Europe, and the whole world, must continue indefinitely to be divided into scores of sovereign states, each with its own currency, armed forces, customs, frontiers, and all the rest of that – that medieval paraphernalia?'

'I don't quarrel with Federation as an *ultimate* objective, though some of my supporters might not agree. My point is that it must come from within, not be superimposed from without. We must work out our own destiny – we have a right to independence. There must be no more interference in human affairs!'

Stormgren sighed. All this he had heard a hundred times before, and he knew that he could only give the old answers that the Freedom League had refused to accept. He had faith in Karellen, and they had not. That was the fundamental difference, and there was nothing he could do about it. Luckily, there was nothing that the Freedom League could do either.

'Let me ask you a few questions,' he said. 'Can you deny that the Overlords have brought security, peace and prosperity to the world?'

'That is true. But they have taken our freedom. Man does not live – '

'By bread alone. Yes, I know – but this is the first age in which every man was sure of getting even that. In any case, what freedom have we lost compared with that which the Overlords have given us for the first time in human history?'

'Freedom to control our own lives, under God's guidance.'

Stormgren shook his head.

'Last month, five hundred bishops, cardinals and rabbis signed a joint declaration pledging support for the Supervisor's policy. The world's religions are against you.'

'Because so few people realize the danger. When they do, it may be too late. Humanity will have lost its initiative and will have become a subject race.'

Stormgren did not seem to hear. He was watching the crowd below, milling aimlessly now that it had lost its leader. How long, he wondered, would it be before men ceased to abandon their reason and identity when more than a few of them were gathered together? Wainwright might be a sincere and honest man, but the same could not be said of many of his followers.

Stormgren turned back to his visitor.

'In three days I shall be meeting the Supervisor again. I shall explain your objections to him, since it is my duty to represent the views of the world. But it will alter nothing.'

There was a slight pause. Then, rather slowly, Wainwright began again.

'That brings me to another point. One of our main objections to the Overlords, as you know, is their secretiveness. You are the only human being who has ever spoken with Karellen – and even you have never seen him. Is it surprising that many of us are suspicious of his motives?'

'You have heard his speeches. Aren't they convincing enough?'

'Frankly, words are not sufficient. I do not know which we resent more – Karellen's omnipotence, or his secrecy.'

Stormgren was silent. There was nothing he could say to this – nothing, at any rate, that would convince the other. He sometimes wondered if he had really convinced himself.

It was, of course, only a very small operation from their point of view, but to Earth it was the biggest thing that had ever happened. There had been no warning, but a sudden shadow had fallen across a score of the world's greatest cities. Looking up from their work, a million men saw in that heart-freezing instant that the human race was no longer alone.

Countless times this day had been described in fiction, but no one had really believed that it would ever come. Now it had dawned at last: the twenty great ships were the symbol of a science man could not hope to match for centuries. For seven days they floated motionless above his cities, giving no hint that they knew of his existence. But none was needed: not by chance alone could those mighty ships have come to rest so precisely over New York, London, Moscow, Canberra, Rome, Capetown, Tokyo . . .

Even before the ending of those unforgettable days, some men had guessed the truth. This was not the first tentative contact by a race which knew nothing of Man. Within those silent, unmoving ships, master psychologists were studying humanity's reactions. When the curve of tension had reached its peak, they would reveal themselves.

And on the eighth day, Karellen, Supervisor for Earth, made himself known to the world. He spoke in English so perfect that the controversy it began was to rage across the Atlantic for half a century. But the context of the speech was more staggering even than its delivery. By any standards, it was a work of superlative genius, showing a complete and absolute mastery of human affairs. There was little doubt but that its scholarship and virtuosity, its tantalizing glimpses of knowledge still untapped, were deliberately designed to convince mankind that it was in the presence of overwhelming intellectual power. When Karellen had finished, the nations of Earth knew that their days of precarious sovereignty were ending. Local, internal governments would still retain their powers, but in the wider field of international affairs the supreme decisions had passed out of human hands. Arguments, protests – all were futile. No weapon could touch those brooding giants, and even if it could their downfall would utterly destroy the cities beneath. Overnight, Earth had become a protectorate in some shadowy, star-strewn empire beyond the knowledge of Man.

In a little while the tumult had subsided, and the world went about its business again. The only change a suddenly awakened Rip Van Winkle would have noticed was a hushed expectancy, a mental glancing-over-the-shoulder, as mankind waited for the Overlords to show themselves and to step down from their gleaming ships.

Five years later, it was still waiting. That, thought Stormgren, was the cause of all the trouble.

The room was small and, save for the single chair and the table beneath the vision-screen, unfurnished. As was intended, it told nothing of the creatures who had built it. There was only the one entrance, and that led directly to the airlock in the curving flank of the great ship. Through that lock only Stormgren, alone of living men, had ever come to meet Karellen, Supervisor for Earth.

The vision-screen was empty now, as it had always been. Behind that rectangle of darkness lay utter mystery

62

– but there too lay affection and an immense and tolerant understanding of mankind. An understanding which, Stormgren knew, could only have been acquired through centuries of study.

From the hidden grille came that calm, never-hurried voice with its undercurrent of humor – the voice which Stormgren knew so well though the world had heard it only thrice in history.

'Yes, Rikki, I was listening. What did you make of Mr Wainwright?'

'He's an honest man, whatever his supporters may be. What are we going to do about him? The League itself isn't dangerous, but some of its more extreme supporters are openly advocating violence. I've been wondering for some time if I should put a guard on my house. But I hope it isn't necessary.'

Karellen evaded the point in the annoying way he sometimes had.

'The details of the European Federation have been out for a month now. Has there been a substantial increase in the seven percent who disapprove of me, or the nine percent who Don't Know?'

'Not yet, despite the press reactions. What I'm worried about is a general feeling, even among your supporters, that it's time this secrecy came to an end.'

Karellen's sigh was technically perfect, yet somehow lacked conviction.

'That's your feeling too, isn't it?'

The question was so rhetorical that Stormgren didn't bother to answer it.

'Do you really appreciate,' he continued earnestly, 'how difficult this state of affairs makes my job?'

'It doesn't exactly help mine,' replied Karellen with some spirit. 'I wish people would stop thinking of me as a world dictator and remember that I'm only a civil servant trying to administer a somewhat idealistic colonial policy.'

'Then can't you at least give us some reason for your concealment? Because we don't understand it, it annoys us and gives rise to all sorts of rumors.'

Karellen gave that deep, rich laugh of his, just too musical to be altogether human.

'What am I supposed to be now? Does the robot theory still hold the field? I'd rather be a mass of cogwheels than crawl around the floor like a centipede, as most of the tabloids seem to imagine.'

Stormgren let out a Finnish oath he was fairly sure Karellen wouldn't know – though one could never be quite certain in these matters.

'Can't you ever be serious?'

'My dear Rikki,' said Karellen, 'it's only by *not* taking the human race seriously that I retain those fragments of my once considerable mental powers that I still possess.'

Despite himself, Stormgren smiled.

'That doesn't help me a great deal, does it? I have to go down there and convince my fellow men that although you won't show yourself, you've got nothing to hide. It's not an easy job. Curiosity is one of the most dominant human characteristics. You can't defy it forever.'

'Of all the problems that faced us when we came to Earth, this was the most difficult,' admitted Karellen. 'You have trusted our wisdom in other things – surely you can trust us in this!'

'*I* trust you,' said Stormgren, 'but Wainwright doesn't, nor do his supporters. Can you really blame them if they put a bad interpretation upon your unwillingness to show yourself?'

'Listen, Rikki,' Karellen answered at length. 'These matters are beyond my control. Believe me, I regret the

64

need for this concealment, but the reasons are – sufficient. However, I will try and get a statement from my superiors which may satisfy you and perhaps placate the Freedom League. Now, please, can we return to the agenda and start recording again? We've only reached Item 23, and I want to make a better job of settling the Jewish question than my predecessors for the last few thousand years . . .'

II

'Any luck, Chief?' asked van Ryberg anxiously.

'I don't know,' Stormgren replied wearily as he threw the files down on his desk and collapsed into the seat. 'Karellen's consulting *his* superiors now, whoever or whatever they may be. He won't make any promises.'

'Listen,' said Pieter abruptly. 'I've just thought of something. What reason have we for believing that there is anyone beyond Karellen? The Overlords may be a myth – you know how he hates the word.'

Tired though he was, Stormgren sat up with a start.

'It's an ingenious theory. But it clashes with what little I do know about Karellen's background.'

'And how much is that?'

'Well, he was a professor of astropolitics on a world he calls Skyrondel, and he put up a terrific fight before they made him take this job. He pretends to hate it, but he's really enjoying himself.'

Stormgren paused for a moment, and a smile of amusement softened his rugged features.

'At any rate, he once remarked that running a private zoo is rather good fun.'

'Hmm – a somewhat dubious compliment. He's immortal, isn't he?'

'Yes, after a fashion, though there's something thousands of years ahead of him which he seems to fear: I can't imagine what it is. And that's really all I know.'

'He could easily have made it up. My theory is that his little fleet's lost in space and looking for a new home. He doesn't want us to know how few he and his comrades are. Perhaps all those other ships are automatic, and there's no one in any of them. They're just an imposing façade.'

'You,' said Stormgren with great severity, 'have been reading science fiction in office hours.'

Van Ryberg grinned.

'The "Invasion from Space" didn't turn out quite as expected, did it? My theory would certainly explain why Karellen never shows himself. He doesn't want us to learn that there are no Overlords.'

Stormgren shook his head in amused disagreement.

'Your explanation, as usual, is much too ingenious to be true. Though we can only infer its existence, there must be a great civilization behind the Supervisor – and one that's known about Man for a very long time. Karellen himself must have been studying us for centuries. Look at his command of English, for example. He taught *me* how to speak it idiomatically!'

'I sometimes think he went a little too far,' laughed van Ryberg. 'Have you ever discovered anything he *doesn't* know?'

'Oh yes, quite often – but only on trivial points. I think he has an absolutely perfect memory, but there are some things he hasn't bothered to learn. For instance, he only understands English, though in the past two years he's picked up a good deal of Finnish just to tease me. And

Finnish isn't the sort of language one learns in a hurry! I think he can quote the whole of the *Kalevala* whereas I'm ashamed to say I know only a few dozen lines. He also knows the biographies of all living statesmen, and sometimes I can spot the references he's used. His knowledge of history and science seems complete: you know how much we've already learned from him. Yet, taken one at a time, I don't think his mental gifts are quite outside the range of human achievement. But no man could possibly do all the things he does.'

'That's more or less what I'd decided already,' agreed van Ryberg. 'We can argue round Karellen forever, but in the end we always come back to the same question – why the devil won't he show himself? Until he does, I'll go on theorizing and the Freedom League will go on fulminating.'

He cocked a rebellious eye at the ceiling.

'One dark night, Mr Supervisor, I'm going to take a rocket up to your ship and climb in through the back door with my camera. What a scoop *that* would be!'

If Karellen was listening, he gave no sign of it. But, of course, he never did.

Stormgren slept badly that night, and in the small hours of the morning rose from his bed and wandered restlessly out on to the veranda. It was warm, almost oppressive, but the sky was clear and a brilliant moon hung low in the southwest. In the far distance the lights of London glowed on the skyline like a frozen dawn.

Stormgren raised his eyes above the sleeping city, climbing again the fifty miles of space he alone of living men had crossed. Far away though it was, the beautiful lines of Karellen's ship were clearly visible in the moonlight. He wondered what the Supervisor was doing, for he did not believe that the Overlords ever slept.

High above, a meteor thrust its shining spear through the dome of the sky. The luminous trail glowed faintly for a while: then only the stars were left. The reminder was brutal: in a hundred years Karellen would still be leading mankind towards the goal that he alone could see, but four months from now another man would be Secretary-General. That in itself Stormgren was far from minding – but there was little time left if he ever hoped to learn what lay behind that darkened screen.

A naturally reticent man himself, the reasons for Karellen's behavior had never worried Stormgren once its initial strangeness had worn off. But now he knew that the mystery which tormented so many minds was beginning to obsess his own: he could understand – in time he might even share – the psychological outlook which had driven many to support the Freedom League. The propaganda about Man's enslavement was just – propaganda. Few people seriously believed it, or really wished for a return to the old days of national rivalries. Men had grown accustomed to Karellen's imperceptible rule; but they were becoming impatient to know who ruled them.

There was a faint 'click' from the teletype in the adjoining room as it ejected the hourly summary from Central News. Stormgren wandered indoors and ruffled half-heartedly through the sheets. On the other side of the world, the Freedom League had thought of a new head-line. 'IS MAN RULED BY MONSTERS?' asked the teletype, and went on to quote: 'Addressing a meeting in Madras today, Dr C. V. Krishnan, President of the Indian Division of the Freedom League, said: "The explanation of the Overlords' behavior is quite simple. Their physical form is so alien and so repulsive that they dare not show themselves to humanity. I challenge the Supervisor to deny this."'

Stormgren threw down the paper with a sigh. Even if it were true, did it really matter? The idea was an old one, but it had never worried him. He did not believe that there was any biological form, however strange, which he could not accept in time and, perhaps, even find beautiful. If he could convince Karellen of this, the Overlords might change their policy. Certainly they could not be half as hideous as the imaginative drawings that had filled the papers soon after their coming to Earth!

Stormgren smiled a little wryly as he turned back to his bedroom. He was honest enough to admit that, in the final analysis, his real motive was ordinary human curiosity.

When Stormgren failed to arrive at his usual hour, Pieter van Ryberg was surprised and a little annoyed. Though the Secretary-General often made a number of calls before reaching his own office, he invariably left word that he was doing so. This morning, to make matters worse, there had been several urgent messages for Stormgren. Van Ryberg rang half a dozen departments to try and locate him, then gave it up in disgust.

By noon he had become alarmed and sent a car to Stormgren's house. Ten minutes later he was startled by the scream of a siren, and a police patrol came racing up Wilson Avenue. The news agencies must have had friends in that machine, for even as van Ryberg watched it approach, the radio was telling the world that he was no longer Assistant, but Acting-Secretary-General of the United Nations.

If van Ryberg had not had so many other matters on his hands, he would have found it very interesting to study the press reactions to Stormgren's disappearance. For the past month, the world's papers had divided themselves into two sharply defined groups. The American press, on the whole, thought that the Federation of Europe was long overdue, but had a nervous feeling that this was only the beginning. The Europeans, on the other hand, were undergoing violent but largely synthetic spasms of national pride. Criticism of the Overlords was widespread and energetic: after an initial period of caution the press had discovered that it could be as rude to Karellen as it liked and nothing would happen. Now it was excelling itself.

Most of these attacks, though very vocal, were not representative of the great mass of the public. Along the frontiers that would soon be gone forever the guards had been doubled – but the soldiers eyed each other with a still inarticulate friendliness. The politicians and the generals might storm and rave, but the silently waiting millions felt that, none too soon, a long and bloody chapter of history was coming to an end.

And now Stormgren had gone, no one knew where or how. The tumult suddenly subsided as the world realized that it had lost the only man through whom the Overlords, for their own strange reasons, would speak to Earth. A paralysis seemed to descend upon press and radio, but in the silence could be heard the voice of the Freedom League, anxiously protesting its innocence.

It was completely dark when Stormgren awoke. How strange that was, he was for a moment too sleepy to realize. Then, as full consciousness dawned, he sat up with a start and felt for the light switch beside his bed. In the darkness his hand encountered a bare stone wall, cold to the touch. He froze instantly, mind and body paralyzed by the impact of the unexpected. Then, scarcely believing his senses, he kneeled on the bed and began to explore with his finger tips that shockingly unfamiliar wall.

He had been doing this for only a moment when there was a sudden 'click' and a section of the darkness slid aside. He caught a glimpse of a man silhouetted against a dimly lit background: then the door closed again and the darkness returned. It happened so swiftly that he saw nothing of the room in which he was lying.

An instant later, he was dazzled by the light of a powerful electric torch. The beam flickered across his face, held him steadily for a moment, then dipped to illuminate the whole bed – which was, he now saw, nothing more than a mattress supported on rough planks.

Out of the darkness a soft voice spoke to him in excellent English but with an accent which at first Stormgren could not identify.

'Ah, Mr Secretary, I'm glad to see you're awake. I hope you feel all right.'

There was something about the last sentence that caught Stormgren's attention, so that the angry questions he was about to ask died upon his lips. He stared back into the darkness, then replied calmly: 'How long have I been unconscious?'

The other chuckled.

'Several days. We were promised that there would be no aftereffects. I'm glad to see it's true.'

Partly to gain time, partly to test his own reactions, Stormgren swung his legs over the side of the bed. He was still wearing his nightclothes, but they were badly crumpled and seemed to have gathered considerable dirt. As he moved he felt a slight dizziness – not enough to be troublesome, but sufficient to convince him that he had indeed been drugged.

He turned towards the light.

'Where am I?' he said sharply. 'Does Wainwright know about this?'

71

'Smart, aren't you?' said the voice admiringly. 'But we won't talk about that now. I guess you'll be pretty hungry. Get dressed and come along to dinner.'

The oval of light slipped across the room and for the first time Stormgren had an idea of its dimensions. It was not really correct to call it a room at all, for the walls seemed bare rock, roughly smoothed into shape. He realized that he was underground, possibly at a great depth. He realized too that if he had been unconscious for several days he might be anywhere on Earth.

The torchlight illuminated a pile of clothes draped over a packing case.

'This should be enough for you,' said the voice from the darkness. 'Laundry's rather a problem here, so we grabbed a couple of your suits and half a dozen shirts.'

'That,' said Stormgren without humor, 'was very considerate of you.'

'We're sorry about the absence of furniture and electric light. This place is convenient in some ways, but it rather lacks amenities.'

'Convenient for what?' asked Stormgren as he climbed into a shirt. The feel of the familiar cloth beneath his fingers was strangely reassuring.

'Just – convenient,' said the voice. 'And by the way, since we're likely to spend a good deal of time together, you'd better call me Joe.'

'Despite your nationality,' retorted Stormgren, 'I think I could pronounce your real name. It won't be worse than many Finnish ones.'

There was a slight pause and the light flickered for an instant.

'Well, I should have expected it,' said Joe resignedly. 'You must have plenty of practice at this sort of thing.'

'It's a useful hobby for a man in my position. I suppose you were born in Poland, and picked up your English in Britain during the War? I should think you were stationed quite a while in Scotland, from your r's.'

'That,' said the other very firmly, 'is quite enough. As you seem to have finished dressing – thank you.'

The door opened as Stormgren walked towards it, and the other stood aside to let him pass. Stormgren wondered if Joe was armed and decided that he probably was. In any case, he would certainly have friends around.

The corridor was dimly lit by oil lamps at intervals, and for the first time Stormgren could see his captor. He was a man of about fifty, and must have weighed well over two hundred pounds. Everything about him was outsize, from the stained battledress that might have come from any of half a dozen armed forces, to the startlingly large signet ring on his left hand. It should not be difficult to trace him, thought Stormgren, if he ever got out of this place. He was a little depressed to think that the other must be perfectly well aware of this.

The walls around them, though occasionally faced with concrete, were mostly bare rock. It was clear to Stormgren that he was in some disused mine, and he could think of few more effective prisons. Until now the thought that he had been kidnapped had somehow failed to worry him greatly. He felt that, whatever happened, the immense resources of the Supervisor would soon locate and rescue him. Now he was not so sure: there must be a limit even to Karellen's powers, and if he was indeed buried in some remote continent all the science of the Overlords might be unable to trace him.

III

There were three other men round the table in the bare but brightly lit room. They looked up with interest and more than a little awe as Stormgren entered, and a substantial pile of meat sandwiches was quickly placed before him. He could have done with a more interesting meal, for he felt extremely hungry, but it was very obvious that his captors had dined no better.

As he ate, he glanced quickly at the four men around him. Joe was by far the most outstanding character – not merely in physical bulk. The others were nondescript individuals, probably Europeans also. He would be able to place them when he heard them talk.

He pushed away the plate, and ignoring the other men spoke directly to the huge Pole.

'Well,' he said evenly, 'now perhaps you'll tell me what this is all about, and what you hope to get out of it.'

Joe cleared his throat.

'I'd like to make one thing clear,' he said. 'This is nothing to do with Wainwright. He'll be as surprised as anyone.'

Stormgren had rather expected this. It gave him relatively little satisfaction to confirm the existence of an extremist movement inside the Freedom League.

'As a matter of interest,' he said, 'how did you kidnap me?'

He hardly expected a reply, and was taken aback by the other's readiness – even eagerness – to answer. Only slowly did he guess the reason.

'It was all rather like one of those old Fritz Lang films,'

said Joe cheerfully. 'We weren't sure if Karellen had a watch on you, so we took somewhat elaborate precautions. You were knocked out by gas in the air conditioner: that was easy. Then we carried you out into the car and drove off – no trouble at all. All this, I might say, wasn't done by any of our people. We hired – er, professionals for the job. Karellen may get them – in fact, he's supposed to – but he'll be no wiser. When it left your house the car drove into a long road tunnel not many miles from the center of London. It came out again on schedule at the other end, still carrying a drugged man extraordinarily like the Secretary-General. About the same time a large truck loaded with metal cases emerged in the opposite direction and drove to a certain airfield where one of the cases was loaded aboard a freighter. Meanwhile the car that had done the job continued elaborate evasive action in the general direction of Scotland. Perhaps Karellen's caught it by now: I don't know. As you'll see – I do hope you appreciate my frankness – our whole plan depended on one thing. We're pretty sure that Karellen can see and hear everything that happens on the surface of the Earth – but unless he uses magic, not science, he can't see underneath it. So he won't know about that transfer in the tunnel. Naturally we've taken a risk, but there were also one or two other stages in your removal which I won't go into now. We may have to use them again one day, and it would be a pity to give them away.'

Joe had related the whole story with such obvious gusto that Stormgren found it difficult to be appropriately furious. Yet he felt very disturbed. The plan was an ingenious one, and it seemed more than likely that whatever watch Karellen kept on him, he would have been tricked by this ruse.

The Pole was watching Stormgren's reactions closely. He would have to appear confident, whatever his real feelings.

'You must be a lot of fools,' said Stormgren scornfully, 'if you think you can trick the Overlords like this. In any case, what conceivable good would it do?'

Joe offered him a cigarette, which Stormgren refused, then lit one himself and sat on the edge of the table. There was an ominous creaking and he jumped off hastily.

'Our motives,' he began, 'should be pretty obvious. We've found that argument's useless, so we have to take other measures. There have been underground movements before, and even Karellen, whatever powers he's got, won't find it easy to deal with us. We're out to fight for our independence. Don't misunderstand me. There'll be nothing violent – at first, anyway. But the Overlords have to use human agents, and we can make it mighty uncomfortable for them.'

Starting with me, I suppose, thought Stormgren. He wondered if the other had given him more than a fraction of the whole story. Did they really think that these gangster methods would influence Karellen in the slightest? On the other hand, it was quite true that a well-organized resistance movement could make things very difficult.

'What do you intend to do with me?' asked Stormgren at length. 'Am I a hostage, or what?'

'Don't worry – we'll look after you. We expect some visitors in a day or two, and until then we'll entertain you as well as we can.'

He added some words in his own language, and one of the others produced a brand-new pack of cards.

'We got these especially for you,' explained Joe. His voice suddenly became grave. 'I hope you've got plenty of

76

cash,' he said anxiously. 'After all, we can hardly accept checks.'

Quite overcome, Stormgren stared blankly at his captors. Then, as the true humor of the situation sank into his mind, it suddenly seemed to him that all the cares and worries of office had lifted from his shoulders. Whatever happened, there was absolutely nothing he could do about it – and now these fantastic criminals wanted to play cards with him.

Abruptly, he threw back his head and laughed as he had not done for years.

There was no doubt, thought van Ryberg morosely, that Wainwright was telling the truth. He might have his suspicions, but he did not know who had kidnapped Stormgren. Nor did he approve of the kidnapping itself. Van Ryberg had a shrewd idea that for some time extremists in the Freedom League had been putting pressure on Wainwright to make him adopt a more active policy. Now they were taking things into their own hands.

The kidnapping had been beautifully organized, there was no doubt of that. Stormgren might be anywhere on earth and there seemed little hope of tracing him. Yet something would have to be done, decided van Ryberg, and done quickly. Despite the jests he had so often made, his real feeling towards Karellen was one of overwhelming awe. The thought of approaching the Supervisor directly filled him with dismay, but there seemed no alternative.

Communication Section had several hundred channels to Karellen's ship. Most of them were operating continuously, handling endless streams of statistics – production figures, census returns and all the bookkeeping of a world economic system. One channel, van Ryberg knew, was reserved for Karellen's personal messages to Stormgren.

No one but the Secretary-General himself had ever used it.

Van Ryberg sat down at the keyboard and, after a moment's hesitation, began to tap out his message with unpracticed fingers. The machine clicked away contentedly and the words gleamed for a few seconds on the darkened screen. Then he waited; he would give the Supervisor ten minutes and after that someone else could bring him any reply.

There was no need. Scarcely a minute later the machine started to whirr again. Not for the first time, van Ryberg wondered if the Supervisor ever slept.

The message was as brief as it was unhelpful.

NO INFORMATION. LEAVE MATTERS
ENTIRELY TO YOUR DISCRETION.

Rather bitterly, and without any satisfaction at all, van Ryberg realized how much greatness had been thrust upon him.

During the last three days Stormgren had analyzed his captors with some thoroughness. Joe was the only one of any importance: the others were nonentities – the riffraff one would expect any illegal movement to gather round itself. The ideals of the Freedom League meant nothing to them: their only concern was earning a living with the minimum of work. They were the gangster types from which civilization might never be wholly free.

Joe was an altogether more complex individual, though sometimes he reminded Stormgren of an overgrown baby. Their interminable canasta games were punctuated with violent political arguments, but it became obvious to Stormgren that the big Pole had never thought seriously about the cause for which he was fighting. Emotion and extreme conservatism clouded all his judgments. His country's long struggle for independence had conditioned him so completely that he still lived in the past. He was a picturesque survival, one of those who had no use for an ordered way of life. When his type had vanished, if it ever did, the world would be a safer but less interesting place.

There was little doubt, as far as Stormgren was concerned, that Karellen had failed to locate him. He had tried to bluff, but his captors were unconvinced. He was fairly certain that they had been holding him here to see if Karellen would act, and now that nothing had happened they could proceed with the next part of their plan.

Stormgren was not surprised when, five or six days after his capture, Joe told him to expect visitors. For some time the little group had shown increasing nervousness, and the prisoner guessed that the leaders of the movement, having seen that the coast was clear, were at last coming to collect him.

They were already waiting, gathered round the rickety table, when Joe waved him politely into the living room. The three thugs had vanished, and even Joe seemed somewhat restrained. Stormgren could see at once that he was now confronted by men of a much higher caliber, and the group opposite reminded him strongly of a picture he had once seen of Lenin and his colleagues in the first days of the Russian Revolution. There was the same intellectual force, iron determination, and ruthlessness in these six men. Joe and his like were harmless: here were the real brains behind the organization.

With a curt nod, Stormgren moved over to the seat and tried to look self-possessed. As he approached, the elderly, thickset man on the far side of the table leaned forward and stared at him with piercing gray eyes. They made Stormgren so uncomfortable that he spoke first – something he had not intended to do.

'I suppose you've come to discuss terms. What's my ransom?'

He noticed that in the background someone was taking down his words in a shorthand notebook. It was all very businesslike.

The leader replied in a musical Welsh accent.

'You could put it that way, Mr Secretary-General. But we're interested in information, not cash.'

So that was it, thought Stormgren. He was a prisoner of war, and this was his interrogation.

'You know what our motives are,' continued the other in his softly lilting voice. 'Call us a resistance movement, if you like. We believe that sooner or later Earth will have to fight for its independence – but we realize that the struggle can only be by indirect methods such as sabotage and disobedience. We kidnapped you partly to show Karellen that we mean business and are well organized, but largely because you are the only man who can tell us anything of the Overlords. You're a reasonable man, Mr Stormgren. Give us your cooperation, and you can have your freedom.'

'Exactly what do you wish to know?' asked Stormgren cautiously.

Those extraordinary eyes seemed to search his mind to its depths: they were unlike any that Stormgren had ever seen in his life. Then the singsong voice replied:

'Do you know who, or what, the Overlords really are?'

Stormgren almost smiled.

'Believe me,' he said, 'I'm quite as anxious as you to discover that.'

'Then you'll answer our questions?'

'I make no promises. But I may.'

There was a slight sigh of relief from Joe and a rustle of anticipation went round the room.

'We have a general idea,' continued the other, 'of the circumstances in which you meet Karellen. Would you go through them carefully, leaving out nothing of importance.'

That was harmless enough, thought Stormgren. He had done it scores of times before, and it would give the appearance of cooperation.

He felt in his pockets and produced a pencil and an old envelope. Sketching rapidly while he spoke, he began:

'You know, of course, that a small flying machine, with no obvious means of propulsion, calls for me at regular intervals and takes me up to Karellen's ship. There is only one small room in that machine, and it's quite bare apart from a couch and table. The layout is something like this.'

He pushed the plan across to the old Welshman, but the strange eyes never turned towards it. They were still fixed on Stormgren's face, and as he watched them something seemed to change in their depths. The room had become completely silent, but behind him he heard Joe take a sudden indrawn breath.

Puzzled and annoyed, Stormgren stared back at the other, and as he did so, understanding slowly dawned. In his confusion, he crumpled the envelope into a ball of paper and ground it underfoot.

For the man opposite him was blind.

IV

Van Ryberg had made no more attempts to contact Karellen. Much of his department's work – the forwarding of statistical information, the abstracting of the world's press, and the like – had continued automatically. In Paris the lawyers were still wrangling over the European Constitution, but that was none of his business for the moment. It was three weeks before the Supervisor wanted the final draft: if it was not ready by then, no doubt Karellen would act accordingly.

And there was still no news of Stormgren.

Van Ryberg was dictating when the 'Emergency Only' telephone started to ring. He grabbed the receiver and listened with mounting astonishment, then threw it down and rushed to the open window. In the distance faint cries of amazement were rising from the street and the traffic had already come to a halt.

It was true: Karellen's ship, that never-changing symbol of the Overlords, was no longer in the sky. He searched the heavens as far as he could see, but found no trace of it. Even as he was doing so, it seemed that night had suddenly fallen. Coming down from the north, its shadowed underbelly black as a thundercloud, the great ship was racing low above the towers of London. Involuntarily, van Ryberg shrank away from the onrushing monster. He had always known how huge the ships of the Overlords really were – but it was one thing to see them far away in space, and quite another to watch them passing overhead, almost close enough to touch.

In the darkness of that partial eclipse, he watched until

the ship and its monstrous shadow had moved to the south. There was no sound, not even the whisper of air; van Ryberg realized that, for all its apparent nearness, the ship was still a thousand feet or more above his head. He watched it vanish over the horizon, still large even when it dropped below the curve of the Earth.

In the office behind him all the telephones had started to ring, but van Ryberg did not move. He leaned against the balcony, still staring into the south, paralyzed by the presence of illimitable power.

As Stormgren talked, it seemed to him that his mind was operating on two levels simultaneously. On the one hand he was trying to defy the men who had captured him, yet on the other he was hoping that they might help him to unravel Karellen's secret. He did not feel that he was betraying the Supervisor, for there was nothing here that he had not told many times before. Moreover, the thought that these men could harm Karellen in any way was fantastic.

The blind Welshman had conducted most of the interrogation. It was fascinating to watch that agile mind trying one opening after another, testing and rejecting all the theories that Stormgren himself had abandoned long ago. Presently he leaned back with a sigh and the shorthand writer laid down his stylus.

'We're getting nowhere,' he said resignedly. 'We want more facts, and that means action -- not argument.' The sightless eyes seemed to stare thoughtfully at Stormgren. For a moment he tapped nervously on the table – the first sign of uncertainty that Stormgren had noticed. Then he continued:

'I'm a little surprised, Mr Secretary, that you've never made an effort to learn more about the Overlords.'

'What do you suggest?' asked Stormgren coldly. 'I've told you that there's only one way out of the room in which I've had my talks with Karellen – and that leads straight to the airlock.'

'It might be possible,' mused the other, 'to devise instruments which could teach us something. I'm no scientist, but we can look into the matter. If we give you your freedom, would you be willing to assist with such a plan?'

'Once and for all,' said Stormgren angrily, 'let me make my position perfectly clear. Karellen is working for a united world, and I'll do nothing to help his enemies. What his ultimate plans may be, I don't know, but I believe that they are good. You may annoy him, you may even delay the achievement of his aims, but it will make no difference in the end. You may be sincere in believing as you do: I can understand your fear that the traditions and cultures of little countries will be overwhelmed when the World State arrives. But you are wrong: it is useless to cling to the past. Even before the Overlords came to Earth, the sovereign state was dying. No one can save it now, and no one should try.'

There was no reply: the man opposite neither moved nor spoke. He sat with lips half open, his eyes now lifeless as well as blind. Around him the others were equally motionless, frozen in strained, unnatural attitudes. With a little gasp of pure horror, Stormgren rose to his feet and backed away towards the door. As he did so the silence was suddenly broken.

'That was a nice speech, Rikki. Now I think we can go.'

'Karellen! Thank God – but what have you done?'

'Don't worry. They're all right. You can call it a paralysis, but it's much subtler than that. They're simply living a few thousand times more slowly than normal. When we've gone they'll never know what happened.'

'You'll leave them here until the police come?'

'No: I've a much better plan. I'm letting them go.'

Stormgren felt an illogical sense of relief which he did not care to analyze. He gave a last valedictory glance at the little room and its frozen occupants. Joe was standing on one foot, staring very stupidly at nothing. Suddenly Stormgren laughed and fumbled in his pockets.

'Thanks for the hospitality, Joe,' he said. 'I think I'll leave a souvenir.'

He ruffled through the scraps of paper until he found the figures he wanted. Then, on a reasonably clean sheet, he wrote carefully:

LOMBARD BANK, LONDON

Pay 'Joe' the sum of One Pound Seventeen Shillings and Six Pence (£1-17-6).

R. Stormgren.

As he laid the strip of paper beside the Pole, Karellen's voice inquired: 'Exactly what are you up to?'

'Paying a debt of honor,' explained Stormgren. 'The other two cheated, but I think Joe played fair. At least, I never caught him out.'

He felt very gay and lightheaded as he walked to the door. Hanging just outside it was a large, featureless metal sphere that moved aside to let him pass. He guessed that it was some kind of robot, and it explained how Karellen had been able to reach him through the unknown layers of rock overhead.

'Carry on for a hundred yards,' said the sphere, speaking in Karellen's voice. 'Then turn to the left until I give you further instructions.'

He ran forward eagerly, though he realized that there was no need for hurry. The sphere remained hanging in the corridor, and Stormgren guessed that it was the generator of the paralysis field.

A minute later he came across a second sphere, waiting for him at a fork in the corridor.

'You've half a mile to go,' it said. 'Keep to the left until we meet again.'

Six times he encountered the spheres on his way to the open. At first he wondered if somehow the first robot had slipped ahead of him; then he guessed that there must be a chain of them maintaining a complete circuit down into the depths of the mine. At the entrance a group of guards formed a piece of improbable still life, watched over by yet another of the ubiquitous spheres. On the hillside a few yards away lay the little flying machine in which Stormgren had made all his journeys to Karellen.

He stood for a moment blinking in the fierce sunlight. Then he saw the ruined mining machinery around him, and beyond that a derelict railway stretching down a mountainside. Several miles away dense forest lapped at the base of the mountain, and very far off Stormgren could see the gleam of a great river. He guessed that he was somewhere in southern France, probably in the Cévennes mountains.

As he climbed into the little ship, he had a last glimpse of the mine entrance and the men frozen round it. Quite suddenly a line of metal spheres raced out of the opening like silver cannon balls. Then the door closed behind him and with a sigh of relief he sank back upon the familiar couch.

For a while Stormgren waited until he had recovered his breath; then he uttered a single, heartfelt syllable:

'Well??'

'I'm sorry I couldn't rescue you before. But you'll see how very important it was to wait until all the leaders had gathered here.'

'Do you mean to say,' spluttered Stormgren, 'that you knew where I was all the time? If I thought – '

'Don't be so hasty,' answered Karellen, 'or at any rate, let me finish explaining.'

'It had better be good,' said Stormgren darkly. He was beginning to suspect that he had been no more than the bait in an elaborate trap.

'I've had a tracer on you for some time,' began Karellen, 'and though your late friends were correct in thinking that I couldn't follow you underground, I was able to keep track until they brought you to the mine. That transfer in the tunnel was ingenious, but when the first car ceased to react it gave the show away and I soon located you again. Then it was merely a matter of waiting. I knew that once they were certain I'd lost you, the leaders would come here and I'd be able to trap them all.'

'But you're letting them go!'

'Until now,' said Karellen, 'I did not know which of the two billion men on this planet were the heads of the organization. Now that they're located, I can trace their movements anywhere on Earth, and can probably watch most of their actions in detail if I want to. That's far better than locking them up. They're effectively neutralized, and they know it. Your rescue will be completely inexplicable to them, for you must have vanished before their eyes.'

That rich laugh echoed round the tiny room.

'In some ways the whole affair was a comedy, but it had a serious purpose. It will be a valuable object lesson for any other plotters. I'm not concerned merely with the few score men of this organization – I have to think of the moral effect on other groups which may exist elsewhere.'

Stormgren was silent for a while. He was not altogether satisfied, but he could see Karellen's point of view and some of his anger had evaporated.

'It's a pity to do it in my last few weeks of office,' he said, 'but from now on I'm going to have a guard on my house. Pieter can be kidnapped next time. How has he managed, by the way? Are things in as big a mess as I expect?'

'You'll be disappointed to find out how little your absence has mattered. I've watched Pieter carefully this past week, and have deliberately avoided helping him. On the whole he's done very well – but he's not the man to take your place.'

'That's lucky for him,' said Stormgren, still rather aggrieved. 'And have you had any word from your superiors about – about showing yourself to us? I'm sure now that it's the strongest argument your enemies have. Again and again they told me: "We'll never trust the Overlords until we can see them."'

Karellen sighed.

'No, I have heard nothing. But I know what the answer must be.'

Stormgren did not press the matter. Once he might have done so, but now for the first time the faint shadow of a plan had come into his mind. What he had refused to do under duress, he might yet attempt of his own free will.

Pierre Duval showed no surprise when Stormgren walked unannounced into his office. They were old friends, and there was nothing unusual in the Secretary-General paying a personal visit to the chief of the Science Bureau. Certainly Karellen would not think it odd, even if by any remote chance he turned his attention to this corner of the world.

For a while the two men talked business and exchanged political gossip; then, rather hesitantly, Stormgren came to the point. As his visitor talked, the old Frenchman leaned back in his chair and his eyebrows rose steadily millimeter by millimeter until they were almost entangled in his forelock. Once or twice he seemed about to speak but each time thought better of it.

When Stormgren had finished, the scientist looked nervously around the room.

'Do you think he was listening?' he said.

'I don't believe he can. This place is supposed to be shielded from everything, isn't it? Karellen's not a magician. He knows where I am, but that's all.'

'I hope you're right. Apart from that, won't there be trouble when he discovers what you're trying to do? Because he will, you know.'

'I'll take that risk. Besides, we understand each other rather well.'

The physicist toyed with his pencil and stared into space for a while.

'It's a very pretty problem. I like it,' he said simply. Then he dived into a drawer and produced an enormous writing pad, quite the biggest that Stormgren had ever seen.

'Right,' he began, scribbling furiously. 'Let me make sure I have all the facts. Tell me everything you can about the room in which you have your interviews. Don't omit any detail, however trivial it seems.'

'There isn't much to describe. It's made of metal, and is about eight yards square and four high. The vision screen is about a yard on a side and there's a desk immediately beneath it – here, it will be quicker if I draw it for you.'

Rapidly Stormgren sketched the little room he knew so well, and pushed the drawing over to Duval. As he did so, he remembered with a slight shiver the last time he had done this sort of thing.

The Frenchman studied the drawing with puckered brow.

'And that's all you can tell me?'

'Yes.'

He snorted in disgust.

'What about lighting? Do you sit in total darkness? And how about heating, ventilation . . .'

Stormgren smiled at the characteristic outburst.

'The whole ceiling is luminous, and as far as I can tell the air comes through the speaker grille. I don't know how it leaves; perhaps the stream reverses at intervals, but I haven't noticed it. There's no sign of any heaters, but the room is always at normal temperature.'

'By that I take it that the carbon dioxide has frozen out, but not the oxygen.'

Stormgren did his best to smile at the well-worn joke.

'I think I've told everything,' he concluded. 'As for the machine that takes me up to Karellen's ship, the room in which I travel is as featureless as an elevator cage. Apart from the couch and table, it might very well be one.'

There was silence for several minutes while the physicist embroidered his writing pad with meticulous and microscopic doodles. No one could have guessed that behind that still almost unfurrowed brow the world's finest technical brain was working with the icy precision that had made it famous.

Then Duval nodded to himself in satisfaction, leaned forward and pointed his pencil at Stormgren.

'What makes you think, Rikki,' he asked, 'that Karellen's vision-screen, as you call it, really is what it pretends to be?'

'I've always taken it for granted – it's exactly like one. What else would it be, anyway?'

'The tendency of otherwise first-class minds to overlook the obvious always saddens me. You know that Karellen can watch your movements, but a television system must have some sort of camera. Where is it?'

'I'd thought of that,' said Stormgren with asperity. 'Couldn't the screen do both jobs? I know our televisors don't, but still – '

Duval didn't like the idea.

'It would be possible,' he admitted. 'But why on earth go to all that trouble? The simplest solution is always best. Doesn't it seem far more probable that your "vision-screen" is really *nothing more complicated than a sheet of one-way glass?*'

Stormgren was so annoyed with himself that for a moment he sat in silence, retracing the past. From the beginning, he had never challenged Karellen's story – yet now he came to look back, when had the Supervisor ever told him that he was using a television system? He had just taken it for granted; the whole thing had been a piece of psychological trickery, and he had been completely deceived. He tried to console himself with the thought that in the same circumstances even Duval would have fallen into the trap.

But he was jumping to conclusions: no one had proved anything yet.

'If you're right,' he said, 'all I have to do is smash the glass – '

Duval sighed.

'These nontechnical laymen! Do you think it's likely to be made of anything you could smash without explosives? And if you succeeded, do you imagine that Karellen is likely to breathe the same air as we do? Won't it be nice

91

for both of you if he flourishes in an atmosphere of chlorine?'

Stormgren turned rather pale.

'Well, what *do* you suggest?' he asked with some exasperation.

'I want to think it over. First of all we've got to find if my theory is correct, and if so learn something about the material of the screen. I'll put some of my best men on the job – by the way, I suppose you carry a briefcase when you visit the Supervisor? Is it the one you've got there?'

'Yes.'

'It's rather small. Will you get one at least ten inches deep, and use it from now on so that he becomes used to seeing it?'

'Very well,' said Stormgren doubtfully. 'Do you want me to carry a concealed X-ray set?'

The physicist grinned.

'I don't know yet, but we'll think of something. I'll let you know what it is in about a month's time.'

He gave a little laugh.

'Do you know what all this reminds me of?'

'Yes,' said Stormgren promptly, 'the time you were building illegal radio sets during the German occupation.'

Duval looked disappointed.

'Well, I suppose I *have* mentioned that once or twice before. But there's one other thing – '

'Yes?'

'When you're caught, *I* didn't know what you wanted the gear for.'

'What, after all the fuss you once made about the scientist's social responsibility for his inventions? Really, Pierre, I'm ashamed of you!'

* * *

Stormgren laid down the thick folder of typescript with a sigh of relief.

'Thank heavens that's settled at last,' he said. 'It's strange to think that those few hundred pages hold the future of Europe.'

'They hold a good deal more than that,' said Karellen quietly.

'So a lot of people have been suggesting. The preamble, and most of the constitution itself, won't need many alterations when it's time for the rest of the world to join. But the first step will be quite enough to get on with.'

Stormgren dropped the file into his briefcase, the back of which was now only six inches from the dark rectangle of the screen. From time to time his fingers played across the locks in a half-conscious nervous reaction, but he had no intention of pressing the concealed switch until the meeting was over. There was a chance that something might go wrong: though Duval had sworn that Karellen would detect nothing, one could never be sure.

'Now, you said you'd some news for me,' Stormgren continued, with scarcely concealed eagerness. 'Is it about – '

'Yes,' said Karellen. 'I received the Policy Board's decision a few hours ago, and am authorized to make an important statement. I don't think that the Freedom League will be very satisfied, but it should help to reduce the tension. We won't record this, by the way.

'You've often told me, Rikki, that no matter how unlike you we are physically, the human race will soon grow accustomed to us. That shows a lack of imagination on your part. It would probably be true in your case, but you must remember that most of the world is still uneducated by any reasonable standards, and is riddled with prejudices

93

and superstitions that may take another hundred years to eradicate.

'You will grant us that we know something of human psychology. We know rather accurately what would happen if we revealed ourselves to the world in its present state of development. I can't go into details, even with you, so you must accept my analysis on trust. We can, however, make this definite promise, which should give you some satisfaction. *In fifty years – two generations from now – we shall come down from our ships and humanity will at last see us as we are.*'

Stormgren was silent for a while. He felt little of the satisfaction that Karellen's statement would have once given him. Indeed, he was somewhat confused by his partial success and for a moment his resolution faltered. The truth would come with the passage of time, and all his plotting was unnecessary and perhaps unwise. If he still went ahead, it would only be for the selfish reason that he would not be alive fifty years from now.

Karellen must have seen his irresolution, for he continued:

'I'm sorry if this disappoints you, but at least the political problems of the near future won't be your responsibility. Perhaps you still think that our fears are unfounded, but believe me we've had convincing proof of the dangers of any other course.'

Stormgren leaned forward, breathing heavily.

'I always thought so! You *have* been seen by Man!'

'I didn't say that,' Karellen answered after a short pause. 'Your world isn't the only planet we've supervised.'

Stormgren was not to be shaken off so easily.

'There have been many legends suggesting that Earth has been visited in the past by other races.'

'I know: I've read the Historical Research Section's report. It makes Earth look like the crossroads of the Universe.'

'There may have been visits about which you know nothing,' said Stormgren, still angling hopefully. 'Though since you must have been observing us for thousands of years, I suppose that's rather unlikely.'

'I suppose it is,' said Karellen in his most unhelpful manner. And at that moment Stormgren made up his mind.

'Karellen,' he said abruptly, 'I'll draft out the statement and send it up to you for approval. But I reserve the right to continue pestering you, and if I see any opportunity, I'll do my best to learn your secret.'

'I'm perfectly well aware of that,' replied the Supervisor, with a slight chuckle.

'And you don't mind?'

'Not in the slightest – though I draw the line at atomic bombs, poison gas, or anything else that might strain our friendship.'

Stormgren wondered what, if anything, Karellen had guessed. Behind the Supervisor's banter he had recognized the note of understanding, perhaps – who could tell? – even of encouragement.

'I'm glad to know it,' Stormgren replied in as level a voice as he could manage. He rose to his feet, bringing down the cover of his case as he did so. His thumb slid along the catch.

'I'll draft that statement at once,' he repeated, 'and send it up on the teletype later today.'

While he was speaking, he pressed the button – and knew that all his fears had been groundless. Karellen's senses were no finer than Man's. The Supervisor could have detected nothing, for there was no change in his voice as he said goodbye and spoke the familiar code words that opened the door of the chamber.

Yet Stormgren still felt like a shoplifter leaving a department store under the eyes of the house detective, and breathed a sigh of relief when the airlock doors had finally closed behind him.

V

'I admit,' said van Ryberg, 'that some of my theories haven't been very bright. But tell me what you think of this one.'

'Must I?'

Pieter didn't seem to notice.

'It isn't really my idea,' he said modestly. 'I got it from a story of Chesterton's. Suppose that the Overlords are hiding the fact that they've got nothing to hide?'

'That sounds a little complicated to me,' said Stormgren, beginning to take slight interest.

'What I mean is this,' van Ryberg continued eagerly. '*I* think that physically they're human beings like us. They realize that we'll tolerate being ruled by creatures we imagine to be – well, alien and super-intelligent. But the human race being what it is, it just won't be bossed around by creatures of the same species.'

'Very ingenious, like all your theories,' said Stormgren. 'I wish you'd give them Opus numbers so that I could keep up with them. The objections to this one – '

But at that moment Alexander Wainwright was ushered in.

Stormgren wondered what he was thinking. He wondered, too, if Wainwright had made any contact with the men who had kidnapped him. He doubted it, for he believed Wainwright's disapproval of violent methods to be perfectly genuine. The extremists in his movement had discredited themselves thoroughly, and it would be a long time before the world heard of them again.

The head of the Freedom League listened in silence while the draft was read to him. Stormgren hoped that he appreciated this gesture, which had been Karellen's idea. Not for another twelve hours would the rest of the world know of the promise that had been made to its grandchildren.

'Fifty years,' said Wainwright thoughtfully. 'That is a long time to wait.'

'Not for Karellen, nor for humanity,' Stormgren answered. Only now was he beginning to realize the neatness of the Overlords' solution. It had given them the breathing space they believed they needed, and it had cut the ground from beneath the Freedom League's feet. He did not imagine that the League would capitulate, but its position would be seriously weakened.

Certainly Wainwright realized this as well, as he must also have realized that Karellen would be watching him. For he said very little and left as quickly as he could: Stormgren knew that he would not see him again in his term of office. The Freedom League might still be a nuisance, but that was a problem for his successor.

There were some things that only time could cure. Evil men could be destroyed, but nothing could be done about good men who were deluded.

'Here's your case,' said Duval. 'It's as good as new.'

'Thanks,' Stormgren answered, inspecting it carefully nonetheless. 'Now perhaps you can tell me what it was all about – and what we are going to do next.'

The physicist seemed more interested in his own thoughts.

'What I can't understand,' he said, 'is the ease with which we've got away with it. Now if *I'd* been Kar –'

'But you're not. Get to the point, man. What *did* we discover?'

'Ah me, these excitable, highly strung Nordic races!' sighed Duval. 'Well, it's rather a long story, but the first piece of equipment you carried was a tiny echo sounder using supersonic waves. We went right up the audio spectrum, so high that I was sure no possible sense organs could detect us. When you pressed the button, a rather complicated set of sound pulses went out in various directions. I won't bother about the details, but the main idea was to measure the thickness of the screen and to find the dimensions of the room, if any, behind it.

'The screen seems to be about five inches thick, and the space behind it is at least ten yards across. We couldn't detect any echo from the further wall, but we hardly expected to. However, we *did* get this.'

He pushed forward a photographic record which to Stormgren looked rather like the autograph of a mild earthquake.

'See that little kink?'

'Yes: what is it?'

'Only Karellen.'

'Good Lord! Are you sure?'

'It's a pretty safe guess. He's sitting, or standing, or whatever he does, about two yards on the other side of the screen. If the resolution had been better, we might even have calculated his size.'

Stormgren's feelings were very mixed as he stared at the scarcely visible deflection of the trace. Until now, there had been no proof that Karellen even had a material body.

The evidence was still indirect, but he accepted it with little question.

Duval's voice cut into his reverie.

'The piece of equipment you carried on your second visit was similar,' he said, 'but used light instead of sound. We had to measure the transmission characteristics of the screen, and that presented considerable difficulties. Obviously we dared not use visible light, so once again we chose frequencies so high that we couldn't imagine any eye focusing them – or any atmosphere transmitting them very far. And again we managed to carry it off.

'You'll realize,' he continued, 'that there's no such thing as a truly one-way glass. Karellen's screen, we found when we analyzed our results, transmits about a hundred times as easily in one direction as the other. We've no particular reason to assume that the figure is very different in the visible spectrum – but we're giving you an enormous safety margin.'

With the air of a conjuror producing a whole litter of rabbits, Duval reached into his desk and pulled out a pistol-like object with a flexible bell mouth. It reminded Stormgren of a rubber blunderbuss, and he couldn't imagine what it was supposed to be.

Duval grinned at his perplexity.

'It isn't as dangerous as it looks. All you have to do is to ram the muzzle against the screen and press the trigger. It gives out a very powerful flash lasting five seconds, and in that time you'll be able to swing it round the room. Enough light will come back to give you a good view.'

'It won't hurt Karellen?'

'Not if you aim low and sweep it upwards. That will give him time to accommodate – I suppose he has reflexes like ours, and we don't want to blind him.'

Stormgren looked at the weapon doubtfully and hefted

it in his hand. For the last few weeks his conscience had been pricking him. Karellen had always treated him with unmistakable affection, despite his occasional devastating frankness, and now that their time together was drawing to its close he did not wish to do anything that might spoil that relationship. But the Supervisor had received due warning, and Stormgren had the conviction that if the choice had been his Karellen would long ago have shown himself. Now the decision would be made for him: when their last meeting came to its end, Stormgren would gaze upon Karellen's face.

If, of course, Karellen had a face.

The nervousness that Stormgren had first felt had long since passed away. Karellen was doing almost all the talking, weaving the long, intricate sentences of which he was so fond. Once this had seemed to Stormgren the most wonderful and certainly the most unexpected of all Karellen's gifts. Now it no longer appeared quite so marvelous, for he knew that like most of the Supervisor's abilities it was the result of sheer intellectual power and not of any special talent.

Karellen had time for any amount of literary composition when he slowed his thoughts down to the pace of human speech.

'Do not worry,' he said, 'about the Freedom League. It has been very quiet for the past month, and though it will revive again it is no longer a real danger. Indeed, since it's always valuable to know what your opponents are doing, the League is a very useful institution. Should it ever get into financial difficulties I might even subsidize it.'

Stormgren had often found it difficult to tell when Karellen was joking. He kept his face impassive and continued to listen.

'Very soon the League will lose another of its strongest arguments. There's been a good deal of criticism, mostly rather childish, of the special position you have held for the past few years. I found it very valuable in the early days of my administration, but now that the world is moving along the line that I planned, it can cease. In the future, all my dealings with Earth will be indirect and the office of Secretary-General can once again become what it was originally intended to be.

'During the next fifty years there will be many crises, but they will pass. Almost a generation from now, I shall reach the nadir of my popularity, for plans must be put into operation which cannot be fully explained at the time. Attempts may even be made to destroy me. But the pattern of the future is clear enough, and one day all these difficulties will be forgotten – even to a race with memories as long as yours.'

The last words were spoken with such a peculiar emphasis that Stormgren immediately froze in his seat. Karellen never made accidental slips and even his indiscretions were calculated to many decimal places. But there was no time to ask questions – which certainly would not be answered – before the Supervisor had changed the subject again.

'You've often asked me about our long-term plans,' he continued. 'The foundation of the World State is, of course, only the first step. You will live to see its completion – but the change will be so imperceptible that few will notice it when it comes. After that there will be a pause for thirty years while the next generation reaches maturity. And then will come the day which we have promised. I am sorry that you will not be there.'

Stormgren's eyes were open, but his gaze was fixed far beyond the dark barrier of the screen. He was looking into the future, imagining the day he would never see, when the great ships of the Overlords came down at last to Earth and were thrown open to the waiting world.

'On that day,' continued Karellen, 'the human mind will experience one of its very rare psychological discontinuities. But no permanent harm will be done: the men of that age will be more stable than their grandfathers. We will always have been part of their lives, and when they meet us we will not seem so – strange – as we would do to you.'

Stormgren had never known Karellen in so contemplative a mood, but this gave him no surprise. He did not believe that he had ever seen more than a few facets of the Supervisor's personality: the real Karellen was unknown and perhaps unknowable to human beings. And once again Stormgren had the feeling that the Supervisor's real interests were elsewhere, and that he ruled Earth with only a fraction of his mind, as effortlessly as a master of three-dimensional chess may play a game of checkers.

Karellen continued his reverie, almost as if Stormgren were not there.

'Then there will be another pause, only a short one this time, for the world will be growing impatient. Men will wish to go out to the stars, to see the other worlds of the Universe and to join us in our work. For it is only beginning: not a thousandth of the suns in the Galaxy have ever been visited by the races of which we know. One day, Rikki, your descendants in their own ships will be bringing civilization to the worlds that are ripe to receive it – just as we are doing now.'

Faintly across the gulf of centuries Stormgren could glimpse the future of which Karellen dreamed, the future towards which he was leading mankind. How far ahead? He could not even guess: there was no way in which he could measure Man's present stature against the standards of the Overlords.

Karellen had fallen silent and Stormgren had the impression that the Supervisor was watching him intently.

'It is a great vision,' he said softly. 'Do you bring it to all your worlds?'

'Yes,' said Karellen, 'all that can understand it.'

Out of nowhere, a strangely disturbing thought came into Stormgren's mind.

'Suppose, after all, your experiment fails with Man? We have known such things in our own dealings with other races. Surely you have had your failures too?'

'Yes,' said Karellen, so softly that Stormgren could scarcely hear him. 'We have had our failures.'

'And what do you do then?'

'We wait – and try again.'

There was a pause lasting perhaps ten seconds. When Karellen spoke again, his words were muffled and so unexpected that for a moment Stormgren did not react.

'Goodbye, Rikki!'

Karellen had tricked him – probably it was already too late. Stormgren's paralysis lasted only for a moment. Then in a single swift, well-practiced movement, he whipped out the flash-gun and jammed it against the screen.

The pine trees came almost to the edge of the lake, leaving along its border only a narrow strip of grass a few yards wide. Every evening when it was warm enough Stormgren would walk slowly along this strip to the landing-stage, watch the sunlight die upon the water, and then return to the house before the chill evening wind came up from the forest. The simple ritual gave him much contentment, and he would continue it as long as he had the strength.

Far away over the lake something was coming in from

103

the west, flying low and fast. Aircraft were uncommon in these parts, unless one counted the transpolar liners which must be passing overhead every hour of the day and night. But there was never any sign of their presence, save an occasional vapor trail high against the blue of the stratosphere. This machine was a small helicopter, and it was coming towards him with ominous determination. Stormgren glanced along the beach and saw that there was no chance of escape. Then he shrugged his shoulders and sat down on the wooden bench at the end of the jetty.

The reporter was so deferential that Stormgren found it surprising. He had almost forgotten that he was not only an elder statesman but, outside his own country, almost a mythical figure.

'Mr Stormgren,' the intruder began, 'I'm very sorry to bother you, but I wonder if you would mind answering a few questions about the Overlords?'

Stormgren frowned slightly. After all these years, he still shared Karellen's dislike for the word.

'I do not think,' he said, 'that I can add a great deal to what has already been written elsewhere.'

The reporter was watching him with a curious intentness.

'I thought that you might,' he answered. 'A rather strange story has just come to our notice. It seems that, nearly thirty years ago, one of the Science Bureau's technicians made some remarkable pieces of equipment for you. We wondered if you could tell us anything about it.'

For a moment Stormgren was silent, his mind going back into the past. He was not surprised that the secret had been discovered: indeed it was amazing that it had taken so long. He wondered how it had happened, not that it mattered now.

He rose to his feet and began to walk back along the jetty, the reporter following a few paces behind.

'The story,' he said, 'contains a certain amount of truth. On my last visit to Karellen's ship I took some apparatus with me, in the hope that I might see the Supervisor. It was rather a foolish thing to do but – well, I was only sixty at the time.'

He chuckled to himself and then continued.

'It's not much of a story to have brought you all this way. You see, it didn't work.'

'You saw nothing?'

'No, nothing at all. I'm afraid you'll have to wait – but after all, there are only twenty years to go.'

Twenty years to go. Yes, Karellen had been right. By then the world would be ready, as it had not been when he had spoken that same lie to Duval thirty years before.

Yet was it a lie? What had he really seen? No more, he was certain, than Karellen had intended. He was as sure as he could be of anything that the Supervisor had known his plan from the beginning, and had foreseen every moment of its final act.

Why else had that enormous chair been already empty when the circle of light blazed upon it? In the same moment he had started to swing the beam, but he was too late. The metal door, twice as high as a man, was closing swiftly when he first caught sight of it – closing swiftly, yet not quite swiftly enough.

Karellen had trusted him, had not wished him to go down into the long evening of his life still haunted by a mystery he could never solve. Karellen dared not defy the unknown powers above him (were they of that same race too?) but he had done all that he could. If he had disobeyed Them, They could never prove it.

'We have had our failures.'

Yes, Karellen, that was true: and were you the one who failed, before the dawn of human history? It must have been a failure indeed, for its echoes to roll down all the ages, to haunt the childhood of every race of man. Even in fifty years, could you overcome the power of all the myths and legends of the world?

Yet Stormgren knew there would be no second failure. When the two races met again, the Overlords would have won the trust and friendship of Mankind, and not even the shock of recognition could undo that work. They would go together into the future, and the unknown tragedy that had darkened the past would be lost forever down the dim corridors of prehistoric time.

And Stormgren knew also that the last thing he would ever see as he closed his eyes on life would be that swiftly turning door, and the long black tail disappearing behind it.

A very famous and unexpectedly beautiful tail.

A barbed tail.

Breaking Strain

'Breaking Strain' was written in the summer of 1948, and although its deliberately low-key treatment was neither thrilling nor wondrous, it appeared in Thrilling Wonder Stories for December 1949. (To justify his existence, the editor changed the title to the unexciting and unimaginative 'Thirty Seconds – Thirty Days.' And to make matters even more confused, he later republished it in The Best From Startling Stories.)

The story caused one friendly critic to remark that I was apparently aspiring to the 'Kipling of the spaceways' – a noble but (at least in 1948) – somewhat premature ambition. And on going through my records I am Thrilled and Startled to see that it was sold to CBS in 1955. I wonder if it was ever used . . .

Grant was writing up the *Star Queen*'s log when he heard the cabin door opening behind him. He didn't bother to look around – it was hardly necessary for there was only one other man aboard the ship. But when nothing happened, and when McNeil neither spoke nor came into the room, the long silence finally roused Grant's curiosity and he swung the seat round in its gimbals.

McNeil was just standing in the doorway, looking as if he had seen a ghost. The trite metaphor flashed into Grant's mind instantly. He did not know for a moment how near the truth it was. In a sense McNeil *had* seen a ghost – the most terrifying of all ghosts – his own.

'What's the matter?' said Grant angrily. 'You sick or something?'

The engineer shook his head. Grant noticed the little beads of sweat that broke away from his forehead and went glittering across the room on their perfectly straight trajectories. His throat muscles moved, but for a while no sound came. It looked as though he was going to cry.

'We're done for,' he whispered at last. 'Oxygen reserve's gone.'

Then he did cry. He looked like a flabby doll, slowly collapsing on itself. He couldn't fall, for there was no gravity, so he just folded up in mid-air.

Grant said nothing. Quite unconsciously he rammed his smoldering cigarette into the ash tray, grinding it viciously until the last tiny spark had died. Already the air seemed to be thickening around him as the oldest terror of the spaceways gripped him by the throat.

He slowly loosed the elastic straps which, while he was seated, gave some illusion of weight, and with an automatic skill launched himself toward the doorway. McNeil did not offer to follow. Even making every allowance for the shock he had undergone, Grant felt that he was behaving very badly. He gave the engineer an angry cuff as he passed and told him to snap out of it.

The hold was a large hemispherical room with a thick central column which carried the controls and cabling to the other half of the dumbbell-shaped spaceship a hundred meters away. It was packed with crates and boxes arranged in a surrealistic three-dimensional array that made very few concessions to gravity.

But even if the cargo had suddenly vanished Grant would scarcely have noticed. He had eyes only for the big oxygen tank, taller than himself, which was bolted against the wall near the inner door of the airlock.

It was just as he had last seen it, gleaming with aluminum paint, and the metal sides still held the faint touch of coldness that gave the only hint of the contents. All the piping seemed in perfect condition. There was no sign of anything wrong apart from one minor detail. The needle of the contents gauge lay mutely against the zero stop.

Grant gazed at the silent symbol as a man in ancient London, returning home one evening at the time of the Plague, might have stared at a rough cross newly scrawled upon his door. Then he banged half a dozen times on the glass in the futile hope that the needle had stuck – though he never really doubted its message. News that is sufficiently bad somehow carries its own guarantee of truth. Only good reports need confirmation.

When Grant got back to the control room, McNeil was

himself again. A glance at the opened medicine chest showed the reason for the engineer's rapid recovery. He even assayed a faint attempt at humor.

'It was a meteor,' he said. 'They tell us a ship this size should get hit once a century. We seem to have jumped the gun with ninety-five years still to go.'

'But what about the alarms? The air pressure's normal – how could we have been holed?'

'We weren't,' McNeil replied. 'You know how the oxygen circulates night-side through the refrigerating coils to keep it liquid? The meteor must have smashed them and the stuff simply boiled away.'

Grant was silent, collecting his thoughts. What had happened was serious – deadly serious – but it need not be fatal. After all, the voyage was more than three quarters over.

'Surely the regenerator can keep the air breathable, even if it does get pretty thick?' he asked hopefully.

McNeil shook his head. 'I've not worked it out in detail, but I know the answer. When the carbon dioxide is broken down and the free oxygen gets cycled back there's a loss of about ten percent. That's why we have to carry a reserve.'

'The space suits!' cried Grant in sudden excitement. 'What about their tanks?'

He had spoken without thinking, and the immediate realization of his mistake left him feeling worse than before.

'We can't keep oxygen in them – it would boil off in a few days. There's enough compressed gas there for about thirty minutes – merely long enough for you to get to the main tank in an emergency.'

'There must be a way out – even if we have to jettison

111

cargo and run for it. Let's stop guessing and work out exactly where we are.'

Grant was as much angry as frightened. He was angry with McNeil for breaking down. He was angry with the designers of the ship for not having foreseen this God-knew-how-many-million-to-one chance. The deadline might be a couple of weeks away and a lot could happen before then. The thought helped for a moment to keep his fears at arm's length.

This was an emergency, beyond doubt, but it was one of those peculiarly protracted emergencies that seem to happen only in space. There was plenty of time to think – perhaps too much time.

Grant strapped himself in the pilot's seat and pulled out a writing-pad.

'Let's get the facts right,' he said with artificial calmness. 'We've got the air that's still circulating in the ship and we lose ten percent of the oxygen every time it goes through the generator. Chuck me over the Manual, will you? I can never remember how many cubic meters we use a day.'

In saying that the *Star Queen* might expect to be hit by a meteor once every century, McNeil had grossly but unavoidably oversimplified the problem. For the answer depended on so many factors that three generations of statisticians had done little but lay down rules so vague that the insurance companies still shivered with apprehension when the great meteor showers went sweeping like a gale through the orbits of the inner worlds.

Everything depends, of course, on what one means by the word meteor. Each lump of cosmic slag that reaches the surface of the Earth has a million smaller brethren that perish utterly in the no-man's-land where the atmosphere has not quite ended and space has yet to begin –

112

that ghostly region where the weird Aurora sometimes walks by night.

These are the familiar shooting stars, seldom larger than a pin's head, and these in turn are outnumbered a million-fold again by particles too small to leave any visible trace of their dying as they drift down from the sky. All of them, the countless specks of dust, the rare boulders and even the wandering mountains that Earth encounters perhaps once every million years – all of them are meteors.

For the purposes of space-flight, a meteor is only of interest if, on penetrating the hull of a ship, it leaves a hole large enough to be dangerous. This is a matter of relative speeds as well as size. Tables have been prepared showing approximate collision times for various parts of the Solar System – and for various sizes of meteors down to masses of a few milligrams.

That which had struck the *Star Queen* was a giant, being nearly a centimeter across and weighing all of ten grams. According to the table the waiting-time for collision with such a monster was of the order of ten to the ninth days – say three million years. The virtual certainty that such an occurrence would not happen again in the course of human history gave Grant and McNeil very little consolation.

However, things might have been worse. The *Star Queen* was 115 days on her orbit and had only thirty still to go. She was traveling, as did all freighters, on the long tangential ellipse kissing the orbits of Earth and Venus on opposite sides of the Sun. The fast liners could cut across from planet to planet at three times her speed – and ten times her fuel consumption – but she must plod along her predetermined track like a streetcar, taking 145 days, more or less, for each journey.

Anything more unlike the early-twentieth-century idea of a spaceship than the *Star Queen* would be hard to

113

imagine. She consisted of two spheres, one fifty and the other twenty meters in diameter, joined by a cylinder about a hundred meters long. The whole structure looked like a match-stick-and-Plasticine model of a hydrogen atom. Crew, cargo, and controls were in the larger sphere, while the smaller one held the atomic motors and was – to put it mildly – out of bounds to living matter.

The *Star Queen* had been built in space and could never have lifted herself even from the surface of the Moon. Under full power her ion drive could produce an acceleration of a twentieth of a gravity, which in an hour would give her all the velocity she needed to change from a satellite of the Earth to one of Venus.

Hauling cargo up from the planets was the job of the powerful little chemical rockets. In a month the tugs would be climbing up from Venus to meet her, but the *Star Queen* would not be stopping for there would be no one at the controls. She would continue blindly on her orbit, speeding past Venus at miles a second – and five months later she would be back at the orbit of the Earth, though Earth itself would then be far away.

It is surprising how long it takes to do a simple addition when your life depends on the answer. Grant ran down the short column of figures half a dozen times before he finally gave up hope that the total would change. Then he sat doodling nervously on the white plastic of the pilot's desk.

'With all possible economies,' he said, 'we can last about twenty days. That means we'll be ten days out of Venus when . . .' His voice trailed off into silence.

Ten days didn't sound much – but it might just as well have been ten years. Grant thought sardonically of all the hack adventure writers who had used just this situation in

114

their stories and radio serials. In these circumstances, according to the carbon-copy experts – few of whom had ever gone beyond the Moon – there were three things that could happen.

The popular solution – which had become almost a cliché – was to turn the ship into a glorified greenhouse or a hydroponic farm and let photosynthesis do the rest. Alternatively one could perform prodigies of chemical or atomic engineering – explained in tedious technical detail – and build an oxygen manufacturing plant which would not only save your life – and of course the heroine's – but also make you the owner of fabulously valuable patents. The third or *deus ex machina* solution was the arrival of a convenient spaceship which happened to be matching your course and velocity exactly.

But that was fiction and things were different in real life. Although the first idea was sound in theory there wasn't even a packet of grass seed aboard the *Star Queen*. As for feats of inventive engineering, two men – however brilliant and however desperate – were not likely to improve in a few days on the work of scores of great industrial research organizations over a full century.

The spaceship that 'happened to be passing' was almost, by definition, impossible. Even if other freighters had been coasting on the same elliptic path – and Grant knew there were none – then by the very laws that governed their movements they would always keep their original separations. It was not quite impossible that a liner, racing on its hyperbolic orbit, might pass within a few hundred thousand kilometers of them – but at a speed so great that it would be as inaccessible as Pluto.

'If we threw out the cargo,' said McNeil at last, 'would we have a chance of changing our orbit?'

Grant shook his head.

'I'd hoped so,' he replied, 'but it won't work. We could reach Venus in a week if we wished – but we'd have no fuel for braking and nothing from the planet could catch us as we went past.'

'Not even a liner?'

'According to *Lloyd's Register* Venus has only a couple of freighters at the moment. In any case it would be a practically impossible maneuver. Even if it could match our speed how would the rescue ship get back? It would need about fifty kilometers a second for the whole job!'

'If we can't figure a way out,' said McNeil, 'maybe someone on Venus can. We'd better talk to them.'

'I'm going to,' Grant replied, 'as soon as I've decided what to say. Go and get the transmitter aligned, will you?'

He watched McNeil as he floated out of the room. The engineer was probably going to give trouble in the days that lay ahead. Until now they had got on well enough – like most stout men McNeil was good-natured and easygoing. But now Grant realized that he lacked fiber. He had become flabby – physically and mentally – living too long in space.

A buzzer sounded on the transmitter switchboard. The parabolic mirror out on the hull was aimed at the gleaming arc-lamp of Venus, only ten million kilometers away and moving on an almost parallel path. The three-millimeter waves from the ship's transmitter would make the trip in little more than half a minute. There was bitterness in the knowledge that they were only thirty seconds from safety.

The automatic monitor on Venus gave its impersonal *Go ahead* signal and Grant began to talk steadily, and he hoped, quite dispassionately. He gave a careful analysis of the situation and ended with a request for advice. His fears concerning McNeil he left unspoken. For one thing he knew that the engineer would be monitoring him at the transmitter.

As yet no one on Venus would have heard the message, even though the transmission time-lag was over. It would still be coiled up in the recorder spools, but in a few minutes an unsuspecting signal officer would arrive to play it over.

He would have no idea of the bombshell that was about to burst, triggering trains of sympathetic ripples on all the inhabited worlds as television and newssheet took up the refrain. An accident in space has a dramatic quality that crowds all other items from the headlines.

Until now Grant had been too preoccupied with his own safety to give much thought to the cargo in his charge. A sea captain of ancient times, whose first thought was for his ship, might have been shocked by the attitude. Grant, however, had reason on his side.

The *Star Queen* could never founder, could never run upon uncharted rocks or pass silently, as so many ships have passed, forever from the knowledge of man. She was safe, whatever might befall her crew. If she was undisturbed she would continue to retrace her orbit with such precision that men might set their calendars by her for centuries to come.

The cargo, Grant suddenly remembered, was insured for over twenty million dollars. There were not many goods valuable enough to be shipped from world to world and most of the crates in the hold were worth more than their weight – or rather their mass – in gold. Perhaps some items might be useful in this emergency and Grant went to the safe to find the loading schedule.

He was sorting the thin, tough sheets when McNeil came back into the cabin.

'I've been reducing the air pressure,' he said. 'The hull

shows some leaks that wouldn't have mattered in the usual way.'

Grant nodded absently as he passed a bundle of sheets over to McNeil.

'Here's our loading schedule. I suggest we both run through it in case there's anything in the cargo that may help.'

If it did nothing else, he might have added, it would at least give them something to occupy their minds.

As he ran down the long columns of numbered items – a complete cross-section of interplanetary commerce – Grant found himself wondering what lay behind these inanimate symbols. *Item 347 – 1 book – 4 kilos gross.*

He whistled as he noticed that it was a starred item, insured for a hundred thousand dollars, and he suddenly remembered hearing on the radio that the Hesperian Museum had just bought a first edition *Seven Pillars of Wisdom*.

A few sheets later was a very contrasting item, *Miscellaneous books – 25 kilos – no intrinsic value.*

It had cost a small fortune to ship those books to Venus, yet they were of 'no intrinsic value.' Grant let his imagination loose on the problem. Perhaps someone who was leaving Earth forever was taking with him to a new world his most cherished treasures – the dozen or so volumes that above all others had most shaped his mind.

Item 564 – 12 reels film.

That, of course, would be the Neronian super-epic, *While Rome Burns*, which had left Earth just one jump ahead of the censor. Venus was waiting for it with considerable impatience.

Medical supplies – 50 kilos. Case of cigars – 1 kilo. Precision instruments – 75 kilos. So the list went on. Each item was something rare or something which the industry

118

and science of a younger civilization could not yet produce.

The cargo was sharply divided into two classes – blatant luxury or sheer necessity. There was little in between. And there was nothing, nothing at all, which gave Grant the slightest hope. He did not see how it could have been otherwise, but that did not prevent him from feeling a quite unreasonable disappointment.

The reply from Venus, when it came at last, took nearly an hour to run through the recorder. It was a questionnaire so detailed that Grant wondered morosely if he'd live long enough to answer it. Most of the queries were technical ones concerning the ship. The experts on two planets were pooling their brains in the attempt to save the *Star Queen* and her cargo.

'Well, what do you think of it?' Grant asked McNeil when the other had finished running through the message. He was watching the engineer carefully for any further sign of strain.

There was a long pause before McNeil spoke. Then he shrugged his shoulders and his first words were an echo of Grant's own thoughts.

'It will certainly keep us busy. I won't be able to do all these tests in under a day. I can see what they're driving at most of the time, but some of the questions are just plain crazy.'

Grant had suspected that, but said nothing as the other continued.

'Rate of hull leakage – that's sensible enough, but why should anyone want to know the efficiency of our radiation screening? I think they're trying to keep up our morale by pretending they have some bright ideas – or else they want to keep us too busy to worry.'

Grant was relieved and yet annoyed by McNeil's calmness – relieved because he had been afraid of another scene and annoyed because McNeil was not fitting at all neatly into the mental category he had prepared for him. Was that first momentary lapse typical of the man or might it have happened to anyone?

Grant, to whom the world was very much a place of blacks and whites, felt angry at being unable to decide whether McNeil was cowardly or courageous. That he might be both was a possibility that never occurred to him.

There is a timelessness about space-flight that is unmatched by any other experience of man. Even on the Moon there are shadows that creep sluggishly from crag to crag as the sun makes its slow march across the sky. Earthward there is always the great clock of the spinning globe, marking the hours with continents for hands. But on a long voyage in a gyro-stabilized ship the same patterns of sunlight lie unmoving on wall or floor as the chronometer ticks off its meaningless hours and days.

Grant and McNeil had long since learned to regulate their lives accordingly. In deep space they moved and thought with a leisureliness that would vanish quickly enough when a voyage was nearing its end and the time for braking maneuvers had arrived. Though they were now under sentence of death, they continued along the well-worn grooves of habit.

Every day Grant carefully wrote up the log, checked the ship's position and carried out his various routine duties. McNeil was also behaving normally as far as could be told, though Grant suspected that some of the technical maintenance was being carried out with a very light hand.

It was now three days since the meteor had struck. For

the last twenty-four hours Earth and Venus had been in conference and Grant wondered when he would hear the result of their deliberations. He did not believe that the finest technical brains in the Solar System could save them now, but it was hard to abandon hope when everything still seemed so normal and the air was still clean and fresh.

On the fourth day Venus spoke again. Shorn of its technicalities, the message was nothing more or less than a funeral oration. Grant and McNeil had been written off, but they were given elaborate instructions concerning the safety of the cargo.

Back on Earth the astronomers were computing all the possible rescue orbits that might make contact with the *Star Queen* in the next few years. There was even a chance that she might be reached from Earth six or seven months later, when she was back at aphelion, but the maneuver could be carried out only by a fast liner with no payload and would cost a fortune in fuel.

McNeil vanished soon after this message came through. At first Grant was a little relieved. If McNeil chose to look after himself that was his own affair. Besides there were various letters to write – though the last-will-and-testament business could come later.

It was McNeil's turn to prepare the 'evening' meal, a duty he enjoyed for he took good care of his stomach. When the usual sounds from the galley were not forthcoming Grant went in search of his crew.

He found McNeil lying in his bunk, very much at peace with the universe. Hanging in the air beside him was a large metal crate which had been roughly forced open. Grant had no need to examine it closely to guess its contents. A glance at McNeil was enough.

'It's a dirty shame,' said the engineer without a trace of

embarrassment, 'to suck this stuff up through a tube. Can't you put on some "g" so that we can drink it properly?'

Grant stared at him with angry contempt, but McNeil returned his gaze unabashed.

'Oh, don't be a sourpuss! Have some yourself – what does it matter now?'

He pushed across a bottle and Grant fielded it deftly as it floated by. It was a fabulously valuable wine – he remembered the consignment now – and the contents of that small crate must be worth thousands.

'I don't think there's any need,' said Grant severely, 'to behave like a pig – even in these circumstances.'

McNeil wasn't drunk yet. He had only reached the brightly lighted anteroom of intoxication and had not lost all contact with the drab outer world.

'I am prepared,' he said with great solemnity, 'to listen to any good argument against my present course of action – a course which seems eminently sensible to me. But you'd better convince me quickly while I'm still amenable to reason.'

He pressed the plastic bulb again and a purple jet shot into his mouth.

'Apart from the fact that you're stealing Company property which will certainly be salvaged sooner or later – you can hardly stay drunk for several weeks.'

'That,' said McNeil thoughtfully, 'remains to be seen.'

'I don't think so,' retorted Grant. Bracing himself against the wall, he gave the crate a vicious shove that sent it flying through the open doorway.

As he dived after it and slammed the door he heard McNeil shout, 'Well, of all the dirty tricks!'

It would take the engineer some time – particularly in his present condition – to unbuckle himself and follow.

Grant steered the crate back to the hold and locked the door. As there was never any need to lock the hold when the ship was in space McNeil wouldn't have a key for it himself and Grant could hide the duplicate that was kept in the control cabin.

McNeil was singing when, some time later, Grant went back past his room. He still had a couple of bottles for company and was shouting:

> 'We don't care *where* the oxygen goes
> If it doesn't get into the wine . . .'

Grant, whose education had been severely technical, couldn't place the quotation. As he paused to listen he suddenly found himself shaken by an emotion which, to do him justice, he did not for a moment recognize.

It passed as swiftly as it had come, leaving him sick and trembling. For the first time, he realized that his dislike of McNeil was slowly turning to hatred.

It is a fundamental rule of space-flight that, for sound psychological reasons, the minimum crew on a long journey shall consist of not less than three men.

But rules are made to be broken and the *Star Queen*'s owners had obtained full authority from the Board of Space Control and the insurance companies when the freighter set off for Venus without her regular captain.

At the last moment he had been taken ill and there was no replacement. Since the planets are disinclined to wait upon man and his affairs, if she did not sail on time she would not sail at all.

Millions of dollars were involved – so she sailed. Grant and McNeil were both highly capable men and they had no objection at all to earning double their normal pay for very little extra work. Despite fundamental differences in temperament, they got on well enough in ordinary circumstances. It was nobody's fault that circumstances were now very far from ordinary.

Three days without food, it is said, is long enough to remove most of the subtle differences between a civilized man and a savage. Grant and McNeil were still in no physical discomfort. But their imaginations had been only too active and they now had more in common with two hungry Pacific Islanders in a lost canoe than either would have cared to admit.

For there was one aspect of the situation, and that the most important of all, which had never been mentioned. When the last figures on Grant's writing-pad had been checked and rechecked, the calculation was still not quite complete. Instantly each man had made the one further step, each had arrived simultaneously at the same unspoken result.

It was terribly simple – a macabre parody of those problems in first-year arithmetic that begin, 'If six men take two days to assemble five helicopters, how long . . .'

The oxygen would last *two* men for about twenty days, and Venus was thirty days away. One did not have to be a calculating prodigy to see at once that one man, and one man only, might yet live to walk the metal streets of Port Hesperus.

The acknowledged deadline was twenty days ahead, but the unmentioned one was only ten days off. Until that time there would still be enough air for two men – and thereafter for one man only for the rest of the voyage. To a sufficiently detached observer the situation would have been very entertaining.

It was obvious that the conspiracy of silence could not last much longer. But it is not easy, even at the best of times, for two people to decide amicably which one of them shall commit suicide. It is still more difficult when they are no longer on speaking terms.

Grant wished to be perfectly fair. Therefore the only thing to do was to wait until McNeil sobered up and then to put the question to him frankly. He could think best at his desk, so he went to the control cabin and strapped himself down in the pilot's chair.

For a while he stared thoughtfully into nothingness. It would be better, he decided, to broach the matter by correspondence, especially while diplomatic relations were in their present state. He clipped a sheet of notepaper on the writing-pad and began, 'Dear McNeil . . .' Then he tore it out and started again, 'McNeil . . .'

It took him the best part of three hours and even then he wasn't wholly satisfied. There were some things it was so darned difficult to put down on paper. But at last he managed to finish. He sealed the letter and locked it away in his safe. It could wait for a day or two.

Few of the waiting millions on Earth and Venus could have any idea of the tensions that were slowly building up aboard the *Star Queen*. For days press and radio had been full of fantastic rescue schemes. On three worlds there was hardly any other topic of conversation. But only the faintest echo of the planet-wide tumult reached the two men who were its cause.

At any time the station on Venus could speak to the *Star Queen*, but there was so little that could be said. One could not with any decency give words of encouragement to men in the condemned cell, even when there was some slight uncertainty about the actual date of execution.

So Venus contented itself with a few routine messages every day and blocked the steady stream of exhortations and newspaper offers that came pouring in from Earth. As a result private radio companies on Earth made frantic attempts to contact the *Star Queen* directly. They failed, simply because it never occurred to Grant and McNeil to focus their receiver anywhere except on Venus, now so tantalizingly near at hand.

There had been an embarrassing interlude when McNeil emerged from his cabin, but though relations were not particularly cordial, life aboard the *Star Queen* continued much as before.

Grant spent most of his waking hours in the pilot's position, calculating approach maneuvers and writing interminable letters to his wife. He could have spoken to her had he wished, but the thought of all those millions of waiting ears had prevented him from doing so. Interplanetary speech circuits were supposed to be private – but too many people would be interested in this one.

In a couple of days, Grant assured himself, he would hand his letter to McNeil and they could decide what was to be done. Such a delay would also give McNeil a chance of raising the subject himself. That he might have other reasons for his hesitation was something Grant's conscious mind still refused to admit.

He often wondered how McNeil was spending his time. The engineer had a large library of microfilm books, for he read widely and his range of interests was unusual. His favorite book, Grant knew, was *Jurgen* and perhaps even now he was trying to forget his doom by losing himself in its strange magic. Others of McNeil's books were less respectable and not a few were of the class curiously described as 'curious.'

The truth of the matter was that McNeil was far too subtle and complicated a personality for Grant to understand. He was a hedonist and enjoyed the pleasures of life all the more for being cut off from them for months at a time. But he was by no means the moral weakling that the unimaginative and somewhat puritanical Grant had supposed.

It was true that he had collapsed completely under the initial shock and that his behavior over the wine was – by Grant's standards – reprehensible. But McNeil had had his breakdown and had recovered. Therein lay the difference between him and the hard but brittle Grant.

Though the normal routine of duties had been resumed by tacit consent, it did little to reduce the sense of strain. Grant and McNeil avoided each other as much as possible except when mealtimes brought them together. When they did meet, they behaved with an exaggerated politeness as if each were striving to be perfectly normal – and inexplicably failing.

Grant had hoped that McNeil would himself broach the subject of suicide, thus sparing him a very awkward duty. When the engineer stubbornly refused to do anything of the sort it added to Grant's resentment and contempt. To make matters worse he was now suffering from nightmares and sleeping very badly.

The nightmare was always the same. When he was a child it had often happened that at bedtime he had been reading a story far too exciting to be left until morning. To avoid detection he had continued reading under the bedclothes by flashlight, curled up in a snug white-walled cocoon. Every ten minutes or so the air had become too stifling to breathe and his emergence into the delicious cool air had been a major part of the fun.

Now, thirty years later, these innocent childhood hours returned to haunt him. He was dreaming that he could not escape from the suffocating sheets while the air was steadily and remorselessly thickening around him.

He had intended to give McNeil the letter after two days, yet somehow he put it off again. This procrastination was very unlike Grant, but he managed to persuade himself that it was a perfectly reasonable thing to do.

He was giving McNeil a chance to redeem himself – to prove that he wasn't a coward by raising the matter himself. That McNeil might be waiting for him to do exactly the same thing somehow never occurred to Grant.

The all-too-literal deadline was only five days off when, for the first time, Grant's mind brushed lightly against the thought of murder. He had been sitting after the 'evening' meal, trying to relax as McNeil clattered around in the galley with, he considered, quite unnecessary noise.

What use, he asked himself, was the engineer to the world? He had no responsibilities and no family – no one would be any the worse off for his death. Grant, on the other hand, had a wife and three children of whom he was moderately fond, though for some obscure reason they responded with little more than dutiful affection.

Any impartial judge would have no difficulty in deciding which of them should survive. If McNeil had a spark of decency in him he would have come to the same conclusion already. Since he appeared to have done nothing of the sort he had forfeited all further claims to consideration.

Such was the elemental logic of Grant's subconscious mind, which had arrived at its answer days before but had only now succeeded in attracting the attention for which it had been clamoring. To Grant's credit he at once rejected the thought with horror.

He was an upright and honorable person with a very strict code of behavior. Even the vagrant homicidal impulses of what is misleadingly called 'normal' man had seldom ruffled his mind. But in the days – the very few days – left to him, they would come more and more often.

The air had now become noticeably fouler. Though there was still no real difficulty in breathing, it was a constant reminder of what lay ahead, and Grant found that it was keeping him from sleep. This was not pure loss, as it helped to break the power of his nightmares, but he was becoming physically run down.

His nerve was also rapidly deteriorating, a state of affairs accentuated by the fact that McNeil seemed to be behaving with unexpected and annoying calmness. Grant realized that he had come to the stage when it would be dangerous to delay the showdown any longer.

McNeil was in his room as usual when Grant went up to the control cabin to collect the letter he had locked away in the safe – it seemed a lifetime ago. He wondered if he need add anything more to it. Then he realized that this was only another excuse for delay. Resolutely he made his way toward McNeil's cabin.

A single neutron begins the chain-reaction that in an instant can destroy a million lives and the toil of generations. Equally insignificant and unimportant are the trigger-events which can sometimes change a man's course of action and so alter the whole pattern of his future.

Nothing could have been more trivial than that which made Grant pause in the corridor outside McNeil's room. In the ordinary way he would not even have noticed it. It was the smell of smoke – tobacco smoke.

The thought that the sybaritic engineer had so little self-control that he was squandering the last precious liters of oxygen in such a manner filled Grant with blinding fury. He stood for a moment quite paralyzed with the intensity of his emotion.

Then slowly, he crumpled the letter in his hand. The

thought which had first been an unwelcome intruder, then a casual speculation, was at last fully accepted. McNeil had had his chance and had proved, by his unbelievable selfishness, unworthy of it. Very well – he could die.

The speed with which Grant had arrived at this conclusion would not have deceived the most amateurish of psychologists. It was relief as much as hatred that drove him away from McNeil's room. He had wanted to convince himself that there would be no need to do the honorable thing, to suggest some game of chance that would give them each an equal probability of life.

This was the excuse he needed, and he had seized upon it to salve his conscience. For though he might plan and even carry out a murder, Grant was the sort of person who would have to do it according to his own particular moral code.

As it happened he was – not for the first time – badly misjudging McNeil. The engineer was a heavy smoker and tobacco was quite essential to his mental well-being even in normal circumstances. How much more essential it was now, Grant, who only smoked occasionally and without much enjoyment, could never have appreciated.

McNeil had satisfied himself by careful calculation that four cigarettes a day would make no measurable difference whatsoever to the ship's oxygen endurance, whereas they would make all the difference in the world to his own nerves and hence indirectly to Grant's.

But it was no use explaining this to Grant. So he had smoked in private and with a self-control he found agreeably, almost voluptuously, surprising. It was sheer bad luck that Grant had detected one of the day's four cigarettes.

For a man who had only at that moment talked himself into murder, Grant's actions were remarkably methodical.

Without hesitation, he hurried back to the control room and opened the medicine chest with its neatly labeled compartments, designed for almost every emergency that could occur in space.

Even the ultimate emergency had been considered, for there behind its retaining elastic bands was the tiny bottle he had been seeking, the image of which had been lying hidden far down in the unknown depths of his mind through all these days. It bore a white label carrying a skull-and-crossbones, and beneath them the words: *Approx. one-half gram will cause painless and almost instantaneous death.*

The poison was painless and instantaneous – that was good. But even more important was a fact unmentioned on the label. It was also tasteless.

The contrast between the meals prepared by Grant and those organized with considerable skill and care by McNeil was striking. Anyone who was fond of food and who spent a good deal of his life in space usually learned the art of cooking in self-defense. McNeil had done this long ago.

To Grant, on the other hand, eating was one of those necessary but annoying jobs which had to be got through as quickly as possible. His cooking reflected this opinion. McNeil had ceased to grumble about it, but he would have been very interested in the trouble Grant was taking over this particular meal.

If he noticed any increasing nervousness on Grant's part as the meal progressed, he said nothing. They ate almost in silence, but that was not unusual for they had long since exhausted most of the possibilities of light conversation. When the last dishes – deep bowls with inturned rims to prevent the contents drifting out – had been cleared away, Grant went into the galley to prepare the coffee.

He took rather a long time, for at the last moment something quite maddening and quite ridiculous happened. He suddenly recalled one of the film classics of the last century in which the fabulous Charlie Chaplin tried to poison an unwanted wife – and then accidentally changed the glasses.

No memory could have been more unwelcome, for it left him shaken with a gust of silent hysteria. Poe's *Imp of the Perverse*, that demon who delights in defying the careful canons of self-preservation, was at work and it was a good minute before Grant could regain his self-control.

He was sure that, outwardly at least, he was quite calm as he carried in the two plastic containers and their drinking-tubes. There was no danger of confusing them, for the engineer's had the letters MAC painted boldly across it.

At the thought Grant nearly relapsed into psychopathic giggles but just managed to regain control with the somber reflection that his nerves must be in even worse condition than he had imagined.

He watched, fascinated, though without appearing to do so, as McNeil toyed with his cup. The engineer seemed in no great hurry and was staring moodily into space. Then he put his lips to the drinking tube and sipped.

A moment later he spluttered slightly – and an icy hand seemed to seize Grant's heart and hold it tight. Then McNeil turned to him and said evenly, 'You've made it properly for once. It's quite hot.'

Slowly, Grant's heart resumed its interrupted work. He did not trust himself to speak, but managed a noncommittal nod. McNeil parked the cup carefully in the air, a few inches away from his face.

He seemed very thoughtful, as if weighing his words for some important remark. Grant cursed himself for having made the drink so hot – that was just the sort of detail that hanged murderers. If McNeil waited much longer he would probably betray himself through nervousness.

'I suppose,' said McNeil in a quietly conversational sort of way, 'it has occurred to you that there's still enough air to last one of us to Venus?'

Grant forced his jangling nerves under control and tore his eyes away from that hypnotic cup. His throat seemed very dry as he answered, 'It – it had crossed my mind.'

McNeil touched his cup, found it still too hot and continued thoughtfully, 'Then wouldn't it be more sensible if one of us decided to walk out of the airlock, say – or to take some of the poison in there?' He jerked his thumb toward the medicine chest, just visible from where they were sitting.

Grant nodded.

'The only trouble, of course,' added the engineer, 'is to decide which of us will be the unlucky one. I suppose it would have to be by picking a card or in some other quite arbitrary way.'

Grant stared at McNeil with a fascination that almost outweighed his mounting nervousness. He had never believed that the engineer could discuss the subject so calmly. Grant was sure he suspected nothing. Obviously McNeil's thoughts had been running on parallel lines to his own and it was scarcely even a coincidence that he had chosen this time, of all times, to raise the matter.

McNeil was watching him intently, as if judging his reactions.

'You're right,' Grant heard himself say. 'We must talk it over.'

'Yes,' said McNeil quite impassively. 'We must.' Then he reached for his cup again, put the drinking tube to his lips and sucked slowly.

Grant could not wait until he had finished. To his surprise the relief he had been expecting did not come. He even felt a stab of regret, though it was not quite remorse. It was a little late to think of it now, but he suddenly remembered that he would be alone in the *Star Queen*, haunted by his thoughts, for more than three weeks before rescue came.

He did not wish to see McNeil die, and he felt rather sick. Without another glance at his victim he launched himself toward the exit.

Immovably fixed, the fierce sun and the unwinking stars looked down upon the *Star Queen*, which seemed as motionless as they. There was no way of telling that the tiny dumbbell of the ship had now almost reached her maximum speed and that millions of horsepower were chained within the smaller sphere, waiting for the moment of its release. There was no way of telling, indeed, that she carried any life at all.

An airlock on the night-side of the ship slowly opened, letting a blaze of light escape from the interior. The brilliant circle looked very strange hanging there in the darkness. Then it was abruptly eclipsed as two figures floated out of the ship.

One was much bulkier than the other, and for a rather important reason – it was wearing a space-suit. Now there are some forms of apparel that may be worn or discarded as the fancy pleases with no other ill-effects than a possible loss of social prestige. But space-suits are not among them.

Something not easy to follow was happening in the darkness. Then the smaller figure began to move, slowly at first but with rapidly mounting speed. It swept out of the shadow of the ship into the full blast of the sun, and now one could see that strapped to its back was a small gas-cylinder from which a fine mist was jetting to vanish almost instantly into space.

It was a crude but effective rocket. There was no danger that the ship's minute gravitational pull would drag the body back to it again.

Rotating slightly, the corpse dwindled against the stars and vanished from sight in less than a minute. Quite motionless, the figure in the airlock watched it go. Then the outer door swung shut, the circle of brilliance vanished and only the pale Earthlight still glinted on the shadowed wall of the ship.

Nothing else whatsoever happened for twenty-three days.

The captain of the *Hercules* turned to his mate with a sigh of relief.

'I was afraid he couldn't do it. It must have been a colossal job to break his orbit single-handed – and with the air as thick as it must be by now. How soon can we get to him?'

'It will take about an hour. He's still got quite a bit of eccentricity but we can correct that.'

'Good. Signal the *Leviathan* and *Titan* that we can make contact and ask them to take off, will you? But I wouldn't drop any tips to your news commentator friends until we're safely locked.'

The mate had the grace to blush. 'I don't intend to,' he said in a slightly hurt voice as he pecked delicately at the keys of his calculator. The answer that flashed instantly on the screen seemed to displease him.

'We'd better board and bring the *Queen* down to circular speed ourselves before we call the other tugs,' he said, 'otherwise we'll be wasting a lot of fuel. She's still got a velocity excess of nearly a kilometer a second.'

'Good idea – tell *Leviathan* and *Titan* to stand by but not to blast until we give them the new orbit.'

While the message was on its way down through the unbroken cloudbanks that covered half the sky below, the mate remarked thoughtfully, 'I wonder what he's feeling like now?'

'I can tell you. He's so pleased to be alive that he doesn't give a hoot about anything else.'

'Still, I'm not sure I'd like to have left my shipmate in space so that I could get home.'

'It's not the sort of thing that anyone would like to do. But you heard the broadcast – they'd talked it over calmly and the loser went out of the airlock. It was the only sensible way.'

'Sensible, perhaps – but it's pretty horrible to let someone else sacrifice himself in such a cold-blooded way so that you can live.'

'Don't be a ruddy sentimentalist. I'll bet that if it happened to us you'd push me out before I could even say my prayers.'

'Unless you did it to me first. Still, I don't think it's ever likely to happen to the *Hercules*. Five days out of port's the longest we've ever been, isn't it? Talk about the romance of the spaceways!'

The captain didn't reply. He was peering into the eyepiece of the navigating telescope, for the *Star Queen* should now be within optical range. There was a long pause while he adjusted the vernier controls. Then he gave a little sigh of satisfaction.

'There she is – about nine-fifty kilometers away. Tell the crew to stand by – and send a message to cheer him up. Say we'll be there in thirty minutes even if it isn't quite true.'

Slowly the thousand-meter nylon ropes yielded beneath the strain as they absorbed the relative momentum of the ships, then slackened again as the *Star Queen* and the *Hercules* rebounded toward each other. The electric winches began to turn and, like a spider crawling up its thread, the *Hercules* drew alongside the freighter.

Men in space-suits sweated with heavy reaction units – tricky work, this – until the airlocks had registered and could be coupled together. The outer doors slid aside and the air in the locks mingled, fresh with foul. As the mate of the *Hercules* waited, oxygen cylinder in hand, he wondered what condition the survivor would be in. Then the *Star Queen*'s inner door slid open.

For a moment, the two men stood looking at each other across the short corridor that now connected the two airlocks. The mate was surprised and a little disappointed to find that he felt no particular sense of drama.

So much had happened to make this moment possible that its actual achievement was almost an anticlimax, even in the instant when it was slipping into the past. He wished – for he was an incurable romantic – that he could think of something memorable to say, some 'Doctor Livingstone, I presume?' phrase that would pass into history.

But all he actually said was, 'Well, McNeil, I'm pleased to see you.'

Though he was considerably thinner and somewhat haggard, McNeil had stood the ordeal well. He breathed gratefully the blast of raw oxygen and rejected the idea that he might like to lie down and sleep. As he explained, he had done very little but sleep for the last week to conserve air. The first mate looked relieved. He had been afraid he might have to wait for the story.

The cargo was being trans-shipped and the other two tugs were climbing up from the great blinding crescent of Venus while McNeil retraced the events of the last few weeks and the mate made surreptitious notes.

He spoke quite calmly and impersonally, as if he were relating some adventure that had happened to another person, or indeed had never happened at all. Which was, of course, to some extent the case, though it would be unfair to suggest that McNeil was telling any lies.

He invented nothing, but he omitted a good deal. He had had three weeks in which to prepare his narrative and he did not think it had any flaws . . .

Grant had already reached the door when McNeil called softly after him, 'What's the hurry? I thought we had something to discuss.'

Grant grabbed at the doorway to halt his headlong flight. He turned slowly and stared unbelievingly at the engineer. McNeil should be already dead – but he was sitting quite comfortably, looking at him with a most peculiar expression.

'Sit down,' he said sharply – and in that moment it suddenly seemed that all authority had passed to him. Grant did so, quite without volition. Something had gone wrong, though what it was he could not imagine.

The silence in the control room seemed to last for ages. Then McNeil said rather sadly, 'I'd hoped better of you, Grant.'

At last Grant found his voice, though he could barely recognize it.

'What do you mean?' he whispered.

'What do you think I mean?' replied McNeil, with what

seemed no more than mild irritation. 'This little attempt of yours to poison me, of course.'

Grant's tottering world collapsed at last, but he no longer cared greatly one way or the other. McNeil began to examine his beautifully kept fingernails with some attention.

'As a matter of interest,' he said, in the way that one might ask the time, 'when did you decide to kill me?'

The sense of unreality was so overwhelming that Grant felt he was acting a part, that this had nothing to do with real life at all.

'Only this morning,' he said, and believed it.

'Hmm,' remarked McNeil, obviously without much conviction. He rose to his feet and moved over to the medicine chest. Grant's eyes followed him as he fumbled in the compartment and came back with the little poison bottle. It still appeared to be full. Grant had been careful about that.

'I suppose I should get pretty mad about this whole business,' McNeil continued conversationally, holding the bottle between thumb and forefinger. 'But somehow I'm not. Maybe it's because I never had many illusions about human nature. And, of course, I saw it coming a long time ago.'

Only the last phrase really reached Grant's consciousness.

'You – saw it coming?'

'Heavens, yes! You're too transparent to make a good criminal, I'm afraid. And now that your little plot's failed it leaves us both in an embarrassing position, doesn't it?'

To this masterly understatement there seemed no possible reply.

'By rights,' continued the engineer thoughtfully, 'I should now work myself into a good temper, call Venus

Central, and denounce you to the authorities. But it would be a rather pointless thing to do, and I've never been much good at losing my temper anyway. Of course, you'll say that's because I'm too lazy – but I don't think so.'

He gave Grant a twisted smile.

'Oh, I know what you think about me – you've got me neatly classified in that orderly mind of yours, haven't you? I'm soft and self-indulgent, I haven't any moral courage – or any morals for that matter – and I don't give a damn for anyone but myself. Well, I'm not denying it. Maybe it's ninety percent true. But the odd ten percent is mighty important, Grant!'

Grant felt in no condition to indulge in psychological analysis, and this seemed hardly the time for anything of the sort. Besides, he was still obsessed with the problem of his failure and the mystery of McNeil's continued existence. McNeil, who knew this perfectly well, seemed in no hurry to satisfy his curiosity.

'Well, what do you intend to do now?' Grant asked, anxious to get it over.

'I would like,' said McNeil calmly, 'to carry on our discussion where it was interrupted by the coffee.'

'You don't mean – '

'But I do. Just as if nothing had happened.'

'That doesn't make sense. You've got something up your sleeve!' cried Grant.

McNeil sighed. He put down the poison bottle and looked firmly at Grant.

'*You're* in no position to accuse me of plotting anything. To repeat my earlier remarks, I am suggesting that we decide which one of us shall take poison – only we don't want any more unilateral decisions. Also' – he picked up the bottle again – 'it will be the real thing this time. The stuff in here merely leaves a bad taste in the mouth.'

A light was beginning to dawn in Grant's mind. 'You changed the poison!'

'Naturally. You may think you're a good actor, Grant, but frankly – from the balcony – I thought the performance stank. I could tell you were plotting something, probably before you knew it yourself. In the last few days I've deloused the ship pretty thoroughly. Thinking of all the ways you might have done me in was quite amusing and helped to pass the time. The poison was so obvious that it was the first thing I fixed. But I rather overdid the danger signals and nearly gave myself away when I took the first sip. Salt doesn't go at all well with coffee.'

He gave that wry grin again. 'Also, I'd hoped for something more subtle. So far I've found fifteen infallible ways of murdering anyone aboard a spaceship. But I don't propose to describe them now.'

This was fantastic, Grant thought. He was being treated, not like a criminal, but like a rather stupid schoolboy who hadn't done his homework properly.

'Yet you're still willing,' said Grant unbelievingly, 'to start all over again? And you'd take the poison yourself if you lost?'

McNeil was silent for a long time. Then he began, slowly, 'I can see that you still don't believe me. It doesn't fit at all nicely into your tidy little picture, does it? But perhaps I can make you understand. It's really quite simple.

'I've enjoyed life, Grant, without many scruples or regrets – but the better part of it's over now and I don't cling to what's left as desperately as you might imagine. Yet while I *am* alive I'm rather particular about some things.

'It may surprise you to know that I've got any ideals at all. But I have, Grant – I've always tried to act like a

141

civilized, rational being. I've not always succeeded. When I've failed I've tried to redeem myself.'

He paused, and when he resumed it was as though he, and not Grant, was on the defensive. 'I've never exactly liked you, Grant, but I've often admired you and that's why I'm sorry it's come to this. I admired you most of all the day the ship was holed.'

For the first time, McNeil seemed to have some difficulty in choosing his words. When he spoke again he avoided Grant's eyes.

'I didn't behave very well then. Something happened that I thought was impossible. I've always been quite sure that I'd never lose my nerve but – well – it was so sudden it knocked me over.'

He attempted to hide his embarrassment by humor. 'The same sort of thing happened on my very first trip. I was sure *I'd* never be spacesick – and as a result I was much worse than if I had not been over-confident. But I got over it then – and again this time. It was one of the biggest surprises of my life, Grant, when I saw that you of all people were beginning to crack.

'Oh, yes – the business of the wines! I can see you're thinking about that. Well, that's one thing I *don't* regret. I said I'd always tried to act like a civilized man – and a civilized man should always know when to get drunk. But perhaps you wouldn't understand.'

Oddly enough, that was just what Grant was beginning to do. He had caught his first real glimpse of McNeil's intricate and tortuous personality and realized how utterly he had misjudged him. No – misjudged was not the right word. In many ways his judgment had been correct. But it had only touched the surface – he had never suspected the depths that lay beneath.

In a moment of insight that had never come before, and

from the nature of things could never come again, Grant understood the reasons behind McNeil's action. This was nothing so simple as a coward trying to reinstate himself in the eyes of the world, for no one need ever know what happened aboard the *Star Queen*.

In any case, McNeil probably cared nothing for the world's opinion, thanks to the sleek self-sufficiency that had so often annoyed Grant. But that very self-sufficiency meant that at all costs he must preserve his own good opinion of himself. Without it life would not be worth living – and McNeil had never accepted life save on his own terms.

The engineer was watching him intently and must have guessed that Grant was coming near the truth, for he suddenly changed his tone as though he was sorry he had revealed so much of his character.

'Don't think I get a quixotic pleasure from turning the other cheek,' he said. 'Just consider it from the point of view of pure logic. After all, we've got to come to *some* agreement.

'Has it occurred to you that if only one of us survives without a covering message from the other, he'll have a very uncomfortable time explaining just what happened?'

In his blind fury, Grant had completely forgotten this. But he did not believe it bulked at all important in McNeil's own thoughts.

'Yes,' he said, 'I suppose you're right.'

He felt far better now. All the hate had drained out of him and he was at peace. The truth was known and he accepted it. That it was so different from what he had imagined did not seem to matter now.

'Well, let's get it over,' he said unemotionally. 'There's a new pack of cards lying around somewhere.'

'I think we'd better speak to Venus first – both of us,'

143

replied McNeil, with peculiar emphasis. 'We want a complete agreement on record in case anyone asks awkward questions later.'

Grant nodded absently. He did not mind very much now one way or the other. He even smiled, ten minutes later, as he drew his card from the pack and laid it, face upward, beside McNeil's.

'So that's the whole story, is it?' said the first mate, wondering how soon he could decently get to the transmitter.

'Yes,' said McNeil evenly, 'that's all there was to it.'

The mate bit his pencil, trying to frame the next question. 'And I suppose Grant took it all quite calmly?'

The captain gave him a glare, which he avoided, and McNeil looked at him coldly as if he could see through to the sensation-mongering headlines ranged behind. He got to his feet and moved over to the observation port.

'You heard his broadcast, didn't you? Wasn't that calm enough?'

The mate sighed. It still seemed hard to believe that in such circumstances two men could have behaved in so reasonable, so unemotional a manner. He could have pictured all sorts of dramatic possibilities – sudden outbursts of insanity, even attempts at murder. Yet according to McNeil nothing at all had happened. It was too bad.

McNeil was speaking again, as if to himself. 'Yes, Grant behaved very well – very well indeed. It was a great pity –'

Then he seemed to lose himself in the ever-fresh, incomparable glory of the approaching planet. Not far beneath, and coming closer by kilometers every second, the snow-white crescent arms of Venus spanned more than

144

half the sky. Down there were life and warmth and civilization – and air.

The future, which not long ago had seemed contracted to a point, had opened out again into all its unknown possibilities and wonders. But behind him McNeil could sense the eyes of his rescuers, probing, questioning – yes, and condemning too.

All his life he would hear whispers. Voices would be saying behind his back, 'Isn't that the man who – ?'

He did not care. For once in his life at least, he had done something of which he could feel unashamed. Perhaps one day his own pitiless self-analysis would strip bare the motives behind his actions, would whisper in his ear, 'Altruism? Don't be a fool! You did it to bolster up your own good opinion of yourself – so much more important than anyone else's!'

But the perverse maddening voices, which all his life had made nothing seem worthwhile, were silent for the moment and he felt content. He had reached the calm at the center of the hurricane. While it lasted he would enjoy it to the full.

The Sentinel

Next to 'The Star' and 'The Nine Billion Names of God,' I suppose 'The Sentinel' is my best-known short story – though not for itself, but as the seed from which 2001: A Space Odyssey sprang, twenty years after it was written in 1948. I wonder if I even noticed Christmas that year; Opus 62 bears the date 23–26 December . . .

Unlike most of my short stories, this one was aimed at a specific target – which it missed completely. The BBC had just announced a Short Story Competition; I submitted 'The Sentinel' hot from the typewriter, and got it back a month later.

Somehow, I've never had any luck with such contests. A few years later I wrote 'The Star' specifically for a London Observer competition on the subject '2500 A.D.' It too was bounced – though the judges were perceptive enough to give an award to one Brian Aldiss.

I am continually annoyed by careless references to 'The Sentinel' as 'the story on which 2001 is based'; it bears about as much relation to the movie as an acorn to the resultant full-grown oak. (Considerably less, in fact, because ideas from several other stories were also incorporated.) Even the elements that Stanley Kubrick and I did actually use were considerably modified. Thus the 'glittering, roughly pyramidal structure . . . set in the rock like a gigantic, many-faceted jewel' became – after several modifications – the famous black monolith. And the locale was moved from the Mare Crisium to the most spectacular of all lunar craters, Tycho – easily visible to the naked eye from Earth at Full Moon.

Some time after 'The Sentinel' was published, I was asked if I had ever read Jack London's 'The Red One' (1918). As I'd never even heard of it, I hastened to do so, and was deeply impressed by his thirty-year-earlier tale of the 'Star-Born,' an enormous sphere lying for ages in the jungles of Guadalcanal. I wonder if this is the first treatment of a theme which has suddenly become topical, now that the focus of the SETI debate has changed from 'Where's Everyone?' to the even more puzzling 'Where Are Their Artifacts?'

The next time you see the full moon high in the south, look carefully at its right-hand edge and let your eye travel upward along the curve of the disk. Round about two o'clock you will notice a small, dark oval: anyone with normal eyesight can find it quite easily. It is the great walled plain, one of the finest on the Moon, known as the Mare Crisium – the Sea of Crises. Three hundred miles in diameter, and almost completely surrounded by a ring of magnificent mountains, it had never been explored until we entered it in the late summer of 1996.

Our expedition was a large one. We had two heavy freighters which had flown our supplies and equipment from the main lunar base in the Mare Serenitatis, five hundred miles away. There were also three small rockets which were intended for short-range transport over regions which our surface vehicles couldn't cross. Luckily, most of the Mare Crisium is very flat. There are none of the great crevasses so common and so dangerous else-where, and very few craters or mountains of any size. As far as we could tell, our powerful caterpillar tractors would have no difficulty in taking us wherever we wished to go.

I was geologist – or selenologist, if you want to be pedantic – in charge of the group exploring the southern region of the Mare. We had crossed a hundred miles of it in a week, skirting the foothills of the mountains along the shore of what was once the ancient sea, some thousand million years before. When life was beginning on Earth, it was already dying here. The waters were retreating down

150

the flanks of those stupendous cliffs, retreating into the empty heart of the Moon. Over the land which we were crossing, the tideless ocean had once been half a mile deep, and now the only trace of moisture was the hoarfrost one could sometimes find in caves which the searing sunlight never penetrated.

We had begun our journey early in the slow lunar dawn, and still had almost a week of Earth-time before nightfall. Half a dozen times a day we would leave our vehicle and go outside in the space-suits to hunt for interesting minerals, or to place markers for the guidance of future travelers. It was an uneventful routine. There is nothing hazardous or even particularly exciting about lunar exploration. We could live comfortably for a month in our pressurized tractors, and if we ran into trouble we could always radio for help and sit tight until one of the spaceships came to our rescue.

I said just now that there was nothing exciting about lunar exploration, but of course that isn't true. One could never grow tired of those incredible mountains, so much more rugged than the gentle hills of Earth. We never knew, as we rounded the capes and promontories of that vanished sea, what new splendors would be revealed to us. The whole southern curve of the Mare Crisium is a vast delta where a score of rivers once found their way into the ocean, fed perhaps by the torrential rains that must have lashed the mountains in the brief volcanic age when the Moon was young. Each of these ancient valleys was an invitation, challenging us to climb into the unknown uplands beyond. But we had a hundred miles still to cover, and could only look longingly at the heights which others must scale.

We kept Earth-time aboard the tractor, and precisely at 22.00 hours the final radio message would be sent out to

Base and we would close down for the day. Outside, the rocks would still be burning beneath the almost vertical sun, but to us it was night until we awoke again eight hours later. Then one of us would prepare breakfast, there would be a great buzzing of electric razors, and someone would switch on the short-wave radio from Earth. Indeed, when the smell of frying sausages began to fill the cabin, it was sometimes hard to believe that we were not back on our own world – everything was so normal and homely, apart from the feeling of decreased weight and the unnatural slowness with which objects fell.

It was my turn to prepare breakfast in the corner of the main cabin that served as a galley. I can remember that moment quite vividly after all these years, for the radio had just played one of my favorite melodies, the old Welsh air, 'David of the White Rock.' Our driver was already outside in his space-suit, inspecting our caterpillar treads. My assistant, Louis Garnett, was up forward in the control position, making some belated entries in yesterday's log.

As I stood by the frying pan waiting, like any terrestrial housewife, for the sausages to brown, I let my gaze wander idly over the mountain walls which covered the whole of the southern horizon, marching out of sight to east and west below the curve of the Moon. They seemed only a mile or two from the tractor, but I knew that the nearest was twenty miles away. On the Moon, of course, there is no loss of detail with distance – none of that almost imperceptible haziness which softens and sometimes transfigures all far-off things on Earth.

Those mountains were ten thousand feet high, and they climbed steeply out of the plain as if ages ago some subterranean eruption had smashed them skyward through the molten crust. The base of even the nearest was hidden from sight by the steeply curving surface of the plain, for the Moon is a very little world, and from where I was standing the horizon was only two miles away.

I lifted my eyes toward the peaks which no man had ever climbed, the peaks which, before the coming of terrestrial life, had watched the retreating oceans sink sullenly into their graves, taking with them the hope and the morning promise of a world. The sunlight was beating against those ramparts with a glare that hurt the eyes, yet only a little way above them the stars were shining steadily in a sky blacker than a winter midnight on Earth.

I was turning away when my eye caught a metallic glitter high on the ridge of a great promontory thrusting out into the sea thirty miles to the west. It was a dimensionless point of light, as if a star had been clawed from the sky by one of those cruel peaks, and I imagined that some smooth rock surface was catching the sunlight and heliographing it straight into my eyes. Such things were not uncommon. When the Moon is in her second quarter, observers on Earth can sometimes see the great ranges in the Oceanus Procellarum burning with a blue-white iridescence as the sunlight flashes from their slopes and leaps again from world to world. But I was curious to know what kind of rock could be shining so brightly up there, and I climbed into the observation turret and swung our four-inch telescope round to the west.

I could see just enough to tantalize me. Clear and sharp in the field of vision, the mountain peaks seemed only half a mile away, but whatever was catching the sunlight was still too small to be resolved. Yet it seemed to have an elusive symmetry, and the summit upon which it rested was curiously flat. I stared for a long time at that glittering enigma, straining my eyes into space, until presently a smell of burning from the galley told me that our breakfast

153

sausages had made their quarter-million-mile journey in vain.

All that morning we argued our way across the Mare Crisium while the western mountains reared higher in the sky. Even when we were out prospecting in the space-suits, the discussion would continue over the radio. It was absolutely certain, my companions argued, that there had never been any form of intelligent life on the Moon. The only living things that had ever existed there were a few primitive plants and their slightly less degenerate ances-tors. I knew that as well as anyone, but there are times when a scientist must not be afraid to make a fool of himself.

'Listen,' I said at last, 'I'm going up there, if only for my own peace of mind. That mountain's less than twelve thousand feet high – that's only two thousand under Earth gravity – and I can make the trip in twenty hours at the outside. I've always wanted to go up into those hills, anyway, and this gives me an excellent excuse.'

'If you don't break your neck,' said Garnett, 'you'll be the laughing-stock of the expedition when we get back to Base. That mountain will probably be called Wilson's Folly from now on.'

'I won't break my neck,' I said firmly. 'Who was the first man to climb Pico and Helicon?'

'But weren't you rather younger in those days?' asked Louis gently.

'That,' I said with great dignity, 'is as good a reason as any for going.'

We went to bed early that night, after driving the tractor to within half a mile of the promontory. Garnett was coming with me in the morning; he was a good climber, and had often been with me on such exploits before. Our driver was only too glad to be left in charge of the machine.

At first sight, those cliffs seemed completely unscaleable, but to anyone with a good head for heights, climbing is easy on a world where all weights are only a sixth of their normal value. The real danger in lunar mountaineering lies in overconfidence; a six-hundred-foot drop on the Moon can kill you just as thoroughly as a hundred-foot fall on Earth.

We made our first halt on a wide ledge about four thousand feet above the plain. Climbing had not been very difficult, but my limbs were stiff with the unaccustomed effort, and I was glad of the rest. We could still see the tractor as a tiny metal insect far down at the foot of the cliff, and we reported our progress to the driver before starting on the next ascent.

Inside our suits it was comfortably cool, for the refrigeration units were fighting the fierce sun and carrying away the body heat of our exertions. We seldom spoke to each other, except to pass climbing instructions and to discuss our best plan of ascent. I do not know what Garnett was thinking, probably that this was the craziest goose-chase he had ever embarked upon. I more than half agreed with him, but the joy of climbing, the knowledge that no man had ever gone this way before and the exhilaration of the steadily widening landscape gave me all the reward I needed.

I don't think I was particularly excited when I saw in front of us the wall of rock I had first inspected through the telescope from thirty miles away. It would level off about fifty feet above our heads, and there on the plateau would be the thing that had lured me over these barren wastes. It was, almost certainly, nothing more than a boulder splintered ages ago by a falling meteor, and with

155

its cleavage planes still fresh and bright in this incorruptible, unchanging silence.

There were no hand-holds on the rock face, and we had to use a grapnel. My tired arms seemed to gain new strength as I swung the three-pronged metal anchor round my head and sent it sailing up toward the stars. The first time it broke loose and came falling slowly back when we pulled the rope. On the third attempt, the prongs gripped firmly and our combined weights could not shift it.

Garnett looked at me anxiously. I could tell that he wanted to go first, but I smiled back at him through the glass of my helmet and shook my head. Slowly, taking my time, I began the final ascent.

Even with my space-suit, I weighed only forty pounds here, so I pulled myself up hand over hand without bothering to use my feet. At the rim I paused and waved to my companion, then I scrambled over the edge and stood upright, staring ahead of me.

You must understand that until this very moment I had been almost completely convinced that there could be nothing strange or unusual for me to find here. Almost, but not quite; it was that haunting doubt that had driven me forward. Well, it was a doubt no longer, but the haunting had scarcely begun.

I was standing on a plateau perhaps a hundred feet across. It had once been smooth – too smooth to be natural – but falling meteors had pitted and scored its surface through immeasurable eons. It had been leveled to support a glittering, roughly pyramidal structure, twice as high as a man, that was set in the rock like a gigantic, many-faceted jewel.

Probably no emotion at all filled my mind in those first few seconds. Then I felt a great lifting of my heart, and a strange, inexpressible joy. For I loved the Moon, and now

I knew that the creeping moss of Aristarchus and Eratosthenes was not the only life she had brought forth in her youth. The old, discredited dream of the first explorers was true. There had, after all, been a lunar civilization – and I was the first to find it. That I had come perhaps a hundred million years too late did not distress me; it was enough to have come at all.

My mind was beginning to function normally, to analyze and to ask questions. Was this a building, a shrine – or something for which my language had no name? If a building, then why was it erected in so uniquely inaccessible a spot? I wondered if it might be a temple, and I could picture the adepts of some strange priesthood calling on their gods to preserve them as the life of the Moon ebbed with the dying oceans, and calling on their gods in vain.

I took a dozen steps forward to examine the thing more closely, but some sense of caution kept me from going too near. I knew a little of archaeology, and tried to guess the cultural level of the civilization that must have smoothed this mountain and raised the glittering mirror surfaces that still dazzled my eyes.

The Egyptians could have done it, I thought, if their workmen had possessed whatever strange materials these far more ancient architects had used. Because of the thing's smallness, it did not occur to me that I might be looking at the handiwork of a race more advanced than my own. The idea that the Moon had possessed intelligence at all was still almost too tremendous to grasp, and my pride would not let me take the final, humiliating plunge.

And then I noticed something that set the scalp crawling at the back of my neck – something so trivial and so innocent that many would never have noticed it at all. I have said that the plateau was scarred by meteors; it was also coated inches-deep with the cosmic dust that is always filtering down upon the surface of any world where there are no winds to disturb it. Yet the dust and the meteor scratches ended quite abruptly in a wide circle enclosing the little pyramid, as though an invisible wall was protecting it from the ravages of time and the slow but ceaseless bombardment from space.

There was someone shouting in my earphones, and I realized that Garnett had been calling me for some time. I walked unsteadily to the edge of the cliff and signaled him to join me, not trusting myself to speak. Then I went back toward that circle in the dust. I picked up a fragment of splintered rock and tossed it gently toward the shining enigma. If the pebble had vanished at that invisible barrier I should not have been surprised, but it seemed to hit a smooth, hemispherical surface and slide gently to the ground.

I knew then that I was looking at nothing that could be matched in the antiquity of my own race. This was not a building, but a machine, protecting itself with forces that had challenged Eternity. Those forces, whatever they might be, were still operating, and perhaps I had already come too close. I thought of all the radiations man had trapped and tamed in the past century. For all I knew, I might be as irrevocably doomed as if I had stepped into the deadly, silent aura of an unshielded atomic pile.

I remember turning then toward Garnett, who had joined me and was now standing motionless at my side. He seemed quite oblivious to me, so I did not disturb him but walked to the edge of the cliff in an effort to marshal my thoughts. There below me lay the Mare Crisium – Sea of Crises, indeed – strange and weird to most men, but reassuringly familiar to me. I lifted my eyes toward the crescent Earth, lying in her cradle of stars, and I wondered what her clouds had covered when these unknown builders had finished their work. Was it the steaming jungle of the Carboniferous, the bleak shoreline over which the first amphibians must crawl to conquer the land – or, earlier still, the long loneliness before the coming of life?

Do not ask me why I did not guess the truth sooner – the truth that seems so obvious now. In the first excitement of my discovery, I had assumed without question that this crystalline apparition had been built by some race belonging to the Moon's remote past, but suddenly, and with overwhelming force, the belief came to me that it was as alien to the Moon as I myself.

In twenty years we had found no trace of life but a few degenerate plants. No lunar civilization, whatever its doom, could have left but a single token of its existence.

I looked at the shining pyramid again, and the more remote it seemed from anything that had to do with the Moon. And suddenly I felt myself shaking with a foolish, hysterical laughter, brought on by excitement and overexertion: for I had imagined that the little pyramid was speaking to me and was saying: 'Sorry, I'm a stranger here myself.'

It had taken us twenty years to crack that invisible shield and to reach the machine inside those crystal walls. What we could not understand, we broke at last with the savage might of atomic power and now I have seen the fragments of the lovely, glittering thing I found up there on the mountain.

They are meaningless. The mechanisms – if indeed they are mechanisms – of the pyramid belong to a technology that lies far beyond our horizon, perhaps to the technology of para-physical forces.

The mystery haunts us all the more now that the other

planets have been reached and we know that only Earth has ever been the home of intelligent life in our Universe. Nor could any lost civilization of our own world have built that machine, for the thickness of the meteoric dust on the plateau has enabled us to measure its age. It was set there upon its mountain before life had emerged from the seas of Earth.

When our world was half its present age, *something* from the stars swept through the Solar System, left this token of its passage, and went again upon its way. Until we destroyed it, that machine was still fulfilling the purpose of its builders; and as to that purpose, here is my guess.

Nearly a hundred thousand million stars are turning in the circle of the Milky Way, and long ago other races on the worlds of other suns must have scaled and passed the heights that we have reached. Think of such civilizations, far back in time against the fading afterglow of Creation, masters of a universe so young that life as yet had come only to a handful of worlds. Theirs would have been a loneliness we cannot imagine, the loneliness of gods looking out across infinity and finding none to share their thoughts.

They must have searched the star clusters as we have searched the planets. Everywhere there would be worlds, but they would be empty or peopled with crawling, mindless things. Such was our own Earth, the smoke of the great volcanoes still staining the skies, when that first ship of the peoples of the dawn came sliding in from the abyss beyond Pluto. It passed the frozen outer worlds, knowing that life could play no part in their destinies. It came to rest among the inner planets, warming themselves around the fire of the Sun and waiting for their stories to begin.

Those wanderers must have looked on Earth, circling safely in the narrow zone between fire and ice, and must have guessed that it was the favorite of the Sun's children. Here, in the distant future, would be intelligence; but there were countless stars before them still, and they might never come this way again.

So they left a sentinel, one of millions they have scattered throughout the Universe, watching over all worlds with the promise of life. It was a beacon that down the ages has been patiently signaling the fact that no one had discovered it.

Perhaps you understand now why that crystal pyramid was set upon the Moon instead of on the Earth. Its builders were not concerned with races still struggling up from savagery. They would be interested in our civilization only if we proved our fitness to survive – by crossing space and so escaping from the Earth, our cradle. That is the challenge that all intelligent races must meet, sooner or later. It is a double challenge, for it depends in turn upon the conquest of atomic energy and the last choice between life and death.

Once we had passed that crisis, it was only a matter of time before we found the pyramid and forced it open. Now its signals have ceased, and those whose duty it is will be turning their minds upon Earth. Perhaps they wish to help our infant civilization. But they must be very, very old, and the old are often insanely jealous of the young.

I can never look now at the Milky Way without wondering from which of those banked clouds of stars the emissaries are coming. If you will pardon so commonplace a simile, we have set off the fire-alarm and have nothing to do but to wait.

I do not think we will have to wait for long.

Jupiter V

'Jupiter V,' written in June 1951, belongs to that typical and often despised category of science fiction, the 'gimmick' story, in which some little-known fact or natural law forms an essential part of the plot. The genre may well have originated (like much else) with Edgar Allan Poe; his 'A Descent into the Maelstrom' is a classic example.

As I wrote on its first appearance in volume form (Reach for Tomorrow, 1956): 'I am by no means sure that I could write "Jupiter V" today; it involved twenty or thirty pages of orbital calculations and should by rights be dedicated to Professor G. C. McVittie, my erstwhile tutor in applied mathematics.' Twenty-seven years later I'm completely sure on this point.

But during those years something has happened that, when I wrote the story, I would have dismissed as completely incredible. The photographer covering the satellites of Jupiter for a 2044 issue of Life Magazine (presumably a holographic, satellite-delivered edition) was sixty-five years too late. The Voyager spacecraft had already done the job, back in 1979 . . .

Or at least the first part of it, for we will never finish unravelling the complexities of the mini-solar-system formed by Jupiter and his moons. And dated though this story has been by the astonishing speed of space exploration (it was written, please remember, when Sputnik I was still six years in the future!), it may yet contain some elements of truth.

Those fuzzy, long-range shots of little Jupiter V (now officially christened Amalthea) look very, very odd indeed . . .

Professor Forster is such a small man that a special space-suit had to be made for him. But what he lacked in physical size he more than made up – as is so often the case – in sheer drive and determination. When I met him, he'd spent twenty years pursuing a dream. What is more to the point, he had persuaded a whole succession of hard-headed business men, World Council Delegates and administrators of scientific trusts to underwrite his expenses and to fit out a ship for him. Despite everything that happened later, I still think that was his most remark-able achievement . . .

The 'Arnold Toynbee' had a crew of six aboard when we left Earth. Besides the Professor and Charles Ashton, his chief assistant, there was the usual pilot-navigator-engineer triumvirate and two graduate students – Bill Hawkins and myself. Neither of us had ever gone into space before, and we were still so excited over the whole thing that we didn't care in the least whether we got back to Earth before the next term started. We had a strong suspicion that our tutor had very similar views. The reference he had produced for us was a masterpiece of ambiguity, but as the number of people who could even begin to read Martian script could be counted, if I may coin a phrase, on the fingers of one hand, we'd got the job.

As we were going to Jupiter, and not to Mars, the purpose of this particular qualification seemed a little obscure, though knowing something about the Professor's theories we had some pretty shrewd suspicions. They were partly confirmed when we were ten days out from Earth.

The Professor looked at us very thoughtfully when we answered his summons. Even under zero g he always managed to preserve his dignity, while the best we could do was to cling to the nearest handhold and float around like drifting seaweed. I got the impression – though I may of course be wrong – that he was thinking: What have *I* done to deserve this? as he looked from Bill to me and back again. Then he gave a sort of 'It's too late to do anything about it now' sigh and began to speak in that slow, patient way he always does when he has something to explain. At least, he always uses it when he's speaking to us, but it's just occurred to me – oh, never mind.

'Since we left Earth,' he said, 'I've not had much chance of telling you the purpose of this expedition. Perhaps you've guessed it already.'

'I think I have,' said Bill.

'Well, go on,' replied the Professor, a peculiar gleam in his eye. I did my best to stop Bill, but have you ever tried to kick anyone when you're in free fall?

'You want to find some proof – I mean, some *more* proof – of your diffusion theory of extraterrestrial culture.'

'And have you any idea why I'm going to Jupiter to look for it?'

'Well, not exactly. I suppose you hope to find something on one of the moons.'

'Brilliant, Bill, brilliant. There are fifteen known satellites, and their total area is about half that of Earth. Where would you start looking if you had a couple of weeks to spare? I'd rather like to know.'

Bill glanced doubtfully at the Professor, as if he almost suspected him of sarcasm.

'I don't know much about astronomy,' he said. 'But there are four big moons, aren't there? I'd start on those.'

'For your information, Io, Europa, Ganymede and Callisto are each about as big as Africa. Would you work through them in alphabetical order?'

'No,' Bill replied promptly. 'I'd start on the one nearest Jupiter and go outward.'

'I don't think we'll waste any more time pursuing your logical processes,' sighed the Professor. He was obviously impatient to begin his set speech. 'Anyway, you're quite wrong. We're not going to the big moons at all. They've been photographically surveyed from space and large areas have been explored on the surface. They've got nothing of archaeological interest. *We're* going to a place that's never been visited before.'

'Not to Jupiter!' I gasped.

'Heavens no, nothing as drastic as that! But we're going nearer to him than anyone else has ever been.'

He paused thoughtfully.

'It's a curious thing, you know – or you probably don't – that it's nearly as difficult to travel between Jupiter's satellites as it is to go between the planets, although the distances are so much smaller. This is because Jupiter's got such a terrific gravitational field and his moons are traveling so quickly. The innermost moon's moving almost as fast as Earth, and the journey to it from Ganymede costs almost as much fuel as the trip from Earth to Venus, even though it takes only a day and a half.

'And it's *that* journey which we're going to make. No one's ever done it before because nobody could think of any good reason for the expense. Jupiter Five is only thirty kilometers in diameter, so it couldn't possibly be of much interest. Even some of the outer satellites, which are far easier to reach, haven't been visited because it hardly seemed worth while to waste the rocket fuel.'

'Then why are *we* going to waste it?' I asked impatiently. The whole thing sounded like a complete wild-goose chase, though as long as it proved interesting, and involved no actual danger, I didn't greatly mind.

Perhaps I ought to confess – though I'm tempted to say nothing, as a good many others have done – that at this time I didn't believe a word of Professor Forster's theories. Of course I realized that he was a very brilliant man in his field, but I did draw the line at some of his more fantastic ideas. After all, the evidence was so slight and the conclusions so revolutionary that one could hardly help being skeptical.

Perhaps you can still remember the astonishment when the first Martian expedition found the remains not of one ancient civilization, but of two. Both had been highly advanced, but both had perished more than five million years ago. The reason was unknown (and still is). It did not seem to be warfare, as the two cultures appear to have lived amicably together. One of the races had been insect-like, the other vaguely reptilian. The insects seem to have been the genuine, original Martians. The reptile-people – usually referred to as 'Culture X' – had arrived on the scene later.

So, at least, Professor Forster maintained. They had certainly possessed the secret of space travel, because the ruins of their peculiar cruciform cities had been found on – of all places – Mercury. Forster believed that they had tried to colonize all the smaller planets – Earth and Venus having been ruled out because of their excessive gravity. It was a source of some disappointment to the Professor that no traces of Culture X had ever been found on the

Moon, though he was certain that such a discovery was only a matter of time.

The 'conventional' theory of Culture X was that it had originally come from one of the smaller planets or satellites, had made peaceful contact with the Martians – the only other intelligent race in the known history of the System – and had died out at the same time as the Martian civilization. But Professor Forster had more ambitious ideas: he was convinced that Culture X had entered the Solar System from interstellar space. The fact that no one else believed this annoyed him, though not very much, for he is one of those people who are happy only when in a minority.

From where I was sitting, I could see Jupiter through the cabin porthole as Professor Forster unfolded his plan. It was a beautiful sight: I could just make out the equatorial cloud belts, and three of the satellites were visible as little stars close to the planet. I wondered which was Ganymede, our first port of call.

'If Jack will condescend to pay attention,' the Professor continued, 'I'll tell you why we're going such a long way from home. You know that last year I spent a good deal of time poking among the ruins in the twilight belt of Mercury. Perhaps you read the paper I gave on the subject at the London School of Economics. You may even have been there – I do remember a disturbance at the back of the hall.

'What I didn't tell anyone then was that while I was on Mercury I discovered an important clue to the origin of Culture X. I've kept quiet about it, although I've been sorely tempted when fools like Dr Haughton have tried to be funny at my expense. But I wasn't going to risk letting someone else get here before I could organize this expedition.

'One of the things I found on Mercury was a rather well preserved bas-relief of the Solar System. It's not the first that's been discovered – as you know, astronomical motifs are common in true Martian and Culture X art. But there were certain peculiar symbols against various planets, including Mars and Mercury. I think the pattern had some historic significance, and the most curious thing about it is that little Jupiter Five – one of the least important of all the satellites – seemed to have the most attention drawn to it. I'm convinced that there's something on Five which is the key to the whole problem of Culture X, and I'm going there to discover what it is.'

As far as I can remember now, neither Bill nor I was particularly impressed by the Professor's story. Maybe the people of Culture X had left some artifacts on Five for obscure reasons of their own. It would be interesting to unearth them, but hardly likely that they would be as important as the Professor thought. I guess he was rather disappointed at our lack of enthusiasm. If so it was his fault since, as we discovered later, he was still holding out on us.

We landed on Ganymede, the largest moon, about a week later. Ganymede is the only one of the satellites with a permanent base on it; there's an observatory and a geophysical station with a staff of about fifty scientists. They were rather glad to see visitors, but we didn't stay long as the Professor was anxious to refuel and set off again. The fact that we were heading for Five naturally aroused a good deal of interest, but the Professor wouldn't talk and we couldn't; he kept too close an eye on us.

Ganymede, by the way, is quite an interesting place and we managed to see rather more of it on the return journey. But as I've promised to write an article for another magazine about that, I'd better not say anything else here.

(You might like to keep your eyes on the *National Astrographic* Magazine next Spring.)

The hop from Ganymede to Five took just over a day and a half, and it gave us an uncomfortable feeling to see Jupiter expanding hour by hour until it seemed as if he was going to fill the sky. I don't know much about astronomy, but I couldn't help thinking of the tremendous gravity field into which we were falling. All sorts of things could go wrong so easily. If we ran out of fuel we'd never be able to get back to Ganymede, and we might even drop into Jupiter himself.

I wish I could describe what it was like seeing that colossal globe, with its raging storm belts spinning in the sky ahead of us. As a matter of fact I did make the attempt, but some literary friends who have read this MS advised me to cut out the result. (They also gave me a lot of other advice which I don't think they could have meant seriously, because if I'd followed it there would have been no story at all.)

Luckily there have been so many color close-ups of Jupiter published by now that you're bound to have seen some of them. You may even have seen the one which, as I'll explain later, was the cause of all our trouble.

At last Jupiter stopped growing: we'd swung into the orbit of Five and would soon catch up with the tiny moon as it raced around the planet. We were all squeezed in the control room waiting for our first glimpse of our target. At least, all of us who could get in were doing so. Bill and I were crowded out into the corridor and could only crane over other people's shoulders. Kingsley Searle, our pilot, was in the control seat looking as unruffled as ever; Eric Fulton, the engineer, was thoughtfully chewing his mustache and watching the fuel gauges, and Tony Groves was doing complicated things with his navigation tables.

171

And the Professor appeared to be rigidly attached to the eyepiece of the teleperiscope. Suddenly he gave a start and we heard a whistle of indrawn breath. After a minute, without a word, he beckoned to Searle, who took his place at the eyepiece. Exactly the same thing happened, and then Searle handed over to Fulton. It got a bit monotonous by the time Groves had reacted identically, so we wormed our way in and took over after a bit of opposition.

I don't know quite what I'd expected to see, so that's probably why I was disappointed. Hanging there in space was a tiny gibbous moon, its 'night' sector lit up faintly by the reflected glory of Jupiter. And that seemed to be all.

Then I began to make out additional markings, in the way that you do if you look through a telescope for long enough. There were faint crisscrossing lines on the surface of the satellite, and suddenly my eye grasped their full pattern. For it *was* a pattern: those lines covered Five with the same geometrical accuracy as the lines of latitude and longitude divide up a globe of the Earth. I suppose I gave my whistle of amazement, for then Bill pushed me out of the way and had his turn to look.

The next thing I remember is Professor Forster looking very smug while we bombarded him with questions.

'Of course,' he explained, 'this isn't as much a surprise to me as it is to you. Besides the evidence I'd found on Mercury, there were other clues. I've a friend at the Ganymede Observatory whom I've sworn to secrecy and who's been under quite a strain this last few weeks. It's rather surprising to anyone who's not an astronomer that the Observatory has never bothered much about the satellites. The big instruments are all used on extra-galactic nebulae, and the little ones spend all their time looking at Jupiter.

'The only thing the Observatory had ever done to Five

was to measure its diameter and take a few photographs. They weren't quite good enough to show the markings we've just observed, otherwise there would have been an investigation before. But my friend Lawton detected them through the hundred-centimeter reflector when I asked him to look, and he also noticed something else that should have been spotted before. Five is only thirty kilometers in diameter, but it's much brighter than it should be for its size. When you compare its reflecting power – its aldeb – its – '

'Its albedo.'

'Thanks, Tony – it's albedo with that of the other Moons, you find that it's a much better reflector than it should be. In fact, it behaves more like polished metal than rock.'

'So that explains it!' I said. 'The people of Culture X must have covered Five with an outer shell – like the domes they built on Mercury, but on a bigger scale.'

The Professor looked at me rather pityingly.

'So you still haven't guessed!' he said.

I don't think this was quite fair. Frankly, would you have done any better in the same circumstances?

We landed three hours later on an enormous metal plain. As I looked through the portholes, I felt completely dwarfed by my surroundings. An ant crawling on the top of an oil-storage tank might have had much the same feelings – and the looming bulk of Jupiter up there in the sky didn't help. Even the Professor's usual cockiness now seemed to be overlaid by a kind of reverent awe.

The plain wasn't quite devoid of features. Running across it in various directions were broad bands where the stupendous metal plates had been joined together. These bands, or the crisscross pattern they formed, were what we had seen from space.

About a quarter of a kilometer away was a low hill – at least, what would have been a hill on a natural world. We had spotted it on our way in after making a careful survey of the little satellite from space. It was one of six such projections, four arranged equidistantly around the equator and the other two at the Poles. The assumption was pretty obvious that they would be entrances to the world below the metal shell.

I know that some people think it must be very entertaining to walk around on an airless, low-gravity planet in space-suits. Well, it isn't. There are so many points to think about, so many checks to make and precautions to observe, that the mental strain outweighs the glamor – at least as far as I'm concerned. But I must admit that this time, as we climbed out of the airlock, I was so excited that for once these things didn't worry me.

The gravity of Five was so microscopic that walking was completely out of the question. We were all roped together like mountaineers and blew ourselves across the metal plain with gentle bursts from our recoil pistols. The experienced astronauts, Fulton and Groves, were at the two ends of the chain so that any unwise eagerness on the part of the people in the middle was restrained.

It took us only a few minutes to reach our objective, which we discovered to be a broad, low dome at least a kilometer in circumference. I wondered if it was a gigantic airlock, large enough to permit the entrance of whole spaceships. Unless we were very lucky, we might be unable to find a way in, since the controlling mechanisms would no longer be functioning, and even if they were, we would not know how to operate them. It would be difficult to imagine anything more tantalizing than being locked out, unable to get at the greatest archaeological find in all history.

We had made a quarter circuit of the dome when we found an opening in the metal shell. It was quite small – only about two meters across – and it was so nearly circular that for a moment we did not realize what it was. Then Tony's voice came over the radio:

'That's not artificial. We've got a meteor to thank for it.'

'Impossible!' protested Professor Forster. 'It's much too regular.'

Tony was stubborn.

'Big meteors always produce circular holes, unless they strike very glancing blows. And look at the edges; you can see there's been an explosion of some kind. Probably the meteor and the shell were vaporized; we won't find any fragments.'

'You'd expect this sort of thing to happen,' put in Kingsley. 'How long has this been here? Five million years? I'm surprised we haven't found any other craters.'

'Maybe you're right,' said the Professor, too pleased to argue. 'Anyway, I'm going in first.'

'Right,' said Kingsley, who as captain has the last say in all such matters. 'I'll give you twenty meters of rope and will sit in the hole so that we can keep radio contact. Otherwise this shell will blanket your signals.'

So Professor Forster was the first man to enter Five, as he deserved to be. We crowded close to Kingsley so that he could relay news of the Professor's progress.

He didn't get very far. There was another shell just inside the outer one, as we might have expected. The Professor had room to stand upright between them, and as far as his torch could throw its beam he could see avenues of supporting struts and girders, but that was about all.

It took us about twenty-four exasperating hours before

175

we got any further. Near the end of that time I remember asking the Professor why he hadn't thought of bringing any explosives. He gave me a very hurt look.

'There's enough aboard the ship to blow us all to glory,' he said. 'But I'm not going to risk doing any damage if I can find another way.'

That's what I call patience, but I could see his point of view. After all, what was another few days in a search that had already taken him twenty years?

It was Bill Hawkins, of all people, who found the way in when we had abandoned our first line of approach. Near the North Pole of the little world he discovered a really giant meteor hole – about a hundred meters across and cutting through both the outer shells surrounding Five. It had revealed still another shell below those, and by one of those chances that must happen if one waits enough eons, a second, smaller, meteor had come down inside the crater and penetrated the innermost skin. The hole was just big enough to allow entrance for a man in a space-suit. We went through head first, one at a time.

I don't suppose I'll ever have a weirder experience than hanging from that tremendous vault, like a spider suspended beneath the dome of St Peter's. We only knew that the space in which we floated was vast. Just *how* big it was we could not tell, for our torches gave us no sense of distance. In this airless, dustless cavern the beams were, of course, totally invisible and when we shone them on the roof above, we could see the ovals of light dancing away into the distance until they were too diffuse to be visible. If we pointed them 'downward' we could see a pale smudge of illumination so far below that it revealed nothing.

Very slowly, under the minute gravity of this tiny world, we fell downward until checked by our safety ropes.

Overhead I could see the tiny glimmering patch through which we had entered; it was remote but reassuring.

And then, while I was swinging with an infinitely sluggish pendulum motion at the end of my cable, with the lights of my companions glimmering like fitful stars in the darkness around me, the truth suddenly crashed into my brain. Forgetting that we were all on open circuit, I cried out involuntarily:

'Professor – I don't believe this is a planet at all! *It's a spaceship!*'

Then I stopped, feeling that I had made a fool of myself. There was a brief, tense silence, then a babble of noise as everyone else started arguing at once. Professor Forster's voice cut across the confusion and I could tell that he was both pleased and surprised.

'You're quite right, Jack. This is the ship that brought Culture X to the Solar System.'

I heard someone – it sounded like Eric Fulton – give a gasp of incredulity.

'It's fantastic! A ship thirty kilometers across!'

'*You* ought to know better than that,' replied the Professor with surprising mildness. 'Suppose a civilization wanted to cross interstellar space – how else would it attack the problem? It would build a mobile planetoid out in space, taking perhaps centuries over the task. Since the ship would have to be a self-contained world, which could support its inhabitants for generations, it would need to be as large as this. I wonder how many suns they visited before they found ours and knew that their search was ended? They must have had smaller ships that could take them down to the planets, and of course they had to leave the parent vessel somewhere in space. So they parked it here, in a close orbit near the largest planet, where it would remain safely forever – or until they needed it

177

again. It was the logical place: if they had set it circling the Sun, in time the pulls of the planets would have disturbed its orbit so much that it might have been lost. That could never happen to it here.'

'Tell me, Professor,' someone asked, 'did you guess all this before we started?'

'I *hoped* it. All the evidence pointed to this answer. There's always been something anomalous about Satellite Five, though no one seems to have noticed it. Why this single tiny moon so close to Jupiter, when all the other small satellites are seventy times further away? Astronomically speaking, it didn't make sense. But enough of this chattering. We've got work to do.'

That, I think, must count as the understatement of the century. There were seven of us faced with the greatest archaeological discovery of all time. Almost a whole world – a small world, an artificial one, but still a world – was waiting for us to explore. All we could perform was a swift and superficial reconnaissance: there might be material here for generations of research workers.

The first step was to lower a powerful floodlight on a power line running from the ship. This would act as a beacon and prevent us getting lost, as well as giving local illumination on the inner surface of the satellite. (Even now, I still find it hard to call Five a ship.) Then we dropped down the line to the surface below. It was a fall of about a kilometer, and in this low gravity it was quite safe to make the drop unretarded. The gentle shock of the impact could be absorbed easily enough by the spring-loaded staffs we carried for that purpose.

I don't want to take up any space here with yet another description of all the wonders of Satellite Five; there have already been enough pictures, maps and books on the subject. (My own, by the way, is being published by

Sidgwick and Jackson next summer.) What I would like to give you instead is some impression of what it was actually *like* to be the first men ever to enter that strange metal world. Yet I'm sorry to say – I know this sounds hard to believe – I simply can't remember what I was feeling when we came across the first of the great mushroom-capped entrance shafts. I suppose I was so excited and so overwhelmed by the wonder of it all that I've forgotten everything else. But I can recall the impression of sheer size, something which mere photographs can never give. The builders of this world, coming as they did from a planet of low gravity, were giants – about four times as tall as men. We were pigmies crawling among their works.

We never got below the outer levels on our first visit so we met few of the scientific marvels which later expeditions discovered. That was just as well; the residential areas provided enough to keep us busy for several lifetimes. The globe we were exploring must once have been lit by artificial sunlight pouring down from the triple shell that surrounded it and kept its atmosphere from leaking into space. Here on the surface the Jovians (I suppose I cannot avoid adopting the popular name for the people of Culture X) had reproduced, as accurately as they could, conditions on the world they had left unknown ages ago. Perhaps they still had day and night, changing seasons, rain and mist. They had even taken a tiny sea with them into exile. The water was still there, forming a frozen lake three kilometers across. I hear that there is a plan afoot to electrolize it and provide Five with a breathable atmosphere again, as soon as the meteor holes in the outer shell have been plugged.

The more we saw of their work, the more we grew to like the race whose possessions we were disturbing for the first time in five million years. Even if they were giants from another sun, they had much in common with man, and it is a great tragedy that our races missed each other by what is, on the cosmic scale, such a narrow margin.

We were, I suppose, more fortunate than any archaeologists in history. The vacuum of space had preserved everything from decay and – this was something which could not have been expected – the Jovians had not emptied their mighty ship of all its treasures when they had set out to colonize the Solar System. Here on the inner surface of Five everything still seemed intact, as it had been at the end of the ship's long journey. Perhaps the travelers had preserved it as a shrine in memory of their lost home, or perhaps they had thought that one day they might have to use these things again.

Whatever the reason, everything was here as its makers had left it. Sometimes it frightened me. I might be photographing, with Bill's help, some great wall carving when the sheer *timelessness* of the place would strike into my heart. I would look round nervously, half expecting to see giant shapes come stalking in through the pointed doorways, to continue the tasks that had been momentarily interrupted.

We discovered the art gallery on the fourth day. That was the only name for it; there was no mistaking its purpose. When Groves and Searle, who had been doing rapid sweeps over the southern hemisphere, reported the discovery we decided to concentrate all our forces there. For, as somebody or other has said, the art of a people reveals its soul, and here we might find the key to Culture X.

The building was huge, even by the standards of this giant race. Like all the other structures on Five, it was made of metal, yet there was nothing cold or mechanical about it. The topmost peak climbed half way to the remote roof of the world, and from a distance – before the details were visible – the building looked not unlike a Gothic cathedral. Misled by this chance resemblance, some later writers have called it a temple; but we have never found any trace of what might be called a religion among the Jovians. Yet there seems something appropriate about the name 'The Temple of Art,' and it's stuck so thoroughly that no one can change it now.

It has been estimated that there are between ten and twenty million individual exhibits in this single building – the harvest garnered during the whole history of a race that may have been much older than Man. And it was here that I found a small, circular room which at first sight seemed to be no more than the meeting place of six radiating corridors. I was by myself (and thus, I'm afraid, disobeying the Professor's orders) and taking what I thought would be a short-cut back to my companions. The dark walls were drifting silently past me as I glided along, the light of my torch dancing over the ceiling ahead. It was covered with deeply cut lettering, and I was so busy looking for familiar character groupings that for some time I paid no attention to the chamber's floor. Then I saw the statue and focused my beam upon it.

The moment when one first meets a great work of art has an impact that can never again be recaptured. In this case the subject matter made the effect all the more overwhelming. I was the first man ever to know what the Jovians had looked like, for here, carved with superb skill and authority, was one obviously modeled from life.

The slender, reptilian head was looking straight toward me, the sightless eyes staring into mine. Two of the hands were clasped upon the breast as if in resignation; the other two were holding an instrument whose purpose is still unknown. The long, powerful tail – which, like a kanga-roo's, probably balanced the rest of the body – was stretched out along the ground, adding to the impression of rest or repose.

There was nothing human about the face or the body. There were, for example, no nostrils – only gill-like openings in the neck. Yet the figure moved me profoundly; the artist had spanned the barriers of time and culture in a way I should never have believed possible. 'Not human – but humane' was the verdict Professor Forster gave. There were many things we could not have shared with the builders of this world, but all that was really important we would have felt in common.

Just as one can read emotions in the alien but familiar face of a dog or a horse, so it seemed that I knew the feelings of the being confronting me. Here was wisdom and authority – the calm, confident power that is shown, for example, in Bellini's famous portrait of the Doge Loredano. Yet there was sadness also – the sadness of a race which had made some stupendous effort, and made it in vain.

We still do not know why this single statue is the only representation the Jovians have ever made of themselves in their art. One would hardly expect to find taboos of this nature among such an advanced race; perhaps we will know the answer when we have deciphered the writing carved on the chamber walls.

Yet I am already certain of the statue's purpose. It was set here to bridge time and to greet whatever beings might one day stand in the footsteps of his makers. That, perhaps, is why they shaped it so much smaller than life. Even then they must have guessed that the future belonged to Earth or Venus, and hence to beings whom they would have dwarfed. They knew that size could be a barrier as well as time.

A few minutes later I was on my way back to the ship with my companions, eager to tell the Professor about the discovery. He had been reluctantly snatching some rest, though I don't believe he averaged more than four hours' sleep a day all the time we were on Five. The golden light of Jupiter was flooding the great metal plain as we emerged through the shell and stood beneath the stars once more.

'Hello!' I heard Bill say over the radio, 'the Prof's moved the ship.'

'Nonsense,' I retorted. 'It's exactly where we left it.'

Then I turned my head and saw the reason for Bill's mistake. We had visitors.

The second ship had come down a couple of kilometers away, and as far as my non-expert eyes could tell it might have been a duplicate of ours. When we hurried through the airlock, we found that the Professor, a little bleary-eyed, was already entertaining. To our surprise, though not exactly to our displeasure, one of the three visitors was an extremely attractive brunette.

'This,' said Professor Forster, a little wearily, 'is Mr Randolph Mays, the science writer. I imagine you've heard of him. And this is – ' He turned to Mays. 'I'm afraid I didn't quite catch the names.'

'My pilot, Donald Hopkins – my secretary, Marianne Mitchell.'

There was just the slightest pause before the word 'secretary,' but it was long enough to set a little signal light flashing in my brain. I kept my eyebrows from going up, but I caught a glance from Bill that said, without any need for words: If you're thinking what I'm thinking, I'm ashamed of you.

183

Mays was a tall, rather cadaverous man with thinning hair and an attitude of bonhomie which one felt was only skin-deep – the protective coloration of a man who has to be friendly with too many people.

'I expect this is as big a surprise to you as it is to me,' he said with unnecessary heartiness. 'I certainly never expected to find anyone here before me; and I certainly didn't expect to find all *this*.'

'What brought you here?' said Ashton, trying to sound not too suspiciously inquisitive.

'I was just explaining that to the Professor. Can I have that folder please, Marianne? Thanks.'

He drew out a series of very fine astronomical paintings and passed them round. They showed the planets from their satellites – a common-enough subject, of course.

'You've all seen this sort of thing before,' Mays continued. 'But there's a difference here. These pictures are nearly a hundred years old. They were painted by an artist named Chesley Bonestell and appeared in *Life* back in 1944 – long before space-travel began, of course. Now what's happened is that *Life* has commissioned me to go round the Solar System and see how well I can match these imaginative paintings against the reality. In the centenary issue, they'll be published side by side with photographs of the real thing. Good idea, eh?'

I had to admit that it was. But it was going to make matters rather complicated, and I wondered what the Professor thought about it. Then I glanced again at Miss Mitchell, standing demurely in the corner, and decided that there would be compensations.

In any other circumstances, we would have been glad to meet another party of explorers, but here there was the question of priority to be considered. Mays would certainly be hurrying back to Earth as quickly as he could, his original mission abandoned and all his film used up here and now. It was difficult to see how we could stop him, and not even certain that we desired to do so. We wanted all the publicity and support we could get, but we would prefer to do things in our own time, after our own fashion. I wondered how strong the Professor was on tact, and feared the worst.

Yet at first diplomatic relations were smooth enough. The Professor had hit upon the bright idea of pairing each of us with one of Mays's team, so that we acted simultaneously as guides and supervisors. Doubling the number of investigating groups also greatly increased the rate at which we could work. It was unsafe for anyone to operate by himself under these conditions, and this had handicapped us a great deal.

The Professor outlined his policy to us the day after the arrival of Mays's party.

'I hope we can get along together,' he said a little anxiously. 'As far as I'm concerned they can go where they like and photograph what they like, as long *as they don't take anything*, and as long as they don't get back to Earth with their records before we do.'

'I don't see how we can stop them,' protested Ashton.

'Well, I hadn't intended to do this, but I've now registered a claim to Five. I radioed it to Ganymede last night, and it will be at The Hague by now.'

'But no one can claim an astronomical body for himself. That was settled in the case of the Moon, back in the last century.'

The Professor gave a rather crooked smile.

'I'm not annexing an *astronomical body*, remember. I've put in a claim for salvage, and I've done it in the name of the World Science Organization. If Mays takes anything out of Five, he'll be stealing it from them.

185

Tomorrow I'm going to explain the situation gently to him, just in case he gets any bright ideas.'

It certainly seemed peculiar to think of Satellite Five as salvage, and I could imagine some pretty legal quarrels developing when we got home. But for the present the Professor's move should have given us some safeguards and might discourage Mays from collecting souvenirs – so we were optimistic enough to hope.

It took rather a lot of organizing, but I managed to get paired off with Marianne for several trips round the interior of Five. Mays didn't seem to mind: there was no particular reason why he should. A space-suit is the most perfect chaperon ever devised, confound it.

Naturally enough I took her to the art gallery at the first opportunity, and showed her my find. She stood looking at the statue for a long time while I held my torch beam upon it.

'It's very wonderful,' she breathed at last. 'Just think of it waiting here in the darkness all those millions of years! But you'll have to give it a name.'

'I have. I've christened it "The Ambassador."'

'Why?'

'Well, because I think it's a kind of envoy, if you like, carrying a greeting to us. The people who made it knew that one day someone else was bound to come here and find this place.'

'I think you're right. "The Ambassador" – yes, that was clever of you. There's something noble about it, and something very sad, too. Don't you feel it?'

I could tell that Marianne was a very intelligent woman. It was quite remarkable the way she saw my point of view, and the interest she took in everything I showed her. But 'The Ambassador' fascinated her most of all, and she kept on coming back to it.

'You know, Jack,' she said (I think this was sometime the next day, when Mays had been to see it as well) 'you must take that statue back to Earth. Think of the sensation it would cause.'

I sighed.

'The Professor would like to, but it must weigh a ton. We can't afford the fuel. It will have to wait for a later trip.'

She looked puzzled.

'But things hardly weigh anything here,' she protested.

'That's different,' I explained. 'There's weight, and there's inertia – two quite different things. Now inertia – oh, never mind. We can't take it back, anyway. Captain Searle's told us that, definitely.'

'What a pity,' said Marianne.

I forgot all about this conversation until the night before we left. We had had a busy and exhausting day packing our equipment (a good deal, of course, we left behind for future use). All our photographic material had been used up. As Charlie Ashton remarked, if we met a *live* Jovian now we'd be unable to record the fact. I think we were all wanting a breathing space, an opportunity to relax and sort out our impressions and to recover from our head-on collision with an alien culture.

Mays's ship, the 'Henry Luce,' was also nearly ready for take-off. We would leave at the same time, an arrangement which suited the Professor admirably as he did not trust Mays alone on Five.

Everything had been settled when, while checking through our records, I suddenly found that six rolls of exposed film were missing. They were photographs of a complete set of transcriptions in the Temple of Art. After a certain amount of thought I recalled that they had been entrusted to my charge, and I had put them very carefully on a ledge in the Temple, intending to collect them later.

It was a long time before take-off, the Professor and Ashton were canceling some arrears of sleep, and there seemed no reason why I should not slip back to collect the missing material. I knew there would be a row if it was left behind, and as I remembered exactly where it was I need be gone only thirty minutes. So I went, explaining my mission to Bill just in case of accidents.

The floodlight was no longer working, of course, and the darkness inside the shell of Five was somewhat oppressive. But I left a portable beacon at the entrance, and dropped freely until my hand torch told me it was time to break the fall. Ten minutes later, with a sigh of relief, I gathered up the missing films.

It was a natural-enough thing to pay my last respects to The Ambassador: it might be years before I saw him again, and that calmly enigmatic figure had begun to exercise an extraordinary fascination over me.

Unfortunately, that fascination had not been confined to me alone. For the chamber was empty and the statue gone.

I suppose I could have crept back and said nothing, thus avoiding awkward explanations. But I was too furious to think of discretion, and as soon as I returned we woke the Professor and told him what had happened.

He sat on his bunk rubbing the sleep out of his eyes, then uttered a few harsh words about Mr Mays and his companions which it would do no good at all to repeat here.

'What I don't understand,' said Searle, 'is how they got the thing out – if they have, in fact. We should have spotted it.'

'There are plenty of hiding places, and they could have

waited until there was no one around before they took it up through the hull. It must have been quite a job, even under this gravity,' remarked Eric Fulton, in tones of admiration.

'There's no time for post-mortems,' said the Professor savagely. 'We've got five hours to think of something. They can't take off before then, because we're only just past opposition with Ganymede. That's correct, isn't it, Kingsley?'

Searle nodded agreement.

'Yes. We must move round to the other side of Jupiter before we can enter a transfer orbit – at least, a reasonably economical one.'

'Good. That gives us a breathing space. Well, has anyone any ideas?'

Looking back on the whole thing now, it often seems to me that our subsequent behavior was, shall I say, a little peculiar and slightly uncivilized. It was not the sort of thing we could have imagined ourselves doing a few months before. But we were annoyed and overwrought, and our remoteness from all other human beings somehow made everything seem different. Since there were no other laws here, we had to make our own . . .

'Can't we do something to stop them from taking off? Could we sabotage their rockets, for instance?' asked Bill.

Searle didn't like this idea at all.

'We mustn't do anything drastic,' he said. 'Besides, Don Hopkins is a good friend of mine. He'd never forgive me if I damaged his ship. There'd be the danger, too, that we might do something that couldn't be repaired.'

'Then pinch their fuel,' said Groves laconically

'Of course! They're probably all asleep, there's no light in the cabin. All we've got to do is to connect up and pump.'

'A very nice idea,' I pointed out, 'but we're two kilometers apart. How much pipeline have we got? Is it as much as a hundred meters?'

The others ignored this interruption as though it was beneath contempt and went on making their plans. Five minutes later the technicians had settled everything: we only had to climb into our space-suits and do the work.

I never thought, when I joined the Professor's expedition, that I should end up like an African porter in one of those old adventure stories, carrying a load on my head. Especially when that load was a sixth of a spaceship (being so short, Professor Forster wasn't able to provide very effective help). Now that its fuel tanks were half empty, the weight of the ship in this gravity was about two hundred kilograms. We squeezed beneath, heaved, and up she went – very slowly, of course, because her inertia was still unchanged. Then we started marching.

It took us quite a while to make the journey, and it wasn't quite as easy as we'd thought it would be. But presently the two ships were lying side by side, and nobody had noticed us. Everyone in the 'Henry Luce' was fast asleep, as they had every reason to expect us to be.

Though I was still rather short of breath, I found a certain schoolboy amusement in the whole adventure as Searle and Fulton drew the refueling pipeline out of our airlock and quietly coupled up to the other ship.

'The beauty of this plan,' explained Groves to me as we stood watching, 'is that they can't do anything to stop us, unless they come outside and uncouple our line. We can drain them dry in five minutes, and it will take them half that time to wake up and get into their space-suits.'

A sudden horrid fear smote me.

'Suppose they turned on their rockets and tried to get away?'

'Then we'd both be smashed up. No, they'll just have to come outside and see what's going on. Ah, there go the pumps.'

The pipeline had stiffened like a fire-hose under pressure, and I knew that the fuel was pouring into our tanks. Any moment now the lights would go on in the 'Henry Luce' and her startled occupants would come scuttling out.

It was something of an anticlimax when they didn't. They must have been sleeping very soundly not to have felt the vibration from the pumps, but when it was all over nothing had happened and we just stood round looking rather foolish. Searle and Fulton carefully uncoupled the pipeline and put it back into the airlock.

'Well?' we asked the Professor.

He thought things over for a minute.

'Let's get back into the ship,' he said.

When we had climbed out of our suits and were gathered together in the control room, or as far in as we could get, the Professor sat down at the radio and punched out the 'Emergency' signal. Our sleeping neighbors would be awake in a couple of seconds as their automatic receiver sounded the alarm.

The TV screen glimmered into life. There, looking rather frightened, was Randolph Mays.

'Hello, Forster,' he snapped. 'What's the trouble?'

'Nothing wrong here,' replied the Professor in his best deadpan manner, 'but you've lost something important. Look at your fuel gauges.'

The screen emptied, and for a moment there was a confused mumbling and shouting from the speaker. Then Mays was back, annoyance and alarm competing for possession of his features.

'What's going on?' he demanded angrily. 'Do you know anything about this?'

The Prof let him sizzle for a moment before he replied.

'I think you'd better come across and talk things over,' he said. 'You won't have far to walk.'

Mays glared back at him uncertainly, then retorted, 'You bet I will!' The screen went blank.

'He'll have to climb down now!' said Bill gleefully. 'There's nothing else he can do!'

'It's not so simple as you think,' warned Fulton. 'If he really wanted to be awkward, he could just sit tight and radio Ganymede for a tanker.'

'What good would that do him? It would waste days and cost a fortune.'

'Yes, but he'd still have the statue, if he wanted it that badly. And he'd get his money back when he sued us.'

The airlock light flashed on and Mays stumped into the room. He was in a surprisingly conciliatory mood; on the way over, he must have had second thoughts.

'Well, well,' he said affably. 'What's all this nonsense in aid of?'

'You know perfectly well,' the Professor retorted coldly. 'I made it quite clear that nothing was to be taken off Five. You've been stealing property that doesn't belong to you.'

'Now, let's be reasonable. Who *does* it belong to? You can't claim everything on this planet as your personal property.'

'This is *not* a planet – it's a ship and the laws of salvage operate.'

'Frankly, that's a very debatable point. Don't you think you should wait until you get a ruling from the lawyers?'

The Professor was being icily polite, but I could see that

the strain was terrific and an explosion might occur at any moment.

'Listen, Mr Mays,' he said with ominous calm. 'What you've taken is the most important single find we've made here. I will make allowances for the fact that you don't appreciate what you've done, and don't understand the viewpoint of an archaeologist like myself. Return that statue, and we'll pump your fuel back and say no more.'

Mays rubbed his chin thoughtfully.

'I really don't see why you should make such a fuss about one statue, when you consider all the stuff that's still here.'

It was then that the Professor made one of his rare mistakes.

'You talk like a man who's stolen the Mona Lisa from the Louvre and argues that nobody will miss it because of all the other paintings. This statue's unique in a way that no terrestrial work of art can ever be. That's why I'm determined to get it back.'

You should never, when you're bargaining, make it obvious that you want something really badly. I saw the greedy glint in Mays's eye and said to myself, 'Uh-huh! He's going to be tough.' And I remembered Fulton's remark about calling Ganymede for a tanker.

'Give me half an hour to think it over,' said Mays, turning to the airlock.

'Very well,' replied the Professor stiffly. 'Half an hour – no more.'

I must give Mays credit for brains. Within five minutes we saw his communications aerial start slewing round until it locked on Ganymede. Naturally we tried to listen in, but he had a scrambler. These newspaper men must trust each other.

The reply came back a few minutes later; that was

scrambled, too. While we were waiting for the next development, we had another council of war. The Professor was now entering the stubborn, stop-at-nothing stage. He realized he'd miscalculated and that had made him fighting mad.

I think Mays must have been a little apprehensive, because he had reinforcements when he returned. Donald Hopkins, his pilot, came with him, looking rather uncomfortable.

'I've been able to fix things up, Professor,' he said smugly. 'It will take me a little longer, but I can get back without your help if I have to. Still, I must admit that it will save a good deal of time and money if we can come to an agreement. I'll tell you what. Give me back my fuel and I'll return the other – er – souvenirs I've collected. But I insist on keeping Mona Lisa, even if it means I won't get back to Ganymede until the middle of next week.'

The Professor then uttered a number of what are usually called deep-space oaths, though I can assure you they're much the same as any other oaths. That seemed to relieve his feelings a lot and he became fiendishly friendly.

'My dear Mr Mays,' he said, 'you're an unmitigated crook, and accordingly I've no compunction left in dealing with you. I'm prepared to use force, knowing that the law will justify me.'

Mays looked slightly alarmed, though not unduly so. We had moved to strategic positions round the door.

'Please don't be so melodramatic,' he said haughtily. 'This is the twenty-first century, not the Wild West back in 1800.'

'1880,' said Bill, who is a stickler for accuracy.

'I must ask you,' the Professor continued, 'to consider yourself under detention while we decide what is to be done. Mr Searle, take him to Cabin B.'

194

Mays sidled along the wall with a nervous laugh.

'Really, Professor, this is *too* childish! You can't detain me against my will.' He glanced for support at the Captain of the 'Henry Luce.'

Donald Hopkins dusted an imaginary speck of fluff from his uniform.

'I refuse,' he remarked for the benefit of all concerned, 'to get involved in vulgar brawls.'

Mays gave him a venomous look and capitulated with bad grace. We saw that he had a good supply of reading matter, and locked him in.

When he was out of the way, the Professor turned to Hopkins, who was looking enviously at our fuel gauges.

'Can I take it, Captain,' he said politely, 'that you don't wish to get mixed up in any of your employer's dirty business?'

'I'm neutral. My job is to fly the ship here and take her home. You can fight this out among yourselves.'

'Thank you. I think we understand each other perfectly. Perhaps it would be best if you returned to your ship and explained the situation. We'll be calling you in a few minutes.'

Captain Hopkins made his way languidly to the door. As he was about to leave he turned to Searle.

'By the way, Kingsley,' he drawled. 'Have you thought of torture? Do call me if you get round to it – I've some jolly interesting ideas.' Then he was gone, leaving us with our hostage.

I think the Professor had hoped he could do a direct exchange. If so, he had not bargained on Marianne's stubbornness.

'It serves Randolph right,' she said. 'But I don't really see that it makes any difference. He'll be just as comfortable in your ship as in ours, and you can't do anything to him. Let me know when you're fed up with having him around.'

It seemed a complete impasse. We had been too clever by half, and it had got us exactly nowhere. We'd captured Mays, but he wasn't any use to us.

The Professor was standing with his back to us, staring morosely out of the window. Seemingly balanced on the horizon, the immense bulk of Jupiter nearly filled the sky.

'We've got to convince her that we really *do* mean business,' he said. Then he turned abruptly to me.

'Do you think she's actually fond of this blackguard?'

'Er – I shouldn't be surprised. Yes, I really believe so.'

The Professor looked very thoughtful. Then he said to Searle, 'Come into my room. I want to talk something over.'

They were gone quite a while. When they returned, they both had an indefinable air of gleeful anticipation, and the Professor was carrying a piece of paper covered with figures. He went to the radio, and called the 'Henry Luce.'

'Hello,' said Marianne, replying so promptly that she'd obviously been waiting for us. 'Have you decided to call it off? I'm getting so bored.'

The Professor looked at her gravely.

'Miss Mitchell,' he replied. 'It's apparent that you have not been taking us seriously. I'm therefore arranging a somewhat – er – drastic little demonstration for your benefit. I'm going to place your employer in a position from which he'll be only too anxious for you to retrieve him as quickly as possible.'

'Indeed?' replied Marianne noncommittally – though I thought I could detect a trace of apprehension in her voice.

'I don't suppose,' continued the Professor smoothly,

'that you know anything about celestial mechanics. No? Too bad, but your pilot will confirm everything I tell you. Won't you, Hopkins?'

'Go ahead,' came a painstakingly neutral voice from the background.

'Then listen carefully, Miss Mitchell. I want to remind you of our curious – indeed our precarious – position on this satellite. You've only got to look out of the window to see how close to Jupiter we are, and I need hardly remind you that Jupiter has by far the most intense gravitational field of all the planets. You follow me?'

'Yes,' replied Marianne, no longer quite so self-possessed. 'Go on.'

'Very well. This little world of ours goes round Jupiter in almost exactly twelve hours. Now there's a well-known theorem stating that if a body *falls* from an orbit to the center of attraction, it will take point one seven seven of a period to make the drop. In other words, anything falling from here to Jupiter would reach the center of the planet in about two hours seven minutes. I'm sure Captain Hopkins can confirm this.'

There was a long pause. Then we heard Hopkins say, 'Well, of course I can't confirm the exact figures, but they're probably correct. It would be something like that, anyway.'

'Good,' continued the Professor. 'Now I'm sure you realize,' he went on with a hearty chuckle, 'that a fall to the *center* of the planet is a very theoretical case. If anything really was dropped from here, it would reach the upper atmosphere of Jupiter in a considerably shorter time. I hope I'm not boring you?'

'No,' said Marianne, rather faintly.

'I'm so glad to hear it. Anyway, Captain Searle has worked out the actual time for me, and it's one hour thirty-five minutes – with a few minutes either way. We can't guarantee complete accuracy, ha, ha!

'Now, it has doubtless not escaped your notice that this satellite of ours has an extremely weak gravitational field. Its escape velocity is only about ten meters a second, and anything thrown away from it at that speed would never come back. Correct, Mr Hopkins?'

'Perfectly correct.'

'Then, if I may come to the point, we propose to take Mr Mays for a walk until he's immediately under Jupiter, remove the reaction pistols from his suit, and – ah – launch him forth. We will be prepared to retrieve him with our ship as soon as you've handed over the property you've stolen. After what I've told you, I'm sure you'll appreciate that time will be rather vital. An hour and thirty-five minutes is remarkably short, isn't it?'

'Professor!' I gasped. 'You can't possibly do this!'

'Shut up!' he barked. 'Well, Miss Mitchell, what about it?'

Marianne was staring at him with mingled horror and disbelief.

'You're simply bluffing!' she cried. 'I don't believe you'd do anything of the kind! Your crew won't let you!'

The Professor sighed.

'Too bad,' he said. 'Captain Searle – Mr Groves – will you take the prisoner and proceed as instructed.'

'Aye-aye, sir,' replied Searle with great solemnity.

Mays looked frightened but stubborn.

'What are you going to do now?' he said, as his suit was handed back to him.

Searle unholstered his reaction pistols. 'Just climb in,' he said. 'We're going for a walk.'

I realized then what the Professor hoped to do. The whole thing was a colossal bluff: of course he wouldn't

198

really have Mays thrown into Jupiter; and in any case Searle and Groves wouldn't do it. Yet surely Marianne would see through the bluff, and then we'd be left looking mighty foolish.

Mays couldn't run away; without his reaction pistols he was quite helpless. Grasping his arms and towing him along like a captive balloon, his escorts set off toward the horizon – and towards Jupiter.

I could see, looking across the space to the other ship, that Marianne was staring out through the observation windows at the departing trio. Professor Forster noticed it too.

'I hope you're convinced, Miss Mitchell, that my men aren't carrying along an empty space-suit. Might I suggest that you follow the proceedings with a telescope? They'll be over the horizon in a minute, but you'll be able to see Mr Mays when he starts to – er – ascend.'

There was a stubborn silence from the loudspeaker. The period of suspense seemed to last for a very long time. Was Marianne waiting to see how far the Professor really would go?

By this time I had got hold of a pair of binoculars and was sweeping the sky beyond the ridiculously close horizon. Suddenly I saw it – a tiny flare of light against the vast yellow back-cloth of Jupiter. I focused quickly, and could just make out the three figures rising into space. As I watched, they separated: two of them decelerated with their pistols and started to fall back toward Five. The other went on ascending helplessly toward the ominous bulk of Jupiter.

I turned on the Professor in horror and disbelief.

'They've really done it!' I cried. 'I thought you were only bluffing!'

'So did Miss Mitchell, I've no doubt,' said the Professor

calmly, for the benefit of the listening microphone. 'I hope I don't need to impress upon you the urgency of the situation. As I've remarked once or twice before, the time of fall from our orbit to Jupiter's surface is ninety-five minutes. But, of course, if one waited even half that time, it would be much too late . . .'

He let that sink in. There was no reply from the other ship.

'And now,' he continued, 'I'm going to switch off our receiver so we can't have any more arguments. We'll wait until you've unloaded that statue – *and* the other items Mr Mays was careless enough to mention – before we'll talk to you again. Goodbye.'

It was a very uncomfortable ten minutes. I'd lost track of Mays, and was seriously wondering if we'd better overpower the Professor and go after him before we had a murder on our hands. But the people who could fly the ship were the ones who had actually carried out the crime. I didn't know *what* to think.

Then the airlock of the 'Henry Luce' slowly opened. A couple of space-suited figures emerged, floating the cause of all the trouble between them.

'Unconditional surrender,' murmured the Professor with a sigh of satisfaction. 'Get it into our ship,' he called over the radio. 'I'll open up the airlock for you.'

He seemed in no hurry at all. I kept looking anxiously at the clock; fifteen minutes had already gone by. Presently there was a clanking and banging in the airlock, the inner door opened, and Captain Hopkins entered. He was followed by Marianne, who only needed a bloodstained axe to make her look like Clytaemnestra. I did my best to avoid her eye, but the Professor seemed to be quite without shame. He walked into the airlock, checked that his property was back, and emerged rubbing his hands.

'Well, that's that,' he said cheerfully. 'Now let's sit down and have a drink to forget all this unpleasantness, shall we?'

I pointed indignantly at the clock.

'Have you gone crazy!' I yelled. 'He's already halfway to Jupiter!'

Professor Forster looked at me disapprovingly.

'Impatience,' he said, 'is a common failing in the young. I see no cause at all for hasty action.'

Marianne spoke for the first time; she now looked really scared.

'But you promised,' she whispered.

The Professor suddenly capitulated. He had had his little joke, and didn't want to prolong the agony.

'I can tell you at once, Miss Mitchell – and you too, Jack – that Mays is in no more danger than we are. We can go and collect him whenever we like.'

'Do you mean that you lied to me?'

'Certainly not. Everything I told you was perfectly true. You simply jumped to the wrong conclusions. When I said that a body would take ninety-five minutes to fall from here to Jupiter, I omitted – not, I must confess, accidentally – a rather important phrase. I should have added "*a body at rest with respect to Jupiter.*" Your friend Mr Mays was sharing the orbital speed of this satellite, and he's still got it. A little matter of twenty-six kilometers a second, Miss Mitchell.

'Oh yes, we threw him completely off Five and toward Jupiter. But the velocity we gave him then was trivial. He's still moving in practically the same orbit as before. The most he can do – I've got Captain Searle to work out the figures – is to drift about a hundred kilometers inward. And in one revolution – twelve hours – *he'll be right back*

201

where he started, without us bothering to do anything at all.'

There was a long, long silence. Marianne's face was a study in frustration, relief, and annoyance at having been fooled. Then she turned on Captain Hopkins.

'You must have known all the time! Why didn't you tell me?'

Hopkins gave her a wounded expression.

'You didn't ask me,' he said.

We hauled Mays down about an hour later. He was only twenty kilometers up, and we located him quickly enough by the flashing light on his suit. His radio had been disconnected, for a reason that hadn't occurred to me. He was intelligent enough to realize that he was in no danger, and if his set had been working he could have called his ship and exposed our bluff. That is, if he wanted to. Personally, I think I'd have been glad enough to call the whole thing off even if I had known that I was perfectly safe. It must have been awfully lonely up there.

To my great surprise, Mays wasn't as mad as I'd expected. Perhaps he was too relieved to be back in our snug little cabin when we drifted up to him on the merest fizzle of rockets and yanked him in. Or perhaps he felt that he'd been worsted in fair fight and didn't bear any grudge. I really think it was the latter.

There isn't much more to tell, except that we did play one other trick on him before we left Five. He had a good deal more fuel in his tanks than he really needed, now that his payload was substantially reduced. By keeping the excess ourselves, we were able to carry The Ambassador back to Ganymede after all. Oh, yes, the Professor gave him a check for the fuel we'd borrowed. Everything was perfectly legal.

There's one amusing sequel I must tell you, though. The day after the new gallery was opened at the British Museum I went along to see The Ambassador, partly to discover if his impact was still as great in these changed surroundings. (For the record, it wasn't – though it's still considerable and Bloomsbury will never be quite the same to me again.) A huge crowd was milling around the gallery, and there in the middle of it were Mays and Marianne.

It ended up with us having a very pleasant lunch together in Holborn. I'll say this about Mays – he doesn't bear any grudges. But I'm still rather sore about Marianne.

And, frankly, I can't imagine *what* she sees in him.

Refugee

Doubtless to the great confusion of anthologists, this story has been published under three other titles: 'Royal Prerogative,' 'This Earth of Majesty' and '?'. (Now, how do you index that?)

It was written in 1954, and I cannot pretend that no resemblance was intended to any living character. Indeed, I have since met the prototype of 'Prince Henry' on three occasions, and on the last – here in Colombo, only a few months ago – we had a conversation uncannily appropriate to this story.

Our first meeting, I mentioned, had been at an exhibition circa 1958 optimistically called 'Britain Enters The Space Age.' His Royal Highness laughed and answered wryly: 'We never did, did we?'

Not quite true, of course, since there are many British satellites in orbit, and there will soon be a few Britons (courtesy the US Space Shuttle) as well. But that isn't exactly what I had in mind.

Well, Sir Isaac Newton invented gravity. Perhaps one day we British may be lucky enough to disinvent it.

'When he comes aboard,' said Captain Saunders, as he waited for the landing ramp to extrude itself, 'what the devil shall I call him?' There was a thoughtful silence while the navigation officer and the assistant pilot considered this problem in etiquette. Then Mitchell locked the main control panel, and the ship's multitudinous mechanisms lapsed into unconsciousness as power was withdrawn from them.

'The correct address,' he drawled slowly, 'is "Your Royal Highness."'

'Huh!' snorted the captain. 'I'll be damned if I'll call anyone *that*!'

'In these progressive days,' put in Chambers helpfully, 'I believe that "Sir" is quite sufficient. But there's no need to worry if you forget: it's been a long time since anyone went to the Tower. Besides, this Henry isn't as tough a proposition as the one who had all the wives.'

'From all accounts,' added Mitchell, 'he's a very pleasant young man. Quite intelligent, too. He's often been known to ask people technical questions that they couldn't answer.'

Captain Saunders ignored the implications of this remark, beyond resolving that if Prince Henry wanted to know how a Field Compensation Drive Generator worked, then Mitchell could do the explaining. He got gingerly to his feet – they'd been operating on half a gravity during flight, and now they were on Earth, he felt like a ton of bricks – and started to make his way along

207

the corridors that led to the lower air lock. With an oily purring, the great curving door side-stepped out of his way. Adjusting his smile, he walked out to meet the television cameras and the heir to the British throne.

The man who would, presumably, one day be Henry IX of England was still in his early twenties. He was slightly below average height, and had fine-drawn, regular features that really lived up to all the genealogical clichés. Captain Saunders, who came from Dallas and had no intention of being impressed by any prince, found himself unexpectedly moved by the wide, sad eyes. They were eyes that had seen too many receptions and parades, that had had to watch countless totally uninteresting things, that had never been allowed to stray far from the carefully planned official routes. Looking at that proud but weary face, Captain Saunders glimpsed for the first time the ultimate loneliness of royalty. All his dislike of that institution became suddenly trivial against its real defect: what was wrong with the Crown was the unfairness of inflicting such a burden on any human being . . .

The passageways of the *Centaurus* were too narrow to allow for general sight-seeing, and it was soon clear that it suited Prince Henry very well to leave his entourage behind. Once they had begun moving through the ship, Saunders lost all his stiffness and reserve, and within a few minutes was treating the prince exactly like any other visitor. He did not realize that one of the earliest lessons royalty has to learn is that of putting people at their ease.

'You know, Captain,' said the prince wistfully, 'this is a big day for us. I've always hoped that one day it would be possible for spaceships to operate from England. But it still seems strange to have a port of our own here, after all these years. Tell me – did you ever have much to do with rockets?'

208

'Well, I had some training on them, but they were already on the way out before I graduated. I was lucky: some older men had to go back to school and start all over again – or else abandon space completely if they couldn't convert to the new ships.'

'It made as much difference as that?'

'Oh yes – when the rocket went, it was as big as the change from sail to steam. That's an analogy you'll often hear, by the way. There was a glamour about the old rockets, just as there was about the old windjammers, which these modern ships haven't got. When the *Centaurus* takes off, she goes up as quietly as a balloon – and as slowly, if she wants to. But a rocket blast-off shook the ground for miles, and you'd be deaf for days if you were too near the launching apron. Still, you'll know all that from the old news recordings.'

The prince smiled.

'Yes,' he said. 'I've often run through them at the Palace. I think I've watched every incident in all the pioneering expeditions. I was sorry to see the end of the rockets, too. But we could never have had a spaceport here on Salisbury Plain – the vibration would have shaken down Stonehenge!'

'Stonehenge?' queried Saunders as he held open a hatch and let the prince through into Hold Number 3.

'Ancient monument – one of the most famous stone circles in the world. It's really impressive, and about three thousand years old. See it if you can – it's only ten miles from here.'

Captain Saunders had some difficulty in suppressing a smile. What an odd country this was: where else, he wondered, would you find contrasts like this? It made him feel very young and raw when he remembered that back home Billy the Kid was ancient history, and there was hardly anything in the whole of Texas as much as five hundred years old. For the first time he began to realize what tradition meant: it gave Prince Henry something that he could never possess. Poise – self-confidence, yes, that was it. And a pride that was somehow free from arrogance because it took itself so much for granted that it never had to be asserted.

It was surprising how many questions Prince Henry managed to ask in the thirty minutes that had been allotted for his tour of the freighter. They were not the routine questions that people asked out of politeness, quite uninterested in the answers. HRH Prince Henry knew a lot about spaceships, and Captain Saunders felt completely exhausted when he handed his distinguished guest back to the reception committee, which had been waiting outside the *Centaurus* with well-simulated patience.

'Thank you very much, Captain,' said the prince as they shook hands in the air lock. 'I've not enjoyed myself so much for ages. I hope you have a pleasant stay in England, and a successful voyage.' Then his retinue whisked him away, and the port officials, frustrated until now, came aboard to check the ship's papers.

'Well,' said Mitchell when it was all over, 'what did you think of our Prince of Wales?'

'He surprised me,' answered Saunders frankly. 'I'd never have guessed he was a prince. I always thought they were rather dumb. But heck, he *knew* the principles of the Field Drive! Has he ever been up in space?'

'Once, I think. Just a hop above the atmosphere in a Space Force ship. It didn't even reach orbit before it came back again – but the Prime Minister nearly had a fit. There were questions in the House and editorials in the *Times*. Everyone decided that the heir to the throne was too valuable to risk in these newfangled inventions. So, though he has the rank of commodore in the Royal Space Force, he's never even been to the moon.'

'The poor guy,' said Captain Saunders.

He had three days to burn, since it was not the captain's job to supervise the loading of the ship or the preflight maintenance. Saunders knew skippers who hung around breathing heavily on the necks of the servicing engineers, but he wasn't that type. Besides, he wanted to see London. He had been to Mars and Venus and the moon, but this was his first visit to England. Mitchell and Chambers filled him with useful information and put him on the monorail to London before dashing off to see their own families. They would be returning to the spaceport a day before he did, to see that everything was in order. It was a great relief having officers one could rely on so implicitly: they were unimaginative and cautious, but thoroughgoing almost to a fault. If *they* said that everything was shipshape, Saunders knew he could take off without qualms.

The sleek, streamlined cylinder whistled across the carefully tailored landscape. It was so close to the ground, and traveling so swiftly, that one could only gather fleeting impressions of the towns and fields that flashed by. Everything, thought Saunders, was so incredibly compact, and on such a Lilliputian scale. There were no open spaces, no fields more than a mile long in any direction. It was enough to give a Texan claustrophobia – particularly a Texan who also happened to be a space pilot.

The sharply defined edge of London appeared like the bulwark of some walled city on the horizon. With few exceptions, the buildings were quite low – perhaps fifteen or twenty stories in height. The monorail shot through a narrow canyon, over a very attractive park, across a river that was presumably the Thames, and then came to rest with a steady, powerful surge of deceleration. A loudspeaker announced, in a modest voice that seemed afraid of being overheard: 'This is Paddington. Passengers for the North please remain seated.' Saunders pulled his baggage down from the rack and headed out into the station.

As he made for the entrance to the Underground, he passed a bookstall and glanced at the magazines on display. About half of them, it seemed, carried photographs of Prince Henry or other members of the royal family. This, thought Saunders, was altogether too much of a good thing. He also noticed that all the evening papers showed the prince entering or leaving the *Centaurus*, and bought copies to read in the subway – he begged its pardon, the 'Tube.'

The editorial comments had a monotonous similarity. At last, they rejoiced, England need no longer take a back seat among the space-going nations. Now it was possible to operate a space fleet without having a million square miles of desert: the silent, gravity-defying ships of today could land, if need be, in Hyde Park, without even disturbing the ducks on the Serpentine. Saunders found it odd that this sort of patriotism had managed to survive into the age of space, but he guessed that the British had felt it pretty badly when they'd had to borrow launching sites from the Australians, the Americans, and the Russians.

The London Underground was still, after a century and a half, the best transport system in the world, and it deposited Saunders safely at his destination less than ten minutes after he had left Paddington. In ten minutes the *Centaurus* could have covered fifty thousand miles; but space, after all, was not quite so crowded as this. Nor were the orbits of space craft so tortuous as the streets

Saunders had to negotiate to reach his hotel. All attempts to straighten out London had failed dismally, and it was fifteen minutes before he completed the last hundred yards of his journey.

He stripped off his jacket and collapsed thankfully on his bed. Three quiet, carefree days all to himself: it seemed too good to be true.

It was. He had barely taken a deep breath when the phone rang.

'Captain Saunders? I'm so glad we found you. This is the BBC. We have a program called "In Town Tonight" and we were wondering . . .'

The thud of the air-lock door was the sweetest sound Saunders had heard for days. Now he was safe; nobody could get at him here in his armored fortress, which would soon be far out in the freedom of space. It was not that he had been treated badly: on the contrary, he had been treated altogether too well. He had made four (or was it five?) appearances on various TV programs; he had been to more parties than he could remember; he had acquired several hundred new friends and (the way his head felt now) forgotten all his old ones.

'Who started the rumor,' he said to Mitchell as they met at the port, 'that the British were reserved and standoffish? Heaven help me if I ever meet a *demonstrative* Englishman.'

'I take it,' replied Mitchell, 'that you had a good time.'

'Ask me tomorrow,' Saunders replied. 'I may have reintegrated my psyche by then.'

'I saw you on that quiz program last night,' remarked Chambers. 'You looked pretty ghastly.'

'Thank you: that's just the sort of sympathetic encouragement I need at the moment. I'd like to see you think of a synonym for "jejune" after you'd been up until three in the morning.'

'Vapid,' replied Chambers promptly.

'Insipid,' said Mitchell, not to be outdone.

'You win. Let's have those overhaul schedules and see what the engineers have been up to.'

Once seated at the control desk, Captain Saunders quickly became his usual efficient self. He was home again, and his training took over. He knew exactly what to do, and would do it with automatic precision. To right and left of him, Mitchell and Chambers were checking their instruments and calling the control tower.

It took them an hour to carry out the elaborate preflight routine. When the last signature had been attached to the last sheet of instructions, and the last red light on the monitor panel had turned to green, Saunders flopped back in his seat and lit a cigarette. They had ten minutes to spare before take-off.

'One day,' he said, 'I'm going to come to England incognito to find what makes the place tick. I don't understand how you can crowd so many people onto one little island without it sinking.'

'Huh,' snorted Chambers. 'You should see Holland. That makes England look as wide open as Texas.'

'And then there's this royal family business. Do you know, wherever I went everybody kept asking me how I got on with Prince Henry – what we'd talked about – didn't I think he was a fine guy, and so on. Frankly, I got fed up with it. I can't imagine how you've managed to stand it for a thousand years.'

'Don't think that the royal family's been popular all the time,' replied Mitchell. 'Remember what happened to Charles the First? And some of the things we said about the early Georges were quite as rude as the remarks your people made later.'

'We just happen to like tradition,' said Chambers. 'We're not afraid to change when the time comes, but as far as the royal family is concerned – well, it's unique and we're rather fond of it. Just the way you feel about the Statue of Liberty.'

'Not a fair example. I don't think it's right to put human beings up on a pedestal and treat them as if they're – well, minor deities. Look at Prince Henry, for instance. Do you think he'll ever have a chance of doing the things he really wants to do? I saw him three times on TV when I was in London. The first time he was opening a new school somewhere; then he was giving a speech to the Worshipful Company of Fishmongers at the Guildhall (I swear I'm not making *that* up), and finally he was receiving an address of welcome from the mayor of Podunk, or whatever your equivalent is.' ('Wigan,' interjected Mitchell.) 'I think I'd rather be in jail than live that sort of life. Why can't you leave the poor guy alone?'

For once, neither Mitchell nor Chambers rose to the challenge. Indeed, they maintained a somewhat frigid silence. That's torn it, thought Saunders. I should have kept my big mouth shut; now I've hurt their feelings. I should have remembered that advice I read somewhere: 'The British have two religions – cricket and the royal family. Never attempt to criticize either.'

The awkward pause was broken by the radio and the voice of the spaceport controller.

'Control to *Centaurus*. Your flight lane clear. OK to lift.'

'Take-off program starting – *now!*' replied Saunders, throwing the master switch. Then he leaned back, his eyes

215

taking in the entire control panel, his hands clear of the board but ready for instant action.

He was tense but completely confident. Better brains than his – brains of metal and crystal and flashing electron streams – were in charge of the *Centaurus* now. If necessary, he could take command, but he had never yet lifted a ship manually and never expected to do so. If the automatics failed, he would cancel the take-off and sit here on Earth until the fault had been cleared up.

The main field went on, and weight ebbed from the *Centaurus*. There were protesting groans from the ship's hull and structure as the strains redistributed themselves. The curved arms of the landing cradle were carrying no load now; the slightest breath of wind would carry the freighter away into the sky.

Control called from the tower: 'Your weight now zero: check calibration.'

Saunders looked at his meters. The upthrust of the field would now exactly equal the weight of the ship, and the meter readings should agree with the totals on the loading schedules. In at least one instance this check had revealed the presence of a stowaway on board a spaceship – the gauges were as sensitive as that.

'One million, five hundred and sixty thousand, four hundred and twenty kilograms,' Saunders read off from the thrust indicators. 'Pretty good – it checks to within fifteen kilos. The first time I've been underweight, though. You could have taken on some more candy for that plump girl friend of yours in Port Lowell, Mitch.'

The assistant pilot gave a rather sickly grin. He had never quite lived down a blind date on Mars which had given him a completely unwarranted reputation for preferring statuesque blondes.

There was no sense of motion, but the *Centaurus* was

now falling up into the summer sky as her weight was not only neutralized but reversed. To the watchers below, she would be a swiftly mounting star, a silver globule climbing through and beyond the clouds. Around her, the blue of the atmosphere was deepening into the eternal darkness of space. Like a bead moving along an invisible wire, the freighter was following the pattern of radio waves that would lead her from world to world.

This, thought Captain Saunders, was his twenty-sixth take-off from Earth. But the wonder would never die nor would he ever outgrow the feeling of power it gave him to sit here at the control panel, the master of forces beyond even the dreams of mankind's ancient gods. No two departures were ever the same; some were into the dawn, some toward the sunset, some above a cloud-veiled Earth, some through clear and sparkling skies. Space itself might be unchanging, but on Earth the same pattern never recurred, and no man ever looked twice at the same landscape or the same sky. Down there the Atlantic waves· were marching eternally toward Europe, and high above them – but so far below the *Centaurus*! – the glittering bands of cloud were advancing before the same winds. England began to merge into the continent, and the European coast line became foreshortened and misty as it sank hull down beyond the curve of the world. At the frontier of the west, a fugitive stain on the horizon was the first hint of America. With a single glance, Captain Saunders could span all the leagues across which Columbus had labored half a thousand years ago.

With the silence of limitless power, the ship shook itself free from the last bonds of Earth. To an outside observer, the only sign of the energies it was expending would have been the dull red glow from the radiation fins around the vessel's equator, as the heat loss from the mass-converters was dissipated into space.

'14:03:45,' wrote Captain Saunders neatly in the log. 'Escape velocity attained. Course deviation negligible.'

There was little point in making the entry. The modest 25,000 miles an hour that had been the most unattainable goal of the first astronauts had no practical significance now, since the *Centaurus* was still accelerating and would continue to gain speed for hours. But it had a profound psychological meaning. Until this moment, if power had failed, they would have fallen back to Earth. But now gravity could never recapture them: they had achieved the freedom of space, and could take their pick of the planets. In practice, of course, there would be several kinds of hell to pay if they did not pick Mars and deliver their cargo according to plan. But Captain Saunders, like all spacemen, was fundamentally a romantic. Even on a milk run like this he would sometimes dream of the ringed glory of Saturn or the somber Neptunian wastes, lit by the distant fires of the shrunken sun.

An hour after take-off, according to the hallowed ritual, Chambers left the course computer to its own devices and produced the three glasses that lived beneath the chart table. As he drank the traditional toast to Newton, Oberth, and Einstein, Saunders wondered how this little ceremony had originated. Space crews had certainly been doing it for at least sixty years: perhaps it could be traced back to the legendary rocket engineer who made the remark, 'I've burned more alcohol in sixty seconds than you've ever sold across this lousy bar.'

Two hours later, the last course correction that the tracking stations on Earth could give them had been fed into the computer. From now on, until Mars came sweeping up ahead, they were on their own. It was a lonely thought, yet a curiously exhilarating one. Saunders savored it in his mind. There were just the three of them here – and no one else within a million miles.

In the circumstances, the detonation of an atomic bomb could hardly have been more shattering than the modest knock on the cabin door . . .

Captain Saunders had never been so startled in his life. With a yelp that had already left him before he had a chance to suppress it, he shot out of his seat and rose a full yard before the ship's residual gravity field dragged him back. Chambers and Mitchell, on the other hand, behaved with traditional British phlegm. They swiveled in their bucket seats, stared at the door, and then waited for their captain to take action.

It took Saunders several seconds to recover. Had he been confronted with what might be called a normal emergency, he would already have been halfway into a space-suit. But a diffident knock on the door of the control cabin, when everybody else in the ship was sitting beside him, was not a fair test.

A stowaway was simply impossible. The danger had been so obvious, right from the beginning of commercial space flight, that the most stringent precautions had been taken against it. One of his officers, Saunders knew, would always have been on duty during loading; no one could possibly have crept in unobserved. Then there had been the detailed preflight inspection, carried out by both Mitchell and Chambers. Finally, there was the weight check at the moment before take-off; *that* was conclusive. No, a stowaway was totally . . .

The knock on the door sounded again. Captain Saunders clenched his fists and squared his jaw. In a few minutes, he thought, some romantic idiot was going to be very, very sorry.

'Open the door, Mr Mitchell,' Saunders growled. In a single long stride, the assistant pilot crossed the cabin and jerked open the hatch.

For an age, it seemed, no one spoke. Then the stowaway, wavering slightly in the low gravity, came into the cabin. He was completely self-possessed, and looked very pleased with himself.

'Good afternoon, Captain Saunders,' he said, 'I must apologize for this sudden intrusion.'

Saunders swallowed hard. Then, as the pieces of the jigsaw fell into place, he looked first at Mitchell, then at Chambers. Both of his officers stared guilelessly back at him with expressions of ineffable innocence. 'So *that's* it,' he said bitterly. There was no need for any explanations: everything was perfectly clear. It was easy to picture the complicated negotiations, the midnight meetings, the falsification of records, the off-loading of nonessential cargoes that his trusted colleagues had been conducting behind his back. He was sure it was a most interesting story, but he didn't want to hear about it now. He was too busy wondering what the *Manual of Space Law* would have to say about a situation like this, though he was already gloomily certain that it would be of no use to him at all.

It was too late to turn back, of course: the conspirators wouldn't have made an elementary miscalculation like that. He would just have to make the best of what looked to be the trickiest voyage in his career.

He was still trying to think of something to say when the PRIORITY signal started flashing on the radio board. The stowaway looked at his watch.

'I was expecting that,' he said. 'It's probably the Prime Minister. I think I'd better speak to the poor man.'

Saunders thought so too.

'Very well, Your Royal Highness,' he said sulkily, and with such emphasis that the title sounded almost like an insult. Then, feeling much put upon, he retired into a corner.

It was the Prime Minister all right, and he sounded very upset. Several times he used the phrase 'your duty to your people' and once there was a distinct catch in his throat as he said something about 'devotion of your subjects to the Crown.' Saunders realized, with some surprise, that he really meant it.

While this emotional harangue was in progress, Mitchell leaned over to Saunders and whispered in his ear:

'The old boy's on a sticky wicket, and he knows it. The people will be behind the prince when they hear what's happened. Everybody knows he's been trying to get into space for years.'

'I wish he hadn't chosen *my* ship,' said Saunders. 'And I'm not sure that this doesn't count as mutiny.'

'The heck it does. Mark my words – when this is all over you'll be the only Texan to have the Order of the Garter. Won't that be nice for you?'

'Shush!' said Chambers. The prince was speaking, his words winging back across the abyss that now sundered him from the island he would one day rule.

'I am sorry, Mr Prime Minister,' he said, 'if I've caused you any alarm. I will return as soon as it is convenient. Someone has to do everything for the first time, and I felt the moment had come for a member of my family to leave Earth. It will be a valuable part of my education, and will make me more fitted to carry out my duty. Goodbye.'

He dropped the microphone and walked over to the observation window – the only spaceward-looking port on the entire ship. Saunders watched him standing there, proud and lonely – but contented now. And as he saw the prince staring out at the stars which he had at last attained, all his annoyance and indignation slowly evaporated.

No one spoke for a long time. Then Prince Henry tore his gaze away from the blinding splendor beyond the port, looked at Captain Saunders, and smiled.

'Where's the galley, Captain?' he asked. 'I may be out of practice, but when I used to go scouting I was the best cook in my patrol.'

Saunders slowly relaxed, then smiled back. The tension seemed to lift from the control room. Mars was still a long way off, but he knew now that this wasn't going to be such a bad trip after all . . .

The Wind From the Sun

'The Wind From the Sun' was written just twenty years ago, but is far more topical now than it was in 1963. I have in front of me at the moment a folder full of technical papers assembled by the World Space Foundation in support of its Solar Sail Project – conducted in cooperation with the University of Utah, the Jet Propulsion Laboratory, and the Radio Amateur Satellite Corporation, with the assistance of the Charles A. Lindbergh Fund.

Let me quote from the Foundation's leaflet, so that you will better appreciate the background of the story that follows:

'In 1924, Fridrikh Tsander, perhaps as a result of suggestion by Konstantin Tsiolkovsky, noted that in the vacuum of space, a large thin sheet of reflective material illuminated by the Sun and controlled in orientation could be used as a propulsion device requiring no propellant. This propulsion device is now called a solar sail. In 1973, NASA sponsored a design study which led to a full-scale evaluation of solar sailing for the proposed Halley's Comet rendezvous mission. Plans for this mission were suspended in 1977, but not before solar sailing had received a thorough technical review confirming its feasibility and unique advantages.'

The World Space Foundation hopes to launch a small solar-sailer, either from the US Shuttle or the European Space Association 'Ariane' rocket, in connection with Vancouver's EXPO '86. Anyone wishing to support this project can contact the WSF at P.O. Box Y, South Pasadena, Calif. 91030.

There is also an enthusiastic French group (U3P – Union pour la Promotion de la Promotion Photonique, 6 rue des Ramparts Coligny, Venerque 31120, Portet-sur-Garonne) planning a solar race around the Moon, hopefully by 1985–6. (Unmanned, of course – again the ESA Ariane would be used as a launcher.)

And a few months ago I received a fascinating letter from Dr V. Beletsky, of the Keldysh Institute of Applied Mathematics, Moscow, enclosing his book Essays on the Motions of Space Bodies. *One whole chapter is devoted to an analysis of 'The Wind From the Sun,' with a detailed integration of the trajectories of 'Diana' and 'Sunbeam.' To my pleased surprise, Dr Beletsky wrote: 'The data mentioned in your story has proved to be quite sufficient to integrate the differential equations of yacht motions. Integration results almost completely agree with situation in your story!! Have you also integrated the equations of yachts' motions? If not, why such close agreement of such unobvious details. If yes, why is such important characteristic as the total flight time not in agreement? – 2 days in your story and 5 in mine . . .'*

I had to confess that any agreement must have been more luck than integration. Though I had done some back-of-the-envelope calculations to make sure that the velocities and accelerations were not ridiculous, I had certainly not computed the orbit in any detail.

Incidentally, the story's original title, under which it first appeared in Boy's Life *(March 1964) was the rather obvious 'Sunjammer.' However, Poul Anderson had the same idea almost simultaneously, so I had to make a quick change of name . . .*

The enormous disc of sail strained at its rigging, already filled with the wind that blew between the worlds. In three minutes the race would begin, yet now John Merton felt more relaxed, more at peace, than at any time for the past year. Whatever happened when the Commodore gave the starting signal, whether *Diana* carried him to victory or defeat, he had achieved his ambition. After a lifetime spent designing ships for others, now he would sail his own.

'T minus two minutes,' said the cabin radio. 'Please confirm your readiness.'

One by one, the other skippers answered. Merton recognized all the voices – some tense, some calm – for they were the voices of his friends and rivals. On the four inhabited worlds, there were scarcely twenty men who could sail a sun yacht; and they were all there, on the starting line or aboard the escort vessels, orbiting twenty-two thousand miles above the equator.

'Number One – *Gossamer* – ready to go.'

'Number Two – *Santa Maria* – all OK.'

'Number Three – *Sunbeam* – OK.'

'Number Four – *Woomera* – all systems GO.'

Merton smiled at that last echo from the early, primitive days of astronautics. But it had become part of the tradition of space; and there were times when a man needed to evoke the shades of those who had gone before him to the stars.

'Number Five – *Lebedev* – we're ready.'

226

'Number Six – *Arachne* – OK.'

Now it was his turn, at the end of the line; strange to think that the words he was speaking in this tiny cabin were being heard by at least five billion people.

'Number Seven – *Diana* – ready to start.'

'One through Seven acknowledged,' answered that impersonal voice from the judge's launch. 'Now T minus one minute.'

Merton scarcely heard it. For the last time, he was checking the tension in the rigging. The needles of all the dynamometers were steady; the immense sail was taut, its mirror surface sparkling and glittering gloriously in the sun.

To Merton, floating weightless at the periscope, it seemed to fill the sky. As well it might – for out there were fifty million square feet of sail, linked to his capsule by almost a hundred miles of rigging. All the canvas of all the tea clippers that had once raced like clouds across the China seas, sewn into one gigantic sheet, could not match the single sail that *Diana* had spread beneath the sun. Yet it was little more substantial than a soap bubble; that two square miles of aluminized plastic was only a few millionths of an inch thick.

'T minus ten seconds. All recording cameras ON.'

Something so huge, yet so frail, was hard for the mind to grasp. And it was harder still to realize that this fragile mirror could tow him free of Earth merely by the power of the sunlight it would trap.

'. . . five, four, three, two, one, CUT!'

Seven knife blades sliced through seven thin lines tethering the yachts to the mother ships that had assembled and serviced them. Until this moment, all had been circling Earth together in a rigidly held formation, but now the yachts would begin to disperse, like dandelion

227

seeds drifting before the breeze. And the winner would be the one that first drifted past the Moon.

Aboard *Diana*, nothing seemed to be happening. But Merton knew better. Though his body could feel no thrust, the instrument board told him that he was now accelerating at almost one thousandth of a gravity. For a rocket, that figure would have been ludicrous – but this was the first time any solar yacht had ever attained it. *Diana*'s design was sound; the vast sail was living up to his calculations. At this rate, two circuits of the Earth would build up his speed to escape velocity, and then he could head out for the Moon, with the full force of the Sun behind him.

The full force of the Sun . . . He smiled wryly, remembering all his attempts to explain solar sailing to those lecture audiences back on Earth. That had been the only way he could raise money, in those early days. He might be Chief Designer of Cosmodyne Corporation, with a whole string of successful spaceships to his credit, but his firm had not been exactly enthusiastic about his hobby.

'Hold your hands out to the Sun,' he'd said. 'What do you feel? Heat, of course. But there's pressure as well – though you've never noticed it, because it's so tiny. Over the area of your hands, it comes to only about a millionth of an ounce.

'But out in space, even a pressure as small as that can be important, for it's acting all the time, hour after hour, day after day. Unlike rocket fuel, it's free and unlimited. If we want to, we can use it. We can build sails to catch the radiation blowing from the Sun.'

At that point, he would pull out a few square yards of sail material and toss it toward the audience. The silvery film would coil and twist like smoke, then drift slowly to the ceiling in the hot-air currents.

'You can see how light it is,' he'd continue. 'A square mile weighs only a ton, and can collect five pounds of radiation pressure. So it will start moving – and we can let it tow us along, if we attach rigging to it.

'Of course, its acceleration will be tiny – about a thousandth of a g. That doesn't seem much, but let's see what it means.

'It means that in the first second, we'll move about a fifth of an inch. I suppose a healthy snail could do better than that. But after a minute, we've covered sixty feet, and will be doing just over a mile an hour. That's not bad, for something driven by pure sunlight! After an hour, we're forty miles from our starting point, and will be moving at eighty miles an hour. Please remember that in space there's no friction; so once you start anything moving, it will keep going forever. You'll be surprised when I tell you what our thousandth-of-a-g sailboat will be doing at the end of a day's run: *almost two thousand miles an hour!* If it starts from orbit – as it has to, of course – it can reach escape velocity in a couple of days. And all without burning a single drop of fuel!'

Well, he'd convinced them, and in the end he'd even convinced Cosmodyne. Over the last twenty years, a new sport had come into being. It had been called the sport of billionaires, and that was true. But it was beginning to pay for itself in terms of publicity and TV coverage. The prestige of four continents and two worlds was riding on this race, and it had the biggest audience in history.

Diana had made a good start; time to take a look at the opposition. Moving very gently – though there were shock absorbers between the control capsule and the delicate rigging, he was determined to run no risks – Merton stationed himself at the periscope.

There they were, looking like strange silver flowers

229

planted in the dark fields of space. The nearest, South America's *Santa Maria*, was only fifty miles away; it bore a close resemblance to a boy's kite, but a kite more than a mile on a side. Farther away, the University of Astrograd's *Lebedev* looked like a Maltese cross; the sails that formed the four arms could apparently be tilted for steering purposes. In contrast, the Federation of Australasia's *Woomera* was a simple parachute, four miles in circumference. General Spacecraft's *Arachne*, as its name suggested, looked like a spider web, and had been built on the same principles, by robot shuttles spiraling out from a central point. Eurospace Corporation's *Gossamer* was an identical design, on a slightly smaller scale. And the Republic of Mars's *Sunbeam* was a flat ring, with a half-mile-wide hole in the center, spinning slowly, so that centrifugal force gave it stiffness. That was an old idea, but no one had ever made it work; and Merton was fairly sure that the colonials would be in trouble when they started to turn.

That would not be for another six hours, when the yachts had moved along the first quarter of their slow and stately twenty-four-hour orbit. Here at the beginning of the race, they were all heading directly away from the Sun – running, as it were, before the solar wind. One had to make the most of this lap, before the boats swung around to the other side of Earth and then started to head back into the Sun.

Time, Merton told himself, for the first check, while he had no navigational worries. With the periscope, he made a careful examination of the sail, concentrating on the points where the rigging was attached to it. The shroud lines – narrow bands of unsilvered plastic film – would have been completely invisible had they not been coated with fluorescent paint. Now they were taut lines of colored light, dwindling away for hundreds of yards toward that gigantic sail. Each had its own electric windlass, not much bigger than a game fisherman's reel. The little windlasses were continually turning, playing lines in or out as the autopilot kept the sail trimmed at the correct angle to the Sun.

The play of sunlight on the great flexible mirror was beautiful to watch. The sail was undulating in slow, stately oscillations, sending multiple images of the Sun marching across it, until they faded away at its edges. Such leisurely vibrations were to be expected in this vast and flimsy structure. They were usually quite harmless, but Merton watched them carefully. Sometimes they could build up to the catastrophic undulations known as the 'wriggles,' which could tear a sail to pieces.

When he was satisfied that everything was shipshape, he swept the periscope around the sky, rechecking the positions of his rivals. It was as he had hoped: the weeding-out process had begun, as the less efficient boats fell astern. But the real test would come when they passed into the shadow of Earth. Then, maneuverability would count as much as speed.

It seemed a strange thing to do, what with the race having just started, but he thought it might be a good idea to get some sleep. The two-man crews on the other boats could take it in turns, but Merton had no one to relieve him. He must rely on his own physical resources, like that other solitary seaman, Joshua Slocum, in his tiny *Spray*. The American skipper had sailed *Spray* singlehanded around the world; he could never have dreamed that, two centuries later, a man would be sailing singlehanded from Earth to Moon – inspired, at least partly, by his example.

Merton snapped the elastic bands of the cabin seat around his waist and legs, then placed the electrodes of

231

the sleep-inducer on his forehead. He set the timer for three hours, and relaxed. Very gently, hypnotically, the electronic pulses throbbed in the frontal lobes of his brain. Colored spirals of light expanded beneath his closed eyelids, widening outward to infinity. Then nothing . . .

The brazen clamor of the alarm dragged him back from his dreamless sleep. He was instantly awake, his eyes scanning the instrument panel. Only two hours had passed – but above the accelerometer, a red light was flashing. Thrust was falling; *Diana* was losing power.

Merton's first thought was that something had happened to the sail; perhaps the antispin devices had failed, and the rigging had become twisted. Swiftly, he checked the meters that showed the tension of the shroud lines. Strange – on one side of the sail they were reading normally, but on the other the pull was dropping slowly, even as he watched.

In sudden understanding, Merton grabbed the periscope, switched to wide-angle vision, and started to scan the edge of the sail. Yes – there was the trouble, and it could have only one cause.

A huge, sharp-edged shadow had begun to slide across the gleaming silver of the sail. Darkness was falling upon *Diana*, as if a cloud had passed between her and the Sun. And in the dark, robbed of the rays that drove her, she would lose all thrust and drift helplessly through space.

But, of course, there were no clouds here, more than twenty thousand miles above the Earth. If there was a shadow, it must be made by man.

Merton grinned as he swung the periscope toward the Sun, switching in the filters that would allow him to look full into its blazing face without being blinded.

'Maneuver 4a,' he muttered to himself. 'We'll see who can play best at *that* game.'

It looked as if a giant planet was crossing the face of the Sun; a great black disc had bitten deep into its edge. Twenty miles astern, *Gossamer* was trying to arrange an artificial eclipse, specially for *Diana*'s benefit.

The maneuver was a perfectly legitimate one. Back in the days of ocean racing, skippers had often tried to rob each other of the wind. With any luck, you could leave your rival becalmed, with his sails collapsing around him – and be well ahead before he could undo the damage.

Merton had no intention of being caught so easily. There was plenty of time to take evasive action; things happened very slowly when you were running a solar sailboat. It would be at least twenty minutes before *Gossamer* could slide completely across the face of the Sun, and leave him in darkness.

Diana's tiny computer – the size of a matchbox, but the equivalent of a thousand human mathematicians – considered the problem for a full second and then flashed the answer. He'd have to open control panels three and four, until the sail had developed an extra twenty degrees of tilt; then the radiation pressure would blow him out of *Gossamer*'s dangerous shadow, back into the full blast of the Sun. It was a pity to interfere with the autopilot, which had been carefully programmed to give the fastest possible run – but that, after all, was why he was here. This was what made solar yachting a sport, rather than a battle between computers.

Out went control lines one and six, slowly undulating like sleepy snakes as they momentarily lost their tension. Two miles away, the triangular panels began to open lazily, spilling sunlight through the sail. Yet, for a long time, nothing seemed to happen. It was hard to grow accustomed to this slow-motion world, where it took minutes for the effects of any action to become visible to the eye. Then Merton saw that the sail was indeed tipping toward the Sun – and that *Gossamer*'s shadow was sliding harmlessly away, its cone of darkness lost in the deeper night of space.

Long before the shadow had vanished, and the disc of the Sun had cleared again, he reversed the tilt and brought *Diana* back on course. Her new momentum would carry her clear of the danger; no need to overdo it, and upset his calculations by side-stepping too far. That was another rule that was hard to learn: the very moment you had started something happening in space, it was already time to think about stopping it.

He reset the alarm, ready for the next natural or manmade emergency. Perhaps *Gossamer*, or one of the other contestants, would try the same trick again. Meanwhile, it was time to eat, though he did not feel particularly hungry. One used little physical energy in space, and it was easy to forget about food. Easy – and dangerous; for when an emergency arose, you might not have the reserves needed to deal with it.

He broke open the first of the meal packets, and inspected it without enthusiasm. The name on the label – SPACETASTIES – was enough to put him off. And he had grave doubts about the promise printed underneath: 'Guaranteed crumbless.' It had been said that crumbs were a greater danger to space vehicles than meteorites; they could drift into the most unlikely places, causing short circuits, blocking vital jets, and getting into instruments that were supposed to be hermetically sealed.

Still, the liverwurst went down pleasantly enough; so did the chocolate and the pineapple puree. The plastic coffee bulb was warming on the electric heater when the outside world broke in upon his solitude, as the radio operator on the Commodore's launch routed a call to him.

'Dr Merton? If you can spare the time, Jeremy Blair would like a few words with you.' Blair was one of the more responsible news commentators, and Merton had been on his program many times. He could refuse to be interviewed, of course, but he liked Blair, and at the moment he could certainly not claim to be too busy. 'I'll take it,' he answered.

'Hello, Dr Merton,' said the commentator immediately. 'Glad you can spare a few minutes. And congratulations – you seem to be ahead of the field.'

'Too early in the game to be sure of *that*,' Merton answered cautiously.

'Tell me, Doctor, why did you decide to sail *Diana* by yourself? Just because it's never been done before?'

'Well, isn't that a good reason? But it wasn't the only one, of course.' He paused, choosing his words carefully. 'You know how critically the performance of a sun yacht depends on its mass. A second man, with all his supplies, would mean another five hundred pounds. That could easily be the difference between winning and losing.'

'And you're quite certain that you can handle *Diana* alone?'

'Reasonably sure, thanks to the automatic controls I've designed. My main job is to supervise and make decisions.'

'But – two square miles of sail! It just doesn't seem possible for one man to cope with all that.'

Merton laughed. 'Why not? Those two square miles produce a maximum pull of just ten pounds. I can exert more force with my little finger.'

'Well, thank you, Doctor. And good luck. I'll be calling you again.'

As the commentator signed off, Merton felt a little ashamed of himself. For his answer had been only part of the truth; and he was sure that Blair was shrewd enough to know it.

There was just one reason why he was here, alone in space. For almost forty years he had worked with teams of hundreds or even thousands of men, helping to design the most complex vehicles that the world had ever seen. For the last twenty years he had led one of those teams, and watched his creations go soaring to the stars. (Sometimes . . . There *were* failures, which he could never forget, even though the fault had not been his.) He was famous, with a successful career behind him. Yet he had never done anything by himself; always he had been one of an army.

This was his last chance to try for individual achievement, and he would share it with no one. There would be no more solar yachting for at least five years, as the period of the Quiet Sun ended and the cycle of bad weather began, with radiation storms bursting through the solar system. When it was safe again for these frail, unshielded craft to venture aloft, he would be too old. If, indeed, he was not too old already . . .

He dropped the empty food containers into the waste disposal and turned once more to the periscope. At first he could find only five of the other yachts; there was no sign of *Woomera*. It took him several minutes to locate her – a dim, star-eclipsing phantom, neatly caught in the shadow of *Lebedev*. He could imagine the frantic efforts the Australasians were making to extricate themselves, and wondered how they had fallen into the trap. It suggested that *Lebedev* was unusually maneuverable. She would bear watching, though she was too far away to menace *Diana* at the moment.

Now the Earth had almost vanished; it had waned to a narrow, brilliant bow of light that was moving steadily toward the Sun. Dimly outlined within that burning bow was the night side of the planet, with the phosphorescent gleams of great cities showing here and there through gaps in the clouds. The disc of darkness had already blanked out a huge section of the Milky Way. In a few minutes, it would start to encroach upon the Sun.

The light was fading; a purple, twilight hue – the glow of many sunsets, thousands of miles below – was falling across the sail as *Diana* slipped silently into the shadow of Earth. The Sun plummeted below that invisible horizon; within minutes, it was night.

Merton looked back along the orbit he had traced, now a quarter of the way around the world. One by one he saw the brilliant stars of the other yachts wink out, as they joined him in the brief night. It would be an hour before the Sun emerged from that enormous black shield, and through all that time they would be completely helpless, coasting without power.

He switched on the external spotlight, and started to search the now-darkened sail with its beam. Already the thousands of acres of film were beginning to wrinkle and become flaccid. The shroud lines were slackening, and must be wound in lest they become entangled. But all this was expected; everything was going as planned.

Fifty miles astern, *Arachne* and *Santa Maria* were not so lucky. Merton learned of their troubles when the radio burst into life on the emergency circuit.

'Number Two and Number Six, this is Control. You are on a collision course; your orbits will intersect in sixty-five minutes! Do you require assistance?'

There was a long pause while the two skippers digested this bad news. Merton wondered who was to blame. Perhaps one yacht had been trying to shadow the other, and had not completed the maneuver before they were both caught in darkness. Now there was nothing that either could do. They were slowly but inexorably converging, unable to change course by a fraction of a degree.

Yet – sixty-five minutes! That would just bring them out into sunlight again, as they emerged from the shadow of the Earth. They had a slim chance, if their sails could snatch enough power to avoid a crash. There must be some frantic calculations going on aboard *Arachne* and *Santa Maria*.

Arachne answered first. Her reply was just what Merton had expected.

'Number Six calling Control. We don't need assistance, thank you. We'll work this out for ourselves.'

I wonder, thought Merton; but at least it will be interesting to watch. The first real drama of the race was approaching, exactly above the line of midnight on the sleeping Earth.

For the next hour, Merton's own sail kept him too busy to worry about *Arachne* and *Santa Maria*. It was hard to keep a good watch on that fifty million square feet of dim plastic out there in the darkness, illuminated only by his narrow spotlight and the rays of the still-distant Moon. From now on, for almost half his orbit around the Earth, he must keep the whole of this immense area edge-on to the Sun. During the next twelve or fourteen hours, the sail would be a useless encumbrance; for he would be heading *into* the Sun, and its rays could only drive him backward along his orbit. It was a pity that he could not furl the sail completely, until he was ready to use it again; but no one had yet found a practical way of doing this.

Far below, there was the first hint of dawn along the edge of the Earth. In ten minutes the Sun would emerge from its eclipse. The coasting yachts would come to life again as the blast of radiation struck their sails. That

238

would be the moment of crisis for *Arachne* and *Santa Maria* – and, indeed, for all of them.

Merton swung the periscope until he found the two dark shadows drifting against the stars. They were very close together – perhaps less than three miles apart. They might, he decided, just be able to make it . . .

Dawn flashed like an explosion along the rim of Earth as the Sun rose out of the Pacific. The sail and shroud lines glowed a brief crimson, then gold, then blazed with the pure white light of day. The needles of the dynamometers began to lift from their zeroes – but only just. *Diana* was still almost completely weightless, for with the sail pointing toward the Sun, her acceleration was now only a few millionths of a gravity.

But *Arachne* and *Santa Maria* were crowding on all the sail that they could manage, in their desperate attempt to keep apart. Now, while there was less than two miles between them, their glittering plastic clouds were unfurling and expanding with agonizing slowness as they felt the first delicate push of the Sun's rays. Almost every TV screen on Earth would be mirroring this protracted drama; and even now, at this last minute, it was possible to tell what the outcome would be.

The two skippers were stubborn men. Either could have cut his sail and fallen back to give the other a chance; but neither would do so. Too much prestige, too many millions, too many reputations were at stake. And so, silently and softly as snowflakes falling on a winter night, *Arachne* and *Santa Maria* collided.

The square kite crawled almost imperceptibly into the circular spider web. The long ribbons of the shroud lines twisted and tangled together with dreamlike slowness. Even aboard *Diana*, Merton, busy with his own rigging,

239

could scarcely tear his eyes away from this silent, long-drawn-out disaster.

For more than ten minutes the billowing, shining clouds continued to merge into one inextricable mass. Then the crew capsules tore loose and went their separate ways, missing each other by hundreds of yards. With a flare of rockets, the safety launches hurried to pick them up.

That leaves five of us, thought Merton. He felt sorry for the skippers who had so thoroughly eliminated each other, only a few hours after the start of the race, but they were young men and would have another chance.

Within minutes, the five had dropped to four. From the beginning, Merton had had doubts about the slowly rotating *Sunbeam*; now he saw them justified.

The Martian ship had failed to tack properly. Her spin had given her too much stability. Her great ring of a sail was turning to face the Sun, instead of being edge-on to it. She was being blown back along her course at almost her maximum acceleration.

That was about the most maddening thing that could happen to a skipper – even worse than a collision, for he could blame only himself. But no one would feel much sympathy for the frustrated colonials, as they dwindled slowly astern. They had made too many brash boasts before the race, and what had happened to them was poetic justice.

Yet it would not do to write off *Sunbeam* completely; with almost half a million miles still to go, she might yet pull ahead. Indeed, if there were a few more casualties, she might be the only one to complete the race. It had happened before.

The next twelve hours were uneventful, as the Earth waxed in the sky from new to full. There was little to do while the fleet drifted around the unpowered half of its orbit, but Merton did not find the time hanging heavily on his hands. He caught a few hours of sleep, ate two meals, wrote his log, and became involved in several more radio interviews. Sometimes, though rarely, he talked to the other skippers, exchanging greetings and friendly taunts. But most of the time he was content to float in weightless relaxation, beyond all the cares of Earth, happier than he had been for many years. He was – as far as any man could be in space – master of his own fate, sailing the ship upon which he had lavished so much skill, so much love, that it had become part of his very being.

The next casualty came when they were passing the line between Earth and Sun, and were just beginning the powered half of the orbit. Aboard *Diana*, Merton saw the great sail stiffen as it tilted to catch the rays that drove it. The acceleration began to climb up from the microgravities, though it would be hours yet before it would reach its maximum value.

It would never reach it for *Gossamer*. The moment when power came on again was always critical, and she failed to survive it.

Blair's radio commentary, which Merton had left running at low volume, alerted him with the news: 'Hello, *Gossamer* has the wriggles!' He hurried to the periscope, but at first could see nothing wrong with the great circular disc of *Gossamer*'s sail. It was difficult to study it because it was almost edge-on to him and so appeared as a thin ellipse; but presently he saw that it was twisting back and forth in slow, irresistible oscillations. Unless the crew could damp out these waves, by properly timed but gentle tugs on the shroud lines, the sail would tear itself to pieces.

They did their best, and after twenty minutes it seemed that they had succeeded. Then, somewhere near the center of the sail, the plastic film began to rip. It was slowly driven outward by the radiation pressure, like smoke coiling upward from a fire. Within a quarter of an hour, nothing was left but the delicate tracery of the radial spars that had supported the great web. Once again there was a flare of rockets, as a launch moved in to retrieve the *Gossamer*'s capsule and her dejected crew.

'Getting rather lonely up here, isn't it?' said a conversational voice over the ship-to-ship radio.

'Not for you, Dimitri,' retorted Merton. 'You've still got company back there at the end of the field. I'm the one who's lonely, up here in front.' It was not an idle boast; by this time *Diana* was three hundred miles ahead of the next competitor, and her lead should increase still more rapidly in the hours to come.

Aboard *Lebedev*, Dimitri Markoff gave a good-natured chuckle. He did not sound, Merton thought, at all like a man who had resigned himself to defeat.

'Remember the legend of the tortoise and the hare,' answered the Russian. 'A lot can happen in the next quarter-million miles.'

It happened much sooner than that, when they had completed their first orbit of Earth and were passing the starting line again – though thousands of miles higher, thanks to the extra energy the Sun's rays had given them. Merton had taken careful sights on the other yachts, and had fed the figures into the computer. The answer it gave for *Woomera* was so absurd that he immediately did a recheck.

There was no doubt of it – the Australasians were catching up at a completely fantastic rate. No solar yacht could possibly have such an acceleration, unless . . .

A swift look through the periscope gave the answer. *Woomera*'s rigging, pared back to the very minimum of mass, had given way. It was her sail alone, still maintaining its shape, that was racing up behind him like a handkerchief blown before the wind. Two hours later it fluttered past, less than twenty miles away; but long before that, the Australasians had joined the growing crowd aboard the Commodore's launch.

So now it was a straight fight between *Diana* and *Lebedev* – for though the Martians had not given up, they were a thousand miles astern and no longer counted as a serious threat. For that matter, it was hard to see what *Lebedev* could do to overtake *Diana*'s lead; but all the way around the second lap, through eclipse again and the long, slow drift against the Sun, Merton felt a growing unease.

He knew the Russian pilots and designers. They had been trying to win this race for twenty years – and, after all, it was only fair that they should, for had not Pyotr Nikolaevich Lebedev been the first man to detect the pressure of sunlight, back at the very beginning of the twentieth century? But they had never succeeded.

And they would never stop trying. Dimitri was up to something – and it would be spectacular.

Aboard the official launch, a thousand miles behind the racing yachts, Commodore van Stratten looked at the radiogram with angry dismay. It had traveled more than a hundred million miles, from the chain of solar observatories swinging high above the blazing surface of the Sun; and it brought the worst possible news.

The Commodore – his title was purely honorary, of course; back on Earth he was Professor of Astrophysics at Harvard – had been half expecting it. Never before had the race been arranged so late in the season. There had been many delays; they had gambled – and now, it seemed, they might all lose.

Deep beneath the surface of the Sun, enormous forces were gathering. At any moment the energies of a million hydrogen bombs might burst forth in the awesome explosion known as a solar flare. Climbing at millions of miles an hour, an invisible fireball many times the size of Earth would leap from the Sun and head out across space.

The cloud of electrified gas would probably miss the Earth completely. But if it did not, it would arrive in just over a day. Spaceships could protect themselves, with their shielding and their powerful magnetic screens; but the lightly built solar yachts, with their paper-thin walls, were defenseless against such a menace. The crews would have to be taken off, and the race abandoned.

John Merton knew nothing of this as he brought *Diana* around the Earth for the second time. If all went well, this would be the last circuit, both for him and for the Russians. They had spiraled upward by thousands of miles, gaining energy from the Sun's rays. On this lap, they should escape from Earth completely, and head outward on the long run to the Moon. It was a straight race now; *Sunbeam*'s crew had finally withdrawn exhausted, after battling valiantly with their spinning sail for more than a hundred thousand miles.

Merton did not feel tired; he had eaten and slept well, and *Diana* was behaving herself admirably. The autopilot, tensioning the rigging like a busy little spider, kept the great sail trimmed to the Sun more accurately than any human skipper could have. Though by this time the two square miles of plastic sheet must have been riddled by hundreds of micrometeorites, the pinhead-sized punctures had produced no falling off of thrust.

He had only two worries. The first was shroud line number eight, which could no longer be adjusted properly. Without any warning, the reel had jammed; even after all these years of astronautical engineering, bearings some-times seized up in vacuum. He could neither lengthen nor shorten the line, and would have to navigate as best he could with the others. Luckily, the most difficult maneu-vers were over; from now on, *Diana* would have the Sun behind her as she sailed straight down the solar wind. And as the old-time sailors had often said, it was easy to handle a boat when the wind was blowing over your shoulder.

His other worry was *Lebedev*, still dogging his heels three hundred miles astern. The Russian yacht had shown remarkable maneuverability, thanks to the four great panels that could be tilted around the central sail. Her flipovers as she rounded the Earth had been carried out with superb precision. But to gain maneuverability she must have sacrificed speed. You could not have it both ways; in the long, straight haul ahead, Merton should be able to hold his own. Yet he could not be certain of victory until, three or four days from now, *Diana* went flashing past the far side of the Moon.

And then, in the fiftieth hour of the race, just after the end of the second orbit around Earth, Markoff sprang his little surprise.

'Hello, John,' he said casually over the ship-to-ship circuit. 'I'd like you to watch this. It should be interesting.'

Merton drew himself across to the periscope and turned up the magnification to the limit. There in the field of view, a most improbable sight against the background of the stars, was the glittering Maltese cross of *Lebedev*, very small but very clear. As he watched, the four arms of the cross slowly detached themselves from the central square, and went drifting away, with all their spars and rigging, into space.

Markoff had jettisoned all unnecessary mass, now that he was coming up to escape velocity and need no longer plod patiently around the Earth, gaining momentum on each circuit. From now on, *Lebedev* would be almost unsteerable – but that did not matter; all the tricky navigation lay behind her. It was as if an old-time yachtsman had deliberately thrown away his rudder and heavy keel, knowing that the rest of the race would be straight downwind over a calm sea.

'Congratulations, Dimitri,' Merton radioed. 'It's a neat trick. But it's not good enough. You can't catch up with me now.'

'I've not finished yet,' the Russian answered. 'There's an old winter's tale in my country about a sleigh being chased by wolves. To save himself, the driver has to throw off the passengers one by one. Do you see the analogy?'

Merton did, all too well. On this final straight lap, Dimitri no longer needed his copilot. *Lebedev* could really be stripped down for action.

'Alexis won't be very happy about this,' Merton replied. 'Besides, it's against the rules.'

'Alexis isn't happy, but I'm the captain. He'll just have to wait around for ten minutes until the Commodore picks him up. And the regulations say nothing about the size of the crew – *you* should know that.'

Merton did not answer; he was too busy doing some hurried calculations, based on what he knew of *Lebedev*'s design. By the time he had finished, he knew that the race was still in doubt. *Lebedev* would be catching up with him at just about the time he hoped to pass the Moon.

But the outcome of the race was already being decided, ninety-two million miles away.

On Solar Observatory Three, far inside the orbit of Mercury, the automatic instruments recorded the whole history of the flare. A hundred million square miles of the

Sun's surface exploded in such blue-white fury that, by comparison, the rest of the disc paled to a dull glow. Out of that seething inferno, twisting and turning like a living creature in the magnetic fields of its own creation, soared the electrified plasma of the great flare. Ahead of it, moving at the speed of light, went the warning flash of ultraviolet and X rays. That would reach Earth in eight minutes, and was relatively harmless. Not so the charged atoms that were following behind at their leisurely four million miles an hour – and which, in just over a day, would engulf *Diana*, *Lebedev*, and their accompanying little fleet in a cloud of lethal radiation.

The Commodore left his decision to the last possible minute. Even when the jet of plasma had been tracked past the orbit of Venus, there was a chance that it might miss the Earth. But when it was less than four hours away, and had already been picked up by the Moonbased radar network, he knew that there was no hope. All solar sailing was over, for the next five or six years – until the Sun was quiet again.

A great sigh of disappointment swept across the solar system. *Diana* and *Lebedev* were halfway between Earth and Moon, running neck and neck – and now no one would ever know which was the better boat. The enthusiasts would argue the result for years; history would merely record: 'Race canceled owing to solar storm.'

When John Merton received the order, he felt a bitterness he had not known since childhood. Across the years, sharp and clear, came the memory of his tenth birthday. He had been promised an exact scale model of the famous spaceship *Morning Star*, and for weeks had been planning how he would assemble it, where he would hang it in his bedroom. And then, at the last moment, his father had broken the news. 'I'm sorry, John – it cost too much money. Maybe next year . . .'

Half a century and a successful lifetime later, he was a heartbroken boy again.

For a moment, he thought of disobeying the Commodore. Suppose he sailed on, ignoring the warning? Even if the race was abandoned, he could make a crossing to the Moon that would stand in the record books for generations.

But that would be worse than stupidity; it would be suicide – and a very unpleasant form of suicide. He had seen men die of radiation poisoning, when the magnetic shielding of their ships had failed in deep space. No – nothing was worth that . . .

He felt as sorry for Dimitri Markoff as for himself. They had both deserved to win, and now victory would go to neither. No man could argue with the Sun in one of its rages, even though he might ride upon its beams to the edge of space.

Only fifty miles astern now, the Commodore's launch was drawing alongside *Lebedev*, preparing to take off her skipper. There went the silver sail, as Dimitri – with feelings that he would share – cut the rigging. The tiny capsule would be taken back to Earth, perhaps to be used again; but a sail was spread for one voyage only.

He could press the jettison button now, and save his rescuers a few minutes of time. But he could not do it; he wanted to stay aboard to the very end, on the little boat that had been for so long a part of his dreams and his life. The great sail was spread now at right angles to the Sun, exerting its utmost thrust. Long ago, it had torn him clear of Earth, and *Diana* was still gaining speed.

Then, out of nowhere, beyond all doubt or hesitation, he knew what must be done. For the last time, he sat down before the computer that had navigated him halfway to the Moon.

When he had finished, he packed the log and his few personal belongings. Clumsily, for he was out of practice, and it was not an easy job to do by oneself, he climbed into the emergency survival suit. He was just sealing the helmet when the Commodore's voice called over the radio.

'We'll be alongside in five minutes, Captain. Please cut your sail, so we won't foul it.'

John Merton, first and last skipper of the sun yacht *Diana*, hesitated a moment. He looked for the last time around the tiny cabin, with its shining instruments and its neatly arranged controls, now all locked in their final positions. Then he said into the microphone: 'I'm abandoning ship. Take your time to pick me up. *Diana* can look after herself.'

There was no reply from the Commodore, and for that he was grateful. Professor van Stratten would have guessed what was happening – and would know that, in these final moments, he wished to be left alone.

He did not bother to exhaust the air lock, and the rush of escaping gas blew him gently out into space. The thrust he gave her then was his last gift to *Diana*. She dwindled away from him, sail glittering splendidly in the sunlight that would be hers for centuries to come. Two days from now she would flash past the Moon; but the Moon, like the Earth, could never catch her. Without his mass to slow her down, she would gain two thousand miles an hour in every day of sailing. In a month, she would be traveling faster than any ship that man had ever built.

As the Sun's rays weakened with distance, so her acceleration would fall. But even at the orbit of Mars, she would be gaining a thousand miles an hour in every day.

Long before then, she would be moving too swiftly for the Sun itself to hold her. Faster than a comet had ever streaked in from the stars, she would be heading out into the abyss.

The glare of rockets, only a few miles away, caught Merton's eye. The launch was approaching to pick him up – at thousands of times the acceleration that *Diana* could ever attain. But its engines could burn for a few minutes only, before they exhausted their fuel – while *Diana* would still be gaining speed, driven outward by the Sun's eternal fires, for ages yet to come.

'Goodbye, little ship,' said John Merton. 'I wonder what eyes will see you next, how many thousand years from now?'

At last he felt at peace, as the blunt torpedo of the launch nosed up beside him. He would never win the race to the Moon; but his would be the first of all man's ships to set sail on the long journey to the stars.

A Meeting with Medusa

'A Meeting with Medusa' was written in January 1971 for one specific purpose. Over the previous decade I had accumulated some 50,000 words of short stories, and needed another 15,000 to make up a complete volume. So I sat down at the typewriter (I still have one gathering dust somewhere, but if this word processor breaks down I'm going back to pen and paper . . .) and 'Medusa' was the result. It was as simple as that.

Well, not really. I had been thinking about Jupiter for a long time; witness the final sequence in the movie 2001: A Space Odyssey. And in some ways the sequel 2010: Odyssey Two *is also a sequel to* this *story;* I had room there to develop in more detail some of the concepts I had first worked out in 'Medusa.'

And by then, of course, our knowledge of Jupiter had been enormously increased, thanks to the marvelous Pioneer and Voyager missions. None of this new information, I am happy to say, has invalidated any of these earlier ideas. On the contrary: there are some very suspicious, sharp-edged blobs floating around in the Jovian atmosphere . . .

'A Meeting with Medusa' was the last story I ever wrote, before concentrating entirely on novels. It won a Playboy editorial award and the Science Fiction Writers of America's annual Nebula, so I am proud to have made it my swan song . . . for the present, at any rate.

And here's a very strange coincidence. Until I started to

write this note, I'd completely forgotten that I used the name 'Kon-Tiki' for the exploring vehicle. And so I was able to autograph a copy of 'Medusa' for Thor Heyerdahl – when I met him this morning, right here in Colombo . . .

1. A Day to remember

The *Queen Elizabeth* was over three miles above the Grand Canyon, dawdling along at a comfortable hundred and eighty, when Howard Falcon spotted the camera platform closing in from the right. He had been expecting it – nothing else was cleared to fly at this altitude – but he was not too happy to have company. Although he welcomed any signs of public interest, he also wanted as much empty sky as he could get. After all, he was the first man in history to navigate a ship three-tenths of a mile long . . .

So far, this first test flight had gone perfectly; ironically enough, the only problem had been the century-old aircraft carrier *Chairman Mao*, borrowed from the San Diego Naval Museum for support operations. Only one of *Mao*'s four nuclear reactors was still operating, and the old battlewagon's top speed was barely thirty knots. Luckily, wind speed at sea level had been less than half this, so it had not been too difficult to maintain still air on the flight deck. Though there had been a few anxious moments during gusts, when the mooring lines had been dropped, the great dirigible had risen smoothly, straight up into the sky, as if on an invisible elevator. If all went well, *Queen Elizabeth IV* would not meet *Chairman Mao* again for another week.

Everything was under control; all test instruments gave normal readings. Commander Falcon decided to go upstairs and watch the rendezvous. He handed over to his second officer, and walked out into the transparent tube-way that led through the heart of the ship. There, as always, he was overwhelmed by the spectacle of the largest single space ever enclosed by man.

The ten spherical gas cells, each more than a hundred feet across, were ranged one behind the other like a line of gigantic soap bubbles. The tough plastic was so clear that he could see through the whole length of the array, and make out details of the elevator mechanism, more than a third of a mile from his vantage point. All around him, like a three-dimensional maze, was the structural framework of the ship – the great longitudinal girders running from nose to tail, the fifteen hoops that were the circular ribs of this sky-borne colossus, and whose varying sizes defined its graceful, streamlined profile.

At this low speed, there was little sound – merely the soft rush of wind over the envelope and an occasional creak of metal as the pattern of stresses changed. The shadowless light from the rows of lamps far overhead gave the whole scene a curiously submarine quality, and to Falcon this was enhanced by the spectacle of the translucent gasbags. He had once encountered a squadron of large but harmless jellyfish, pulsing their mindless way above a shallow tropical reef, and the plastic bubbles that gave *Queen Elizabeth* her lift often reminded him of these – especially when changing pressures made them crinkle and scatter new patterns of reflected light.

He walked down the axis of the ship until he came to the forward elevator, between gas cells one and two. Riding up to the Observation Deck, he noticed that it was uncomfortably hot, and dictated a brief memo to himself on his pocket recorder. The *Queen* obtained almost a quarter of her buoyancy from the unlimited amounts of waste heat produced by her fusion power plant. On this lightly loaded flight, indeed, only six of the ten gas cells contained helium; the remaining four were full of air. Yet she still carried two hundred tons of water as ballast. However, running the cells at high temperatures did produce problems in refrigerating the access ways; it was obvious that a little more work would have to be done there.

A refreshing blast of cooler air hit him in the face when he stepped out onto the Observation Deck and into the dazzling sunlight streaming through the plexiglass roof. Half a dozen workmen, with an equal number of super-chimp assistants, were busily laying the partly completed dance floor, while others were installing electric wiring and fixing furniture. It was a scene of controlled chaos, and Falcon found it hard to believe that everything would be ready for the maiden voyage, only four weeks ahead. Well, that was not *his* problem, thank goodness. He was merely the Captain, not the Cruise Director.

The human workers waved to him, and the 'simps' flashed toothy smiles, as he walked through the confusion, into the already completed Skylounge. This was his favorite place in the whole ship, and he knew that once she was operating he would never again have it all to himself. He would allow himself just five minutes of private enjoyment.

He called the bridge, checked that everything was still in order, and relaxed into one of the comfortable swivel chairs. Below, in a curve that delighted the eye, was the unbroken silver sweep of the ship's envelope. He was perched at the highest point, surveying the whole immensity of the largest vehicle ever built. And when he had tired of that – all the way out to the horizon was the fantastic wilderness carved by the Colorado River in half a billion years of time.

Apart from the camera platform (it had now fallen back and was filming from amidships) he had the sky to himself. It was blue and empty, clear down to the horizon. In his grandfather's day, Falcon knew, it would have been streaked with vapor trails and stained with smoke. Both had gone: the aerial garbage had vanished with the primitive technologies that spawned it, and the long-distance transportation of this age arced too far beyond the stratosphere for any sight or sound of it to reach Earth. Once again, the lower atmosphere belonged to the birds and the clouds – and now to *Queen Elizabeth IV*.

It was true, as the old pioneers had said at the beginning of the twentieth century: this was the only way to travel – in silence and luxury, breathing the air around you and not cut off from it, near enough to the surface to watch the everchanging beauty of land and sea. The subsonic jets of the 1980s, packed with hundreds of passengers seated ten abreast, could not even begin to match such comfort and spaciousness.

Of course, the *Queen* would never be an economic proposition, and even if her projected sister ships were built, only a few of the world's quarter of a billion inhabitants would ever enjoy this silent gliding through the sky. But a secure and prosperous global society could afford such follies and indeed needed them for their novelty and entertainment. There were at least a million men on Earth whose discretionary income exceeded a thousand new dollars a year, so the *Queen* would not lack for passengers.

Falcon's pocket communicator beeped. The copilot was calling from the bridge.

'OK for rendezvous, Captain? We've got all the data we need from this run, and the TV people are getting impatient.'

257

Falcon glanced at the camera platform, now matching his speed a tenth of a mile away.

'OK,' he replied. 'Proceed as arranged. I'll watch from here.'

He walked back through the busy chaos of the Observation Deck so that he could have a better view amidships. As he did so, he could feel the change of vibration underfoot; by the time he had reached the rear of the lounge, the ship had come to rest. Using his master key, he let himself out onto the small external platform flaring from the end of the deck; half a dozen people could stand here, with only low guardrails separating them from the vast sweep of the envelope – and from the ground, thousands of feet below. It was an exciting place to be, and perfectly safe even when the ship was traveling at speed, for it was in the dead air behind the huge dorsal blister of the Observation Deck. Nevertheless, it was not intended that the passengers would have access to it; the view was a little too vertiginous.

The covers of the forward cargo hatch had already opened like giant trap doors, and the camera platform was hovering above them, preparing to descend. Along this route, in the years to come, would travel thousands of passengers and tons of supplies. Only on rare occasions would the *Queen* drop down to sea level and dock with her floating base.

A sudden gust of cross wind slapped Falcon's cheek, and he tightened his grip on the guardrail. The Grand Canyon was a bad place for turbulence, though he did not expect much at this altitude. Without any real anxiety, he focused his attention on the descending platform, now about a hundred and fifty feet above the ship. He knew that the highly skilled operator who was flying the remotely controlled vehicle had performed this simple maneuver a dozen times already; it was inconceivable that he would have any difficulties.

Yet he seemed to be reacting rather sluggishly. That last gust had drifted the platform almost to the edge of the open hatchway. Surely the pilot could have corrected before this . . . Did he have a control problem? It was very unlikely; these remotes had multiple-redundancy, fail-safe takeovers, and any number of backup systems. Accidents were almost unheard of.

But there he went again, off to the left. Could the pilot be *drunk*? Improbable though that seemed, Falcon considered it seriously for a moment. Then he reached for his microphone switch.

Once again, without warning, he was slapped violently in the face. He hardly felt it, for he was staring in horror at the camera platform. The distant operator was fighting for control, trying to balance the craft on its jets – but he was only making matters worse. The oscillations increased – twenty degrees, forty, sixty, ninety . . .

'Switch to automatic, you fool!' Falcon shouted uselessly into his microphone. 'Your manual control's not working!'

The platform flipped over on its back. The jets no longer supported it, but drove it swiftly downward. They had suddenly become allies of the gravity they had fought until this moment.

Falcon never heard the crash, though he felt it; he was already inside the Observation Deck, racing for the elevator that would take him down to the bridge. Workmen shouted at him anxiously, asking what had happened. It would be many months before he knew the answer to that question.

Just as he was stepping into the elevator cage, he changed his mind. What if there was a power failure? Better be on the safe side, even if it took longer and time was the essence. He began to run down the spiral stairway enclosing the shaft.

Halfway down he paused for a second to inspect the damage. That damned platform had gone clear through the ship, rupturing two of the gas cells as it did so. They were still collapsing slowly, in great falling veils of plastic. He was not worried about the loss of lift – the ballast could easily take care of that, as long as eight cells remained intact. Far more serious was the possibility of structural damage. Already he could hear the great latticework around him groaning and protesting under its abnormal loads. It was not enough to have sufficient lift; unless it was properly distributed, the ship would break her back.

He was just resuming his descent when a superchimp, shrieking with fright, came racing down the elevator shaft, moving with incredible speed, hand over hand, along the *outside* of the latticework. In its terror, the poor beast had torn off its company uniform, perhaps in an unconscious attempt to regain the freedom of its ancestors.

Falcon, still descending as swiftly as he could, watched its approach with some alarm. A distraught simp was a powerful and potentially dangerous animal, especially if fear overcame its conditioning. As it overtook him, it started to call out a string of words, but they were all jumbled together, and the only one he could recognize was a plaintive, frequently repeated 'boss.' Even now, Falcon realized, it looked toward humans for guidance. He felt sorry for the creature, involved in a man-made disaster beyond its comprehension, and for which it bore no responsibility.

It stopped opposite him, on the other side of the lattice; there was nothing to prevent it from coming through the open framework if it wished. Now its face was only inches from his, and he was looking straight into the terrified eyes. Never before had he been so close to a simp, and able to study its features in such detail. He felt that strange mingling of kinship and discomfort that all men experience when they gaze thus into the mirror of time.

His presence seemed to have calmed the creature. Falcon pointed up the shaft, back toward the Observation Deck, and said very clearly and precisely: 'Boss – boss – go.' To his relief, the simp understood; it gave him a grimace that might have been a smile, and at once started to race back the way it had come. Falcon had given it the best advice he could. If any safety remained aboard the *Queen*, it was in that direction. But his duty lay in the other.

He had almost completed his descent when, with a sound of rending metal, the vessel pitched nose down, and the lights went out. But he could still see quite well, for a shaft of sunlight streamed through the open hatch and the huge tear in the envelope. Many years ago he had stood in a great cathedral nave watching the light pouring through the stained-glass windows and forming pools of multicolored radiance on the ancient flagstones. The dazzling shaft of sunlight through the ruined fabric high above reminded him of that moment. He was in a cathedral of metal, falling down the sky.

When he reached the bridge, and was able for the first time to look outside, he was horrified to see how close the ship was to the ground. Only three thousand feet below were the beautiful and deadly pinnacles of rock and the red rivers of mud that were still carving their way down into the past. There was no level area anywhere in sight where a ship as large as the *Queen* could come to rest on an even keel.

A glance at the display board told him that all the ballast

had gone. However, rate of descent had been reduced to a few yards a second; they still had a fighting chance.

Without a word, Falcon eased himself into the pilot's seat and took over such control as still remained. The instrument board showed him everything he wished to know; speech was superfluous. In the background, he could hear the Communications Officer giving a running report over the radio. By this time, all the news channels of Earth would have been preempted, and he could imagine the utter frustration of the program controllers. One of the most spectacular wrecks in history was occurring – without a single camera to record it. The last moments of the *Queen* would never fill millions with awe and terror, as had those of the *Hindenburg*, a century and a half before.

Now the ground was only about seventeen hundred feet away, still coming up slowly. Though he had full thrust, he had not dared to use it, lest the weakened structure collapse; but now he realized that he had no choice. The wind was taking them toward a fork in the canyon, where the river was split by a wedge of rock like the prow of some gigantic, fossilized ship of stone. If she continued on her present course, the *Queen* would straddle that triangular plateau and come to rest with at least a third of her length jutting out over nothingness; she would snap like a rotten stick.

Far away, above the sound of straining metal and escaping gas, came the familiar whistle of the jets as Falcon opened up the lateral thrusters. The ship staggered, and began to slew to port. The shriek of tearing metal was now almost continuous – and the rate of descent had started to increase ominously. A glance at the damage-control board showed that cell number five had just gone.

The ground was only yards away. Even now, he could

262

not tell whether his maneuver would succeed or fail. He switched the thrust vectors over to vertical, giving maximum lift to reduce the force of impact.

The crash seemed to last forever. It was not violent – merely prolonged, and irresistible. It seemed that the whole universe was falling about them.

The sound of crunching metal came nearer, as if some great beast were eating its way through the dying ship.

Then floor and ceiling closed upon him like a vise.

2. 'Because it's there'

'Why do you want to go to Jupiter?'

'As Springer said when he lifted for Pluto – "because it's there."'

'Thanks. Now we've got *that* out of the way – the real reason.'

Howard Falcon smiled, though only those who knew him well could have interpreted the slight, leathery grimace. Webster was one of them; for more than twenty years they had shared triumphs and disasters – including the greatest disaster of all.

'Well, Springer's cliché is still valid. We've landed on all the terrestrial planets, but none of the gas giants. They are the only real challenge left in the solar system.'

'An expensive one. Have you worked out the cost?'

'As well as I can; here are the estimates. Remember, though – this isn't a one-shot mission, but a transportation system. Once it's proved out, it can be used over and over again. And it will open up not merely Jupiter, but *all* the giants.'

Webster looked at the figures, and whistled.

'Why not start with an easier planet – Uranus, for example? Half the gravity, and less than half the escape velocity. Quieter weather, too – if that's the right word for it.'

Webster had certainly done his homework. But that, of course, was why he was head of Long-Range Planning.

'There's very little saving – when you allow for the extra distance and the logistics problems. For Jupiter, we can use the facilities of Ganymede. Beyond Saturn, we'd have to establish a new supply base.'

Logical, thought Webster; but he was sure that it was not the important reason. Jupiter was lord of the solar system; Falcon would be interested in no lesser challenge.

'Besides,' Falcon continued, 'Jupiter is a major scientific scandal. It's more than a hundred years since its radio storms were discovered, but we still don't know what causes them – and the Great Red Spot is as big a mystery as ever. That's why I can get matching funds from the Bureau of Astronautics. Do you know how many probes they have dropped into that atmosphere?'

'A couple of hundred, I believe.'

'*Three* hundred and twenty-six, over the last fifty years – about a quarter of them total failures. Of course, they've learned a hell of a lot, but they've barely scratched the planet. Do you realize how *big* it is?'

'More than ten times the size of Earth.'

'Yes, yes – but do you know what that really means?'

Falcon pointed to the large globe in the corner of Webster's office.

'Look at India – how small it seems. Well, if you skinned Earth and spread it out on the surface of Jupiter, it would look about as big as India does here.'

There was a long silence while Webster contemplated the equation: Jupiter is to Earth as Earth is to India.

Falcon had – deliberately, of course – chosen the best possible example . . .

Was it already ten years ago? Yes, it must have been. The crash lay seven years in the past (*that* date was engraved on his heart), and those initial tests had taken place three years before the first and last flight of the *Queen Elizabeth*.

Ten years ago, then, Commander (no, Lieutenant) Falcon had invited him to a preview – a three-day drift across the northern plains of India, within sight of the Himalayas. 'Perfectly safe,' he had promised. 'It will get you away from the office – and will teach you what this whole thing is about.'

Webster had not been disappointed. Next to his first journey to the Moon, it had been the most memorable experience of his life. And yet, as Falcon had assured him, it had been perfectly safe, and quite uneventful.

They had taken off from Srinagar just before dawn, with the huge silver bubble of the balloon already catching the first light of the Sun. The ascent had been made in total silence; there were none of the roaring propane burners that had lifted the hot-air balloons of an earlier age. All the heat they needed came from the little pulsed-fusion reactor, weighing only about two hundred and twenty pounds, hanging in the open mouth of the envelope. While they were climbing, its laser was zapping ten times a second, igniting the merest whiff of deuterium fuel. Once they had reached altitude, it would fire only a few times a minute, making up for the heat lost through the great gasbag overhead.

And so, even while they were almost a mile above the ground, they could hear dogs barking, people shouting, bells ringing. Slowly the vast, Sun-smitten landscape expanded around them. Two hours later, they had leveled out at three miles and were taking frequent draughts of oxygen. They could relax and admire the scenery; the on-board instrumentation was doing all the work – gathering the information that would be required by the designers of the still-unnamed liner of the skies.

It was a perfect day. The southwest monsoon would not break for another month, and there was hardly a cloud in the sky. Time seemed to have come to a stop; they resented the hourly radio reports which interrupted their reverie. And all around, to the horizon and far beyond, was that infinite, ancient landscape, drenched with history – a patchwork of villages, fields, temples, lakes, irrigation canals . . .

With a real effort, Webster broke the hypnotic spell of that ten-year-old memory. It had converted him to lighter-than-air flight – and it had made him realize the enormous size of India, even in a world that could be circled within ninety minutes. And yet, he repeated to himself, Jupiter is to Earth as Earth is to India . . .

'Granted your argument,' he said, 'and supposing the funds are available, there's another question you have to answer. Why should you do better than the – what is it – three hundred and twenty-six robot probes that have already made the trip?'

'I am better qualified than they were – as an observer, and as a pilot. *Especially* as a pilot. Don't forget – I've more experience of lighter-than-air flight than anyone in the world.'

'You could still serve as controller, and sit safely on Ganymede.'

'*But that's just the point!* They've already done that. Don't you remember what killed the *Queen*?'

Webster knew perfectly well; but he merely answered: 'Go on.'

'*Time lag – time lag!* That idiot of a platform controller thought he was using a local radio circuit. But he'd been accidentally switched through a satellite – oh, maybe it wasn't his fault, but he should have noticed. That's a half-second time lag for the round trip. Even then it wouldn't have mattered flying in calm air. It was the turbulence over the Grand Canyon that did it. When the platform tipped, and he corrected for that – it had already tipped the other way. Ever tried to drive a car over a bumpy road with a half-second delay in the steering?'

'No, and I don't intend to try. But I can imagine it.'

'Well, Ganymede is a million kilometers from Jupiter. That means a round-trip delay of six seconds. No, you need a controller on the spot – to handle emergencies in real time. Let me show you something. Mind if I use this?'

'Go ahead.'

Falcon picked up a postcard that was lying on Webster's desk; they were almost obsolete on Earth, but this one showed a 3-D view of a Martian landscape, and was decorated with exotic and expensive stamps. He held it so that it dangled vertically.

'This is an old trick, but helps to make my point. Place your thumb and finger on either side, not quite touching. That's right.'

Webster put out his hand, almost but not quite gripping the card.

'Now catch it.'

Falcon waited for a few seconds; then, without warning, he let go of the card. Webster's thumb and finger closed on empty air.

'I'll do it again, just to show there's no deception. You see?'

Once again, the falling card had slipped through Webster's fingers.

'Now you try it on me.'

This time, Webster grasped the card and dropped it without warning. It had scarcely moved before Falcon had caught it. Webster almost imagined he could hear a click, so swift was the other's reaction.

'When they put me together again,' Falcon remarked in an expressionless voice, 'the surgeons made some improvements. This is one of them – and there are others. I want to make the most of them. Jupiter is the place where I can do it.'

Webster stared for long seconds at the fallen card, absorbing the improbable colors of the Trivium Charontis Escarpment. Then he said quietly: 'I understand. How long do you think it will take?'

'With your help, plus the Bureau, plus all the science foundation we can drag in – oh, three years. Then a year for trials – we'll have to send in at least two test models. So, with luck – five years.'

'That's about what I thought. I hope you get your luck; you've earned it. But there's one thing I won't do.'

'What's that?'

'Next time you go ballooning, don't expect *me* as passenger.'

3. The world of the gods

The fall from Jupiter V to Jupiter itself takes only three and a half hours. Few men could have slept on so awesome a journey. Sleep was a weakness that Howard Falcon hated, and the little he still required brought dreams that time had not yet been able to exorcize. But he could expect no rest in the three days that lay ahead, and must

268

seize what he could during the long fall down into that ocean of clouds, some sixty thousand miles below.

As soon as *Kon-Tiki* had entered her transfer orbit and all the computer checks were satisfactory, he prepared for the last sleep he might ever know. It seemed appropriate that at almost the same moment Jupiter eclipsed the bright and tiny Sun as he swept into the monstrous shadow of the planet. For a few minutes a strange golden twilight enveloped the ship; then a quarter of the sky became an utterly black hole in space, while the rest was a blaze of stars. No matter how far one traveled across the solar system, *they* never changed; these same constellations now shone on Earth, millions of miles away. The only novelties here were the small, pale crescents of Callisto and Ganymede; doubtless there were a dozen other moons up there in the sky, but they were all much too tiny, and too distant, for the unaided eye to pick them out.

'Closing down for two hours,' he reported to the mother ship, hanging almost a thousand miles above the desolate rocks of Jupiter V, in the radiation shadow of the tiny satellite. If it never served any other useful purpose, Jupiter V was a cosmic bulldozer perpetually sweeping up the charged particles that made it unhealthy to linger close to Jupiter. Its wake was almost free of radiation, and there a ship could park in perfect safety, while death sleeted invisibly all around.

Falcon switched on the sleep inducer, and consciousness faded swiftly out as the electric pulses surged gently through his brain. While *Kon-Tiki* fell toward Jupiter, gaining speed second by second in that enormous gravitational field, he slept without dreams. They always came when he awoke; and he had brought his nightmares with him from Earth.

Yet he never dreamed of the crash itself, though he

269

often found himself again face to face with that terrified superchimp, as he descended the spiral stairway between the collapsing gasbags. None of the simps had survived; those that were not killed outright were so badly injured that they had been painlessly 'euthed.' He sometimes wondered why he dreamed only of this doomed creature – which he had never met before the last minutes of its life – and not of the friends and colleagues he had lost aboard the dying *Queen*.

The dreams he feared most always began with his first return to consciousness. There had been little physical pain; in fact, there had been no sensation of any kind. He was in darkness and silence, and did not even seem to be breathing. And – strangest of all – he could not locate his limbs. He could move neither his hands nor his feet, because he did not know where they were.

The silence had been the first to yield. After hours, or days, he had become aware of a faint throbbing, and eventually, after long thought, he deduced that this was the beating of his own heart. That was the first of his many mistakes.

Then there had been faint pinpricks, sparkles of light, ghosts of pressures upon still-unresponsive limbs. One by one his senses had returned, and pain had come with them. He had had to learn everything anew, recapitulating infancy and babyhood. Though his memory was unaffected, and he could understand words that were spoken to him, it was months before he was able to answer except by the flicker of an eyelid. He could remember the moments of triumph when he had spoken the first word, turned the page of a book – and, finally, learned to move under his own power. *That* was a victory indeed, and it had taken him almost two years to prepare for it. A hundred times he had envied that dead superchimp, but *he* had been given no choice. The doctors had made their decision – and now, twelve years later, he was where no human being had ever traveled before, and moving faster than any man in history.

Kon-Tiki was just emerging from shadow, and the Jovian dawn bridged the sky ahead in a titanic bow of light, when the persistent buzz of the alarm dragged Falcon up from sleep. The inevitable nightmares (he had been trying to summon a nurse, but did not even have the strength to push the button) swiftly faded from consciousness. The greatest – and perhaps last – adventure of his life was before him.

He called Mission Control, now almost sixty thousand miles away and falling swiftly below the curve of Jupiter, to report that everything was in order. His velocity had just passed thirty-one miles a second (*that* was one for the books) and in half an hour *Kon-Tiki* would hit the outer fringes of the atmosphere, as he started on the most difficult re-entry in the entire solar system. Although scores of probes had survived this flaming ordeal, they had been tough, solidly packed masses of instrumentation, able to withstand several hundred gravities of drag. *Kon-Tiki* would hit peaks of thirty g's, and would average more than ten, before she came to rest in the upper reaches of the Jovian atmosphere. Very carefully and thoroughly, Falcon began to attach the elaborate system of restraints that would anchor him to the walls of the cabin. When he had finished, he was virtually a part of the ship's structure.

The clock was counting backward; one hundred seconds to re-entry. For better or worse, he was committed. In a minute and a half, he would graze the Jovian atmosphere, and would be caught irrevocably in the grip of the giant.

The countdown was three seconds late – not at all bad, considering the unknowns involved. From beyond the

271

walls of the capsule came a ghostly sighing, which rose steadily to a high-pitched, screaming roar. The noise was quite different from that of a re-entry on Earth or Mars; in this thin atmosphere of hydrogen and helium, all sounds were transformed a couple of octaves upward. On Jupiter, even thunder would have falsetto overtones.

With the rising scream came mounting weight; within seconds, he was completely immobilized. His field of vision contracted until it embraced only the clock and the accelerometer; fifteen g, and four hundred and eighty seconds to go . . .

He never lost consciousness; but then, he had not expected to. *Kon-Tiki*'s trail through the Jovian atmosphere must be really spectacular – by this time, thousands of miles long. Five hundred seconds after entry, the drag began to taper off: ten g, five g, two . . . Then weight vanished almost completely. He was falling free, all his enormous orbital velocity destroyed.

There was a sudden jolt as the incandescent remnants of the heat shield were jettisoned. It had done its work and would not be needed again; Jupiter could have it now. He released all but two of the restraining buckles, and waited for the automatic sequencer to start the next, and most critical, series of events.

He did not see the first drogue parachute pop out, but he could feel the slight jerk, and the rate of fall diminished immediately. *Kon-Tiki* had lost all her horizontal speed and was going straight down at almost a thousand miles an hour. Everything depended on what happened in the next sixty seconds.

There went the second drogue. He looked up through the overhead window and saw, to his immense relief, that clouds of glittering foil were billowing out behind the falling ship. Like a great flower unfurling, the thousands of cubic yards of the balloon spread out across the sky, scooping up the thin gas until it was fully inflated. *Kon-Tiki*'s rate of fall dropped to a few miles an hour and remained constant. Now there was plenty of time; it would take him days to fall all the way down to the surface of Jupiter.

But he would get there eventually, even if he did nothing about it. The balloon overhead was merely acting as an efficient parachute. It was providing no lift; nor could it do so, while the gas inside and out was the same.

With its characteristic and rather disconcerting crack the fusion reactor started up, pouring torrents of heat into the envelope overhead. Within five minutes, the rate of fall had become zero; within six, the ship had started to rise. According to the radar altimeter, it had leveled out at about two hundred and sixty-seven miles above the surface – or whatever passed for a surface on Jupiter.

Only one kind of balloon will work in an atmosphere of hydrogen, which is the lightest of all gases – and that is a hot-hydrogen balloon. As long as the fuser kept ticking over, Falcon could remain aloft, drifting across a world that could hold a hundred Pacifics. After traveling over three hundred million miles, *Kon-Tiki* had at last begun to justify her name. She was an aerial raft, adrift upon the currents of the Jovian atmosphere.

Though a whole new world was lying around him, it was more than an hour before Falcon could examine the view. First he had to check all the capsule's systems and test its response to the controls. He had to learn how much extra heat was necessary to produce a desired rate of ascent, and how much gas he must vent in order to descend. Above all, there was the question of stability. He must adjust the length of the cables attaching his capsule to the huge, pear-shaped balloon, to damp out vibrations and get the smoothest possible ride. Thus far, he was lucky; at this level, the wind was steady, and the Doppler reading on the invisible surface gave him a ground speed of two hundred seventeen and a half miles an hour. For Jupiter, that was modest; winds of up to a thousand had been observed. But mere speed was, of course, unimportant; the real danger was turbulence. If he ran into that, only skill and experience and swift reaction could save him – and these were not matters that could yet be programed into a computer.

Not until he was satisfied that he had got the feel of his strange craft did Falcon pay any attention to Mission Control's pleadings. Then he deployed the booms carrying the instrumentation and the atmospheric samplers. The capsule now resembled a rather untidy Christmas tree, but still rode smoothly down the Jovian winds while it radioed its torrents of information to the recorders on the ship miles above. And now, at last, he could look around . . .

His first impression was unexpected, and even a little disappointing. As far as the scale of things was concerned, he might have been ballooning over an ordinary cloud-scape on Earth. The horizon seemed at a normal distance; there was no feeling at all that he was on a world eleven times the diameter of his own. Then he looked at the infrared radar, sounding the layers of atmosphere beneath him – and knew how badly his eyes had been deceived.

That layer of clouds apparently about three miles away was really more than thirty-seven miles below. And the horizon, whose distance he would have guessed at about one hundred and twenty-five, was actually eighteen hundred miles from the ship.

The crystalline clarity of the hydrohelium atmosphere and the enormous curvature of the planet had fooled him completely. It was even harder to judge distances here than on the Moon; everything he saw must be multiplied by at least ten.

It was a simple matter, and he should have been prepared for it. Yet somehow, it disturbed him profoundly. He did not feel that Jupiter was huge, but that *he* had shrunk – to a tenth of his normal size. Perhaps, with time, he would grow accustomed to the inhuman scale of this world; yet as he stared toward that unbelievably distant horizon, he felt as if a wind colder than the atmosphere around him was blowing through his soul. Despite all his arguments, this might never be a place for man. He could well be both the first and the last to descend through the clouds of Jupiter.

The sky above was almost black, except for a few wisps of ammonia cirrus perhaps twelve miles overhead. It was cold up there, on the fringes of space, but both pressure and temperature increased rapidly with depth. At the level where *Kon-Tiki* was drifting now, it was fifty below zero, and the pressure was five atmospheres. Sixty-five miles farther down, it would be as warm as equatorial Earth, and the pressure about the same as at the bottom of one of the shallower seas. Ideal conditions for life . . .

A quarter of the brief Jovian day had already gone; the sun was halfway up the sky, but the light on the unbroken cloudscape below had a curious mellow quality. That extra three hundred million miles had robbed the Sun of all its power. Though the sky was clear, Falcon found himself continually thinking that it was a heavily overcast day. When night fell, the onset of darkness would be swift indeed; though it was still morning, there was a sense of autumnal twilight in the air. But autumn, of course, was something that never came to Jupiter. There were no seasons here.

Kon-Tiki had come down in the exact center of the equatorial zone – the least colorful part of the planet. The sea of clouds that stretched out to the horizon was tinted a pale salmon; there were none of the yellows and pinks and even reds that banded Jupiter at higher altitudes. The Great Red Spot itself – most spectacular of all of the planet's features – lay thousands of miles to the south. It had been a temptation to descend there, but the south tropical disturbance was unusually active, with currents reaching over nine hundred miles an hour. It would have been asking for trouble to head into that maelstrom of unknown forces. The Great Red Spot and its mysteries would have to wait for future expeditions.

The Sun, moving across the sky twice as swiftly as it did on Earth, was now nearing the zenith and had become eclipsed by the great silver canopy of the balloon. *Kon-Tiki* was still drifting swiftly and smoothly westward at a steady two hundred and seventeen and a half, but only the radar gave any indication of this. Was it always as calm here? Falcon asked himself. The scientists who had talked learnedly of the Jovian doldrums, and had predicted that the equator would be the quietest place, seemed to know what they were talking about, after all. He had been profoundly skeptical of all such forecasts, and had agreed with one unusually modest researcher who had told him bluntly: 'There are no experts on Jupiter.' Well, there would be at least one by the end of this day.

If he managed to survive until then.

4. The Voices of the Deep

That first day, the Father of the Gods smiled upon him. It was as calm and peaceful here on Jupiter as it had been, years ago, when he was drifting with Webster across the plains of northern India. Falcon had time to master his new skills, until *Kon-Tiki* seemed an extension of his own body. Such luck was more than he had dared to hope for, and he began to wonder what price he might have to pay for it.

The five hours of daylight were almost over; the clouds below were full of shadows, which gave them a massive solidity they had not possessed when the Sun was higher. Color was swiftly draining from the sky, except in the west itself, where a band of deepening purple lay along the horizon. Above this band was the thin crescent of a closer moon, pale and bleached against the utter blackness beyond.

With a speed perceptible to the eye, the Sun went straight down over the edge of Jupiter, over eighteen hundred miles away. The stars came out in their legions – and there was the beautiful evening star of Earth, on the very frontier to twilight, reminding him how far he was from home. It followed the Sun down into the west. Man's first night on Jupiter had begun.

With the onset of darkness, *Kon-Tiki* started to sink. The balloon was no longer heated by the feeble sunlight and was losing a small part of its buoyancy. Falcon did nothing to increase lift; he had expected this and was planning to descend.

The invisible cloud deck was still over thirty miles

277

below, and he would reach it about midnight. It showed up clearly on the infrared radar, which also reported that it contained a vast array of complex carbon compounds, as well as the usual hydrogen, helium, and ammonia. The chemists were dying for samples of that fluffy, pinkish stuff; though some atmospheric probes had already gathered a few grams, they had only whetted their appetites. Half the basic molecules of life were here, floating high above the surface of Jupiter. And where there was food, could life be far away? That was the question that, after more than a hundred years, no one had been able to answer.

The infrared was blocked by the clouds, but the microwave radar sliced right through and showed layer after layer, all the way down to the hidden surface almost two hundred and fifty miles below. That was barred to him by enormous pressures and temperatures; not even robot probes had ever reached it intact. It lay in tantalizing inaccessibility at the bottom of the radar screen, slightly fuzzy, and showing a curious granular structure that his equipment could not resolve.

An hour after sunset, he dropped his first probe. It fell swiftly for about sixty miles, then began to float in the denser atmosphere, sending back torrents of radio signals, which he relayed to Mission Control. Then there was nothing else to do until sunrise, except to keep an eye on the rate of descent, monitor the instruments, and answer occasional queries. While she was drifting in this steady current, *Kon-Tiki* could look after herself.

Just before midnight, a woman controller came on watch and introduced herself with the usual pleasantries. Ten minutes later she called again, her voice at once serious and excited.

'Howard! Listen in on channel forty-six – high gain.'

Channel forty-six? There were so many telemetering circuits that he knew the numbers of only those that were critical; but as soon as he threw the switch, he recognized this one. He was plugged in to the microphone on the probe, floating more than eighty miles below him in an atmosphere now almost as dense as water.

At first, there was only a soft hiss of whatever strange winds stirred down in the darkness of that unimaginable world. And then, out of the background noise, there slowly emerged a booming vibration that grew louder and louder, like the beating of a gigantic drum. It was so low that it was felt as much as heard, and the beats steadily increased their tempo, though the pitch never changed. Now it was a swift, almost infrasonic throbbing. Then, suddenly, in mid-vibration, it stopped – so abruptly that the mind could not accept the silence, but memory continued to manufacture a ghostly echo in the deepest caverns of the brain.

It was the most extraordinary sound that Falcon had ever heard, even among the multitudinous noises of Earth. He could think of no natural phenomenon that could have caused it; nor was it like the cry of any animal, not even one of the great whales . . .

It came again, following exactly the same pattern. Now that he was prepared for it, he estimated the length of the sequence; from first faint throb to final crescendo, it lasted just over ten seconds.

And this time there was a real echo, very faint and far away. Perhaps it came from one of the many reflecting layers, deeper in this stratified atmosphere; perhaps it was another, more distant source. Falcon waited for a second echo, but it never came.

Mission Control reacted quickly and asked him to drop another probe at once. With two microphones operating, it would be possible to find the approximate location of the sources. Oddly enough, none of *Kon-Tiki*'s own external mikes could detect anything except wind noises. The boomings, whatever they were, must have been trapped and channeled beneath an atmospheric reflecting layer far below.

They were coming, it was soon discovered, from a cluster of sources about twelve hundred miles away. The distance gave no indication of their power; in Earth's oceans, quite feeble sounds could travel equally far. And as for the obvious assumption that living creatures were responsible, the Chief Exobiologist quickly ruled that out.

'I'll be very disappointed,' said Dr Brenner, 'if there are no microorganisms or plants here. But nothing like animals, because there's no free oxygen. All biochemical reactions on Jupiter must be low-energy ones – there's just no way an active creature could generate enough power to function.'

Falcon wondered if this was true; he had heard the argument before, and reserved judgment.

'In any case,' continued Brenner, 'some of those sound waves are a hundred yards long! Even an animal as big as a whale couldn't produce them. They *must* have a natural origin.'

Yes, that seemed plausible, and probably the physicists would be able to come up with an explanation. What would a blind alien make, Falcon wondered, of the sounds he might hear when standing beside a stormy sea, or a geyser, or a volcano, or a waterfall? He might well attribute them to some huge beast.

About an hour before sunrise the voices of the deep died away, and Falcon began to busy himself with preparation for the dawn of his second day. *Kon-Tiki* was now only three miles above the nearest cloud layer; the external pressure had risen to ten atmospheres, and the temperature was a tropical thirty degrees. A man could be comfortable here with no more equipment than a breathing mask and the right grade of heliox mixture.

'We've some good news for you,' Mission Control reported, soon after dawn. 'The cloud layer's breaking up. You'll have partial clearing in an hour – but watch out for turbulence.'

'I've already noticed some,' Falcon answered. 'How far down will I be able to see?'

'At least twelve miles, down to the second thermocline. *That* cloud deck is solid – it never breaks.'

And it's out of my reach, Falcon told himself; the temperature down there must be over a hundred degrees. This was the first time that any balloonist had ever had to worry, not about his ceiling, but about his basement!

Ten minutes later he could see what Mission Control had already observed from its superior vantage point. There was a change in color near the horizon, and the cloud layer had become ragged and humpy, as if something had torn it open. He turned up his little nuclear furnace and gave *Kon-Tiki* another three miles of altitude, so that he could get a better view.

The sky below was clearing rapidly, completely, as if something was dissolving the solid overcast. An abyss was opening before his eyes. A moment later he sailed out over the edge of a cloud canyon about twelve miles deep and six hundred miles wide.

A new world lay spread beneath him; Jupiter had stripped away one of its many veils. The second layer of clouds, unattainably far below, was much darker in color than the first. It was almost salmon pink, and curiously mottled with little islands of brick red. They were all oval-shaped, with their long axes pointing east-west, in the direction of the prevailing wind. There were hundreds of them, all about the same size, and they reminded Falcon of puffy little cumulus clouds in the terrestrial sky.

He reduced buoyancy, and *Kon-Tiki* began to drop down the face of the dissolving cliff. It was then that he noticed the snow.

White flakes were forming in the air and drifting slowly downward. Yet it was much too warm for snow – and, in any event, there was scarcely a trace of water at this altitude. Moreover, there was no glitter or sparkle about these flakes as they went cascading down into the depths. When, presently, a few landed on an instrument boom outside the main viewing port, he saw that they were a dull, opaque white – not crystalline at all – and quite large – several inches across. They looked like wax, and Falcon guessed that this was precisely what they were. Some chemical reaction was taking place in the atmosphere around him, condensing out the hydrocarbons floating in the Jovian air.

About sixty miles ahead, a disturbance was taking place in the cloud layer. The little red ovals were being jostled around, and were beginning to form a spiral – the familiar cyclonic pattern so common in the meteorology of Earth. The vortex was emerging with astonishing speed; if that was a storm ahead, Falcon told himself, he was in big trouble.

And then his concern changed to wonder – and to fear. What was developing in his line of flight was not a storm at all. Something enormous – something scores of miles across – was rising through the clouds.

The reassuring thought that it, too, might be a cloud – a thunderhead boiling up from the lower levels of the atmosphere – lasted only a few seconds. No; this was *solid*. It shouldered its way through the pink-and-salmon overcast like an iceberg rising from the deeps.

An *iceberg* floating on hydrogen? That was impossible, of course; but perhaps it was not too remote an analogy. As soon as he focused the telescope upon the enigma, Falcon saw that it was a whitish, crystalline mass, threaded with streaks of red and brown. It must be, he decided, the same stuff as the 'snowflakes' falling around him – a mountain range of wax. And it was not, he soon realized, as solid as he had thought; around the edges it was continually crumbling and reforming . . .

'I know what it is,' he radioed Mission Control, which for the last few minutes had been asking anxious questions. 'It's a mass of bubbles – some kind of foam. Hydrocarbon froth. Get the chemists working on . . . *Just a minute!*'

'What is it?' called Mission Control. 'What is it?'

He ignored the frantic pleas from space and concentrated all his mind upon the image in the telescope field. He had to be sure; if he made a mistake, he would be the laughingstock of the solar system.

Then he relaxed, glanced at the clock, and switched off the nagging voice from Jupiter V.

'Hello, Mission Control,' he said, very formally. 'This is Howard Falcon aboard *Kon-Tiki*. Ephemeris Time nineteen hours twenty-one minutes fifteen seconds. Latitude zero degrees five minutes North. Longitude one hundred five degrees forty-two minutes, System One.

'Tell Dr Brenner that there is life on Jupiter. And it's *big* . . .'

5. The wheels of Poseidon

'I'm very happy to be proved wrong,' Dr Brenner radioed back cheerfully. 'Nature always has something up her sleeve. Keep the long-focus camera on target and give us the steadiest pictures you can.'

The things moving up and down those waxen slopes were still too far away for Falcon to make out many details, and they must have been very large to be visible at all at such a distance. Almost black, and shaped like arrowheads, they maneuvered by slow undulations of their entire bodies, so that they looked rather like giant manta rays, swimming above some tropical reef.

Perhaps they were sky-borne cattle, browsing on the cloud pastures of Jupiter, for they seemed to be feeding along the dark, red-brown streaks that ran like driedup river beds down the flanks of the floating cliffs. Occasionally, one of them would dive headlong into the mountain of foam and disappear completely from sight.

Kon-Tiki was moving only slowly with respect to the cloud layer below; it would be at least three hours before she was above those ephemeral hills. She was in a race with the Sun. Falcon hoped that darkness would not fall before he could get a good view of the mantas, as he had christened them, as well as the fragile landscape over which they flapped their way.

It was a long three hours. During the whole time, he kept the external microphones on full gain, wondering if here was the source of that booming in the night. The mantas were certainly large enough to have produced it;

when he could get an accurate measurement, he discovered that they were almost a hundred yards across the wings. That was three times the length of the largest whale – though he doubted if they could weigh more than a few tons.

Half an hour before sunset, *Kon-Tiki* was almost above the 'mountains.'

'No,' said Falcon, answering Mission Control's repeated questions about the mantas, 'they're still showing no reaction to me. I don't think they're intelligent – they look like harmless vegetarians. And even if they try to chase me, I'm sure they can't reach my altitude.'

Yet he was a little disappointed when the mantas showed not the slightest interest in him as he sailed high above their feeding ground. Perhaps they had no way of detecting his presence. When he examined and photographed them through the telescope, he could see no signs of any sense organs. The creatures were simply huge black deltas, rippling over hills and valleys that, in reality, were little more substantial than the clouds of Earth. Though they looked solid, Falcon knew that anyone who stepped on those white mountains would go crashing through them as if they were made of tissue paper.

At close quarters he could see the myriads of cellules or bubbles from which they were formed. Some of these were quite large – a yard or so in diameter – and Falcon wondered in what witches' cauldron of hydrocarbons they had been brewed. There must be enough petrochemicals deep down in the atmosphere of Jupiter to supply all Earth's needs for a million years.

The short day had almost gone when he passed over the crest of the waxen hills, and the light was fading rapidly along their lower slopes. There were no mantas on this western side, and for some reason the topography was very different. The foam was sculptured into long, level terraces, like the interior of a lunar crater. He could almost imagine that they were gigantic steps leading down to the hidden surface of the planet.

And on the lowest of those steps, just clear of the swirling clouds that the mountain had displaced when it came surging skyward, was a roughly oval mass, one or two miles across. It was difficult to see, since it was only a little darker than the gray-white foam on which it rested. Falcon's first thought was that he was looking at a forest of pallid trees, like giant mushrooms that had never seen the Sun.

Yes, it must be a forest – he could see hundreds of thin trunks, springing from the white waxy froth in which they were rooted. But the trees were packed astonishingly close together; there was scarcely any space between them. Perhaps it was not a forest, after all, but a single enormous tree – like one of the giant multi-trunked banyans of the East. Once he had seen a banyan tree in Java that was over six hundred and fifty yards across; this monster was at least ten times that size.

The light had almost gone. The cloudscape had turned purple with refracted sunlight, and in a few seconds that, too, would have vanished. In the last light of his second day on Jupiter, Howard Falcon saw – or thought he saw – something that cast the gravest doubts on his interpretation of the white oval.

Unless the dim light had totally deceived him, those hundreds of thin trunks were beating back and forth, in perfect synchronism, like fronds of kelp rocking in the surge.

And the tree was no longer in the place where he had first seen it.

* * *

'Sorry about this,' said Mission Control, soon after sunset, 'but we think Source Beta is going to blow within the next hour. Probability seventy percent.'

Falcon glanced quickly at the chart. Beta – Jupiter latitude one hundred and forty degrees – was over eighteen thousand six hundred miles away and well below his horizon. Even though major eruptions ran as high as ten megatons, he was much too far away for the shock wave to be a serious danger. The radio storm that it would trigger was, however, quite a different matter.

The decameter outbursts that sometimes made Jupiter the most powerful radio source in the whole sky had been discovered back in the 1950s, to the utter astonishment of the astronomers. Now, more than a century later, their real cause was still a mystery. Only the symptoms were understood; the explanation was completely unknown.

The 'volcano' theory had best stood the test of time, although no one imagined that this word had the same meaning on Jupiter as on Earth. At frequent intervals – often several times a day – titanic eruptions occurred in the lower depths of the atmosphere, probably on the hidden surface of the planet itself. A great column of gas, more than six hundred miles high, would start boiling upward as if determined to escape into space.

Against the most powerful gravitational field of all the planets, it had no chance. Yet some traces – a mere few million tons – usually managed to reach the Jovian ionosphere; and when they did, all hell broke loose.

The radiation belts surrounding Jupiter completely dwarf the feeble Van Allen belts of Earth. When they are short-circuited by an ascending column of gas, the result is an electrical discharge millions of times more powerful than any terrestrial flash of lightning; it sends a colossal

287

thunderclap of radio noise flooding across the entire solar system and on out to the stars.

It had been discovered that these radio outbursts came from four main areas of the planet. Perhaps there were weaknesses there that allowed the fires of the interior to break out from time to time. The scientists on Ganymede, largest of Jupiter's many moons, now thought that they could predict the onset of a decameter storm; their accuracy was about as good as a weather forecaster's of the early 1900s.

Falcon did not know whether to welcome or to fear a radio storm; it would certainly add to the value of the mission – if he survived it. His course had been planned to keep as far as possible from the main centers of disturbance, especially the most active one, Source Alpha. As luck would have it, the threatening Beta was the closest to him. He hoped that the distance, almost three-fourths the circumference of Earth, was safe enough.

'Probability ninety percent,' said Mission Control with a distinct note of urgency. 'And forget that hour. Ganymede says it may be any moment.'

The radio had scarcely fallen silent when the reading on the magnetic field-strength meter started to shoot upward. Before it could go off scale, it reversed and began to drop as rapidly as it had risen. Far away and thousands of miles below, something had given the planet's molten core a titanic jolt.

'There she blows!' called Mission Control.

'Thanks, I already know. When will the storm hit me?'

'You can expect onset in five minutes. Peak in ten.'

Far around the curve of Jupiter, a funnel of gas as wide as the Pacific Ocean was climbing spaceward at thousands of miles an hour. Already the thunderstorms of the lower atmosphere would be raging around it – but they were nothing compared with the fury that would explode when the radiation belt was reached and began dumping its surplus electrons onto the planet. Falcon began to retract all the instrument booms that were extended out from the capsule. There were no other precautions he could take. It would be four hours before the atmospheric shock wave reached him – but the radio blast, traveling at the speed of light, would be here in a tenth of a second, once the discharge had been triggered.

The radio monitor, scanning back and forth across the spectrum, still showed nothing unusual, just the normal mush of background static. Then Falcon noticed that the noise level was slowly creeping upward. The explosion was gathering its strength.

At such a distance he had never expected to *see* anything. But suddenly a flicker as of far-off heat lightning danced along the eastern horizon. Simultaneously, half the circuit breakers jumped out of the main switchboard, the lights failed, and all communications channels went dead.

He tried to move, but was completely unable to do so. The paralysis that gripped him was not merely psychological; he seemed to have lost all control of his limbs and could feel a painful tingling sensation over his entire body. It was impossible that the electric field could have penetrated this shielded cabin. Yet there was a flickering glow over the instrument board, and he could hear the unmistakable crackle of a brush discharge.

With a series of sharp bangs, the emergency systems went into operation, and the overloads reset themselves. The lights flickered on again. And Falcon's paralysis disappeared as swiftly as it had come.

After glancing at the board to make sure that all circuits

were back to normal, he moved quickly to the viewing ports.

There was no need to switch on the inspection lamps – the cables supporting the capsule seemed to be on fire. Lines of light glowing an electric blue against the darkness stretched upward from the main lift ring to the equator of the giant balloon; and rolling slowly along several of them were dazzling balls of fire.

The sight was so strange and so beautiful that it was hard to read any menace in it. Few people, Falcon knew, had ever seen ball lightning from such close quarters – and certainly none had survived if they were riding a hydrogen-filled balloon back in the atmosphere of Earth. He remembered the flaming death of the *Hindenburg*, destroyed by a stray spark when she docked at Lakehurst in 1937; as it had done so often in the past, the horrifying old newsreel film flashed through his mind. But at least that could not happen here, though there was more hydrogen above his head than had ever filled the last of the Zeppelins. It would be a few billion years yet, before anyone could light a fire in the atmosphere of Jupiter.

With a sound like briskly frying bacon, the speech circuit came back to life.

'Hello, *Kon-Tiki* – are you receiving? Are you receiving?'

The words were chopped and badly distorted, but intelligible. Falcon's spirits lifted; he had resumed contact with the world of men.

'I receive you,' he said. 'Quite an electrical display, but no damage – so far.'

'Thanks – thought we'd lost you. Please check telemetry channels three, seven, twenty-six. Also gain on camera two. And we don't quite believe the readings on the external ionization probes . . .'

Reluctantly Falcon tore his gaze away from the fascinating pyrotechnic display around *Kon-Tiki*, though from time to time he kept glancing out of the windows. The ball lightning disappeared first, the fiery globes slowly expanding until they reached a critical size, at which they vanished in a gentle explosion. But even an hour later, there were still faint glows around all the exposed metal on the outside of the capsule; and the radio circuits remained noisy until well after midnight.

The remaining hours of darkness were completely uneventful – until just before dawn. Because it came from the east, Falcon assumed that he was seeing the first faint hint of sunrise. Then he realized that it was twenty minutes too early for this – and the glow that had appeared along the horizon was moving toward him even as he watched. It swiftly detached itself from the arch of stars that marked the invisible edge of the planet, and he saw that it was a relatively narrow band, quite sharply defined. The beam of an enormous searchlight appeared to be swinging beneath the clouds.

Perhaps sixty miles behind the first racing bar of light came another, parallel to it and moving at the same speed. And beyond that another, and another – until all the sky flickered with alternating sheets of light and darkness.

By this time, Falcon thought, he had been inured to wonders, and it seemed impossible that this display of pure, soundless luminosity could present the slightest danger. But it was so astonishing, and so inexplicable, that he felt cold, naked fear gnawing at his self-control. No man could look upon such a sight without feeling like a helpless pygmy in the presence of forces beyond his comprehension. Was it possible that, after all, Jupiter carried not only life but also intelligence? And, perhaps, an intelligence that only now was beginning to react to his alien presence?

'Yes, we see it,' said Mission Control, in a voice that echoed his own awe. 'We've no idea what it is. Stand by, we're calling Ganymede.'

The display was slowly fading; the bands racing in from the far horizon were much fainter, as if the energies that powered them were becoming exhausted. In five minutes it was all over; the last faint pulse of light flickered along the western sky and then was gone. Its passing left Falcon with an overwhelming sense of relief. The sight was so hypnotic, and so disturbing, that it was not good for any man's peace of mind to contemplate it too long.

He was more shaken than he cared to admit. The electrical storm was something that he could understand; but *this* was totally incomprehensible.

Mission Control was still silent. He knew that the information banks up on Ganymede were now being searched as men and computers turned their minds to the problem. If no answer could be found there, it would be necessary to call Earth; that would mean a delay of almost an hour. The possibility that even Earth might be unable to help was one that Falcon did not care to contemplate.

He had never before been so glad to hear the voice of Mission Control as when Dr Brenner finally came on the circuit. The biologist sounded relieved, yet subdued – like a man who has just come through some great intellectual crisis.

'Hello, *Kon-Tiki*. We've solved your problem, but we can still hardly believe it.

'What you've been seeing is bioluminescence, very similar to that produced by microorganisms in the tropical seas of Earth. Here they're in the atmosphere, not the ocean, but the principle is the same.'

'But the pattern,' protested Falcon, 'was so regular – so *artificial*. And it was hundreds of miles across!'

'It was even larger than you imagine; you observed only a small part of it. The whole pattern was over three thousand miles wide and looked like a revolving wheel. You merely saw the spokes, sweeping past you at about six-tenths of a mile a second . . .'

'A *second!*' Falcon could not help interjecting. 'No animals could move that fast!'

'Of course not. Let me explain. What you saw was triggered by the shock wave from Source Beta, moving at the speed of sound.'

'But what about the pattern?' Falcon insisted.

'That's the surprising part. It's a very rare phenomenon, but identical wheels of light – except that they're a thousand times smaller – have been observed in the Persian Gulf and the Indian Ocean. Listen to this: British India Company's *Patna*, Persian Gulf, May 1880, 11:30 P.M. – "an enormous luminous wheel, whirling round, the spokes of which appeared to brush the ship along. The spokes were 200 or 300 yards long . . . each wheel contained about sixteen spokes . . ." And here's one from the Gulf of Omar, dated May 23, 1906: "The intensely bright luminescence approached us rapidly, shooting sharply defined light rays to the west in rapid succession, like the beam from the searchlight of a warship . . . To the left of us, a gigantic fiery wheel formed itself, with spokes that reached as far as one could see. The whole wheel whirled around for two or three minutes . . ." The archive computer on Ganymede dug up about five hundred cases. It would have printed out the lot if we hadn't stopped it in time.'

'I'm convinced – but still baffled.'

'I don't blame you. The full explanation wasn't worked

out until late in the twentieth century. It seems that these luminous wheels are the results of submarine earthquakes, and always occur in shallow waters where the shock waves can be reflected and cause standing wave patterns. Sometimes bars, sometimes rotating wheels – the "Wheels of Poseidon," they've been called. The theory was finally proved by making underwater explosions and photographing the results from a satellite. No wonder sailors used to be superstitious. Who would have believed a thing like *this?*'

So that was it, Falcon told himself. When Source Beta blew its top, it must have sent shock waves in all directions – through the compressed gas of the lower atmosphere, through the solid body of Jupiter itself. Meeting and crisscrossing, those waves must have canceled here, reinforced there; the whole planet must have rung like a bell.

Yet the explanation did not destroy the sense of wonder and awe; he would never be able to forget those flickering bands of light, racing through the unattainable depths of the Jovian atmosphere. He felt that he was not merely on a strange planet, but in some magical realm between myth and reality.

This was a world where absolutely anything could happen, and no man could possibly guess what the future would bring.

And he still had a whole day to go.

6. Medusa

When the true dawn finally arrived, it brought a sudden change of weather. *Kon-Tiki* was moving through a blizzard; waxen snowflakes were falling so thickly that visibility was reduced to zero. Falcon began to worry about the weight that might be accumulating on the envelope. Then he noticed that any flakes settling outside the windows quickly disappeared; *Kon-Tiki*'s continual outpouring of heat was evaporating them as swiftly as they arrived.

If he had been ballooning on Earth, he would also have worried about the possibility of collision. At least that was no danger here; any Jovian mountains were several hundred miles below him. And as for the floating islands of foam, hitting them would probably be like plowing into slightly hardened soap bubbles.

Nevertheless, he switched on the horizontal radar, which until now had been completely useless; only the vertical beam, giving his distance from the invisible surface, had thus far been of any value. Then he had another surprise.

Scattered across a huge sector of the sky ahead were dozens of large and brilliant echoes. They were completely isolated from one another and apparently hung unsupported in space. Falcon remembered a phrase the earliest aviators had used to describe one of the hazards of their profession: 'clouds stuffed with rocks.' That was a perfect description of what seemed to lie in the track of *Kon-Tiki*.

It was a disconcerting sight; then Falcon again reminded himself that nothing *really* solid could possibly hover in this atmosphere. Perhaps it was some strange meteorological phenomenon. In any case, the nearest echo was about a hundred and twenty-five miles.

He reported to Mission Control, which could provide no explanation. But it gave the welcome news that he would be clear of the blizzard in another thirty minutes.

It did not warn him, however, of the violent cross wind that abruptly grabbed *Kon-Tiki* and swept it almost at right angles to its previous track. Falcon needed all his skill and the maximum use of what little control he had over his ungainly vehicle to prevent it from being capsized. Within minutes he was racing northward at over three hundred miles an hour. Then, as suddenly as it had started, the turbulence ceased; he was still moving at high speed, but in smooth air. He wondered if he had been caught in the Jovian equivalent of a jet stream.

The snow storm dissolved; and he saw what Jupiter had been preparing for him.

Kon-Tiki had entered the funnel of a gigantic whirlpool, some six hundred miles across. The balloon was being swept along a curving wall of cloud. Overhead, the sun was shining in a clear sky; but far beneath, this great hole in the atmosphere drilled down to unknown depths until it reached a misty floor where lightning flickered almost continuously.

Though the vessel was being dragged downward so slowly that it was in no immediate danger, Falcon increased the flow of heat into the envelope until *Kon-Tiki* hovered at a constant altitude. Not until then did he abandon the fantastic spectacle outside and consider again the problem of the radar.

The nearest echo was now only about twenty-five miles away. All of them, he quickly realized, were distributed along the wall of the vortex, and were moving with it, apparently caught in the whirlpool like *Kon-Tiki* itself. He aimed the telescope along the radar bearing and found himself looking at a curious mottled cloud that almost filled the field of view.

It was not easy to see, being only a little darker than the whirling wall of mist that formed its background. Not until he had been staring for several minutes did Falcon realize that he had met it once before.

The first time it had been crawling across the drifting mountains of foam, and he had mistaken it for a giant, many-trunked tree. Now at last he could appreciate its real size and complexity and could give it a better name to fix its image in his mind. It did not resemble a tree at all, but a jellyfish – a medusa, such as might be met trailing its tentacles as it drifted along the warm eddies of the Gulf Stream.

This medusa was more than a mile across and its scores of dangling tentacles were hundreds of feet long. They swayed slowly back and forth in perfect unison, taking more than a minute for each complete undulation – almost as if the creature was clumsily rowing itself through the sky.

The other echoes were more distant medusae. Falcon focused the telescope on half a dozen and could see no variations in shape or size. They all seemed to be of the same species, and he wondered just why they were drifting lazily around in this six-hundred-mile orbit. Perhaps they were feeding upon the aerial plankton sucked in by the whirlpool, as *Kon-Tiki* itself had been.

'Do you realize, Howard,' said Dr Brenner, when he had recovered from his initial astonishment, 'that this thing is about a hundred thousand times as large as the biggest whale? And even if it's only a gasbag, it must still weigh a million tons! I can't even guess at its metabolism.

297

It must generate megawatts of heat to maintain its buoyancy.'

'But if it's just a gasbag, why is it such a damn good radar reflector?'

'I haven't the faintest idea. Can you get any closer?'

Brenner's question was not an idle one. If he changed altitude to take advantage of the differing wind velocities, Falcon could approach the medusa as closely as he wished. At the moment, however, he preferred his present twenty-five miles and said so, firmly.

'I see what you mean,' Brenner answered, a little reluctantly. 'Let's stay where we are for the present.' That 'we' gave Falcon a certain wry amusement; an extra sixty thousand miles made a considerable difference in one's point of view.

For the next two hours *Kon-Tiki* drifted uneventfully in the gyre of the great whirlpool, while Falcon experimented with filters and camera contrast, trying to get a clear view of the medusa. He began to wonder if its elusive coloration was some kind of camouflage; perhaps, like many animals of Earth, it was trying to lose itself against its background. That was a trick used by both hunters and hunted.

In which category was the medusa? That was a question he could hardly expect to have answered in the short time that was left to him. Yet just before noon, without the slightest warning, the answer came . . .

Like a squadron of antique jet fighters, five mantas came sweeping through the wall of mist that formed the funnel of the vortex. They were flying in a V formation directly toward the pallid gray cloud of the medusa; and there was no doubt, in Falcon's mind, that they were on the attack. He had been quite wrong to assume that they were harmless vegetarians.

Yet everything happened at such a leisurely pace that it

was like watching a slow-motion film. The mantas undulated along at perhaps thirty miles an hour; it seemed ages before they reached the medusa, which continued to paddle imperturbably along at an even slower speed. Huge though they were, the mantas looked tiny beside the monster they were approaching. When they flapped down on its back, they appeared about as large as birds landing on a whale.

Could the medusa defend itself? Falcon wondered. He did not see how the attacking mantas could be in danger as long as they avoided those huge clumsy tentacles. And perhaps their host was not even aware of them; they could be insignificant parasites, tolerated as are fleas upon a dog.

But now it was obvious that the medusa was in distress. With agonizing slowness, it began to tip over like a capsizing ship. After ten minutes it had tilted forty-five degrees; it was also rapidly losing altitude. It was impossible not to feel a sense of pity for the beleaguered monster, and to Falcon the sight brought bitter memories. In a grotesque way, the fall of the medusa was almost a parody of the dying *Queen*'s last moments.

Yet he knew that his sympathies were on the wrong side. High intelligence could develop only among predators – not among the drifting browsers of either sea or air. The mantas were far closer to him than was this monstrous bag of gas. And anyway, who could *really* sympathize with a creature a hundred thousand times larger than a whale?

Then he noticed that the medusa's tactics seemed to be having some effect. The mantas had been disturbed by its slow roll and were flapping heavily away from its back – like gorging vultures interrupted at mealtime. But they did not move very far, continuing to hover a few yards from the still-capsizing monster.

There was a sudden, blinding flash of light synchronized with a crash of static over the radio. One of the mantas, slowly twisting end over end, was plummeting straight downward. As it fell, a plume of black smoke trailed behind it. The resemblance to an aircraft going down in flames was quite uncanny.

In unison, the remaining mantas dived steeply away from the medusa, gaining speed by losing altitude. They had, within minutes, vanished back into the wall of cloud from which they had emerged. And the medusa, no longer falling, began to roll back toward the horizontal. Soon it was sailing along once more on an even keel, as if nothing had happened.

'Beautiful!' said Dr Brenner, after a moment of stunned silence. 'It's developed electric defenses, like some of our eels and rays. But that must have been about a million volts! Can you see any organs that might produce the discharge? Anything looking like electrodes?'

'No,' Falcon answered, after switching to the highest power of the telescope. 'But here's something odd. Do you see this pattern? Check back on the earlier images. I'm sure it wasn't there before.'

A broad, mottled band had appeared along the side of the medusa. It formed a startlingly regular checkerboard, each square of which was itself speckled in a complex subpattern of short horizontal lines. They were spaced at equal distances in a geometrically perfect array of rows and columns.

'You're right,' said Dr Brenner, with something very much like awe in his voice. 'That's just appeared. And I'm afraid to tell you what I think it is.'

'Well, I have no reputation to lose – at least as a biologist. Shall I give my guess?'

'Go ahead.'

'That's a large meter-band radio array. The sort of thing they used back at the beginning of the twentieth century.'

'I was afraid you'd say that. Now we know why it gave such a massive echo.'

'But why has it just appeared?'

'Probably an aftereffect of the discharge.'

'I've just had another thought,' said Falcon, rather slowly. 'Do you suppose it's *listening* to us?'

'On this frequency? I doubt it. Those are meter – no, *decameter* antennas – judging by their size. Hmm . . . that's an idea!'

Dr Brenner fell silent, obviously contemplating some new line of thought. Presently he continued: 'I bet they're tuned to the radio outbursts! That's something nature never got around to do on Earth . . . We have animals with sonar and even electric senses, but nothing ever developed a radio sense. Why bother where there was so much light?

'But it's different here. Jupiter is *drenched* with radio energy. It's worth while using it – maybe even tapping it. That thing could be a floating power plant!'

A new voice cut into the conversation.

'Mission Commander here. This is all very interesting, but there's a much more important matter to settle. *Is it intelligent?* If so, we've got to consider the First Contact directives.'

'Until I came here,' said Dr Brenner, somewhat rue-fully, 'I would have sworn that anything that could make a shortwave antenna system *must* be intelligent. Now, I'm not sure. This could have evolved naturally. I suppose it's no more fantastic than the human eye.'

'Then we have to play safe and assume intelligence. For the present, therefore, this expedition comes under all the clauses of the Prime directive.'

There was a long silence while everyone on the radio circuit absorbed the implications of this. For the first time in the history of space flight, the rules that had been established through more than a century of argument might have to be applied. Man had – it was hoped – profited from his mistakes on Earth. Not only moral considerations, but also his own self-interest demanded that he should not repeat them among the planets. It could be disastrous to treat a superior intelligence as the American settlers had treated the Indians, or as almost everyone had treated the Africans . . .

The first rule was: keep your distance. Make no attempt to approach, or even to communicate, until 'they' have had plenty of time to study you. Exactly what was meant by 'plenty of time,' no one had ever been able to decide. It was left to the discretion of the man on the spot.

A responsibility of which he had never dreamed had descended upon Howard Falcon. In the few hours that remained to him on Jupiter, he might become the first ambassador of the human race.

And *that* was an irony so delicious that he almost wished the surgeons had restored to him the power of laughter.

7. Prime directive

It was growing darker, but Falcon scarcely noticed as he strained his eyes toward that living cloud in the field of the telescope. The wind that was steadily sweeping *Kon-Tiki* around the funnel of the great whirlpool had now brought him within twelve miles of the creature. If he got much closer than six, he would take evasive action. Though he felt certain that the medusa's electric weapons were short-ranged, he did not wish to put the matter to the test. That would be a problem for future explorers, and he wished them luck.

Now it was quite dark in the capsule. That was strange, because sunset was still hours away. Automatically, he glanced at the horizontally scanning radar, as he had done every few minutes. Apart from the medusa he was studying, there was no other object within about sixty miles of him.

Suddenly, with startling power, he heard the sound that had come booming out of the Jovian night – the throbbing beat that grew more and more rapid, then stopped in mid-crescendo. The whole capsule vibrated with it like a pea in a kettledrum.

Falcon realized two things almost simultaneously during the sudden, aching silence. *This* time the sound was not coming from thousands of miles away, over a radio circuit. It was in the very atmosphere around him.

The second thought was even more disturbing. He had quite forgotten – it was inexcusable, but there had been other apparently more important things on his mind – that most of the sky above him was completely blanked out by *Kon-Tiki*'s gasbag. Being lightly silvered to conserve its heat, the great balloon was an effective shield both to radar and to vision.

He had known this, of course; it had been a minor defect of the design, tolerated because it did not appear important. It seemed very important to Howard Falcon now – as he saw that fence of gigantic tentacles, thicker than the trunks of any tree, descending all around the capsule.

He heard Brenner yelling: 'Remember the Prime directive! Don't alarm it!' Before he could make an appropriate answer that overwhelming drumbeat started again and drowned all other sounds.

The sign of a really skilled test pilot is how he reacts not to foreseeable emergencies, but to ones that nobody could have anticipated. Falcon did not hesitate for more than a second to analyze the situation. In a lightning-swift movement, he pulled the rip cord.

That word was an archaic survival from the days of the first hydrogen balloons; on *Kon-Tiki*, the rip cord did not tear open the gasbag, but merely operated a set of louvers around the upper curve of the envelope. At once the hot gas started to rush out; *Kon-Tiki*, deprived of her lift, began to fall swiftly in this gravity field two and a half times as strong as Earth's.

Falcon had a momentary glimpse of great tentacles whipping upward and away. He had just time to note that they were studded with large bladders or sacs, presumably to give them buoyancy, and that they ended in multitudes of thin feelers like the roots of a plant. He half expected a bolt of lightning – but nothing happened.

His precipitous rate of descent was slackening as the atmosphere thickened and the deflated envelope acted as a parachute. When *Kon-Tiki* had dropped about two miles, he felt that it was safe to close the louvers again. By the time he had restored buoyancy and was in equilibrium once more, he had lost another mile of altitude and was getting dangerously near his safety limit.

He peered anxiously through the overhead windows, though he did not expect to see anything except the obscuring bulk of the balloon. But he had sideslipped during his descent, and part of the medusa was just visible a couple of miles above him. It was much closer than he expected – and it was still coming down, faster than he would have believed possible.

Mission Control was calling anxiously. He shouted: 'I'm OK – but it's still coming after me. I can't go any deeper.'

That was not quite true. He could go a lot deeper – about one hundred and eighty miles. But it would be a one-way trip, and most of the journey would be of little interest to him.

Then, to his great relief, he saw that the medusa was leveling off, not quite a mile above him. Perhaps it had decided to approach this strange intruder with caution; or perhaps it, too, found this deeper layer uncomfortably hot. The temperature was over fifty degrees centigrade, and Falcon wondered how much longer his life-support system could handle matters.

Dr Brenner was back on the circuit, still worrying about the Prime directive.

'Remember – it may only be inquisitive!' he cried, without much conviction. 'Try not to frighten it!'

Falcon was getting rather tired of this advice and recalled a TV discussion he had once seen between a space lawyer and an astronaut. After the full implications of the Prime directive had been carefully spelled out, the incredulous spacer had exclaimed: 'Then if there was no alternative, I must sit still and let myself be eaten?' The lawyer had not even cracked a smile when he answered: 'That's an *excellent* summing up.'

It had seemed funny at the time; it was not at all amusing now.

And then Falcon saw something that made him even more unhappy. The medusa was still hovering about a mile above him – but one of its tentacles was becoming incredibly elongated, and was stretching down toward *Kon-Tiki*, thinning out at the same time. As a boy he had once seen the funnel of a tornado descending from a storm cloud over the Kansas plains. The thing coming toward him now evoked vivid memories of that black, twisting snake in the sky.

'I'm rapidly running out of options,' he reported to Mission Control. 'I now have only a choice between frightening it – and giving it a bad stomach-ache. I don't think it will find *Kon-Tiki* very digestible, if that's what it has in mind.'

He waited for comments from Brenner, but the biologist remained silent.

'Very well. It's twenty-seven minutes ahead of time, but I'm starting the ignition sequencer. I hope I'll have enough reserve to correct my orbit later.'

He could no longer see the medusa; once more it was directly overhead. But he knew that the descending tentacle must now be very close to the balloon. It would take almost five minutes to bring the reactor up to full thrust . . .

The fuser was primed. The orbit computer had not rejected the situation as wholly impossible. The air scoops were open, ready to gulp in tons of the surrounding hydrohelium on demand. Even under optimum conditions, this would have been the moment of truth – for there had been no way of testing how a nuclear ramjet would *really* work in the strange atmosphere of Jupiter.

Very gently something rocked *Kon-Tiki*. Falcon tried to ignore it.

Ignition had been planned at six miles higher, in an atmosphere of less than a quarter of the density and thirty degrees cooler. Too bad.

What was the shallowest dive he could get away with, for the air scoops to work? When the ram ignited, he'd be heading toward Jupiter with two and a half g's to help him get there. Could he possibly pull out in time?

A large, heavy hand patted the balloon. The whole

306

vessel bobbed up and down, like one of the Yo-yos that had just become the craze on Earth.

Of course, Brenner *might* be perfectly right. Perhaps it was just trying to be friendly. Maybe he should try to talk to it over the radio. Which should it be: 'Pretty pussy'? 'Down, Fido'? Or 'Take me to your leader'?

The tritium-deuterium ratio was correct. He was ready to light the candle, with a hundred-million-degree match.

The thin tip of the tentacle came slithering around the edge of the balloon some sixty yards away. It was about the size of an elephant's trunk, and by the delicate way it was moving appeared to be almost as sensitive. There were little palps at its end, like questing mouths. He was sure that Dr Brenner would be fascinated.

This seemed about as good a time as any. He gave a swift scan of the entire control board, started the final four-second ignition count, broke the safety seal, and pressed the JETTISON switch.

There was a sharp explosion and an instant loss of weight. *Kon-Tiki* was falling freely, nose down. Overhead, the discarded balloon was racing upward, dragging the inquisitive tentacle with it. Falcon had no time to see if the gasbag actually hit the medusa, because at that moment the ramjet fired and he had other matters to think about.

A roaring column of hot hydrohelium was pouring out of the reactor nozzles, swiftly building up thrust – but *toward* Jupiter, not away from it. He could not pull out yet, for vector control was too sluggish. Unless he could gain complete control and achieve horizontal flight within the next five seconds, the vehicle would dive too deeply into the atmosphere and would be destroyed.

With agonizing slowness – those five seconds seemed like fifty – he managed to flatten out, then pull the nose upward. He glanced back only once and caught a final glimpse of the medusa, many miles away. *Kon-Tiki*'s discarded gasbag had apparently escaped from its grasp, for he could see no sign of it.

Now he was master once more – no longer drifting helplessly on the winds of Jupiter, but riding his own column of atomic fire back to the stars. He was confident that the ramjet would steadily give him velocity and altitude until he had reached near-orbital speed at the fringes of the atmosphere. Then, with a brief burst of pure rocket power, he would regain the freedom of space.

Halfway to orbit, he looked south and saw the tremendous enigma of the Great Red Spot – that floating island twice the size of Earth – coming up over the horizon. He stared into its mysterious beauty until the computer warned him that conversion to rocket thrust was only sixty seconds ahead. He tore his gaze reluctantly away.

'Some other time,' he murmured.

'What's that?' said Mission Control. 'What did you say?'

'It doesn't matter,' he replied.

8. Between two worlds

'You're a hero now, Howard,' said Webster, not just a celebrity. You've given them something to think about – injected some excitement into their lives. Not one in a million will actually travel to the Outer Giants, but the whole human race will go in imagination. And that's what counts.'

'I'm glad to have made your job a little easier.'

Webster was too old a friend to take offense at the note of irony. Yet it surprised him. And this was not the first change in Howard that he had noticed since the return from Jupiter.

The Administrator pointed to the famous sign on his desk, borrowed from an impresario of an earlier age: ASTONISH ME!

'I'm not ashamed of my job. New knowledge, new resources – they're all very well. But men also need novelty and excitement. Space travel has become routine; you've made it a great adventure once more. It will be a long, long time before we get Jupiter pigeonholed. And maybe longer still before we understand those medusae. I still think that one *knew* where your blind spot was. Anyway, have you decided on your next move? Saturn, Uranus, Neptune – you name it.'

'I don't know. I've thought about Saturn, but I'm not really needed there. It's only one gravity, not two and a half like Jupiter. So men can handle it.'

Men, thought Webster. He said 'men.' He's never done that before. And when did I last hear him use the word 'we'? He's changing, slipping away from us . . .

'Well,' he said aloud, rising from his chair to conceal his slight uneasiness, 'let's get the conference started. The cameras are all set up and everyone's waiting. You'll meet a lot of old friends.'

He stressed the last word, but Howard showed no response. The leather mask of his face was becoming more and more difficult to read. Instead, he rolled back from the Administrator's desk, unlocked his undercarriage so that it no longer formed a chair, and rose on his hydraulics to his full seven feet of height. It had been good psychology on the part of the surgeons to give him that extra twelve inches, to compensate somewhat for all that he had lost when the *Queen* had crashed.

Falcon waited until Webster had opened the door, then

pivoted neatly on his balloon tires and headed for it at a smooth and silent twenty miles an hour. The display of speed and precision was not flaunted arrogantly; rather, it had become quite unconscious.

Howard Falcon, who had once been a man and could still pass for one over a voice circuit, felt a calm sense of achievement – and, for the first time in years, something like peace of mind. Since his return from Jupiter, the nightmares had ceased. He had found his role at last.

He now knew why he had dreamed about that super-chimp aboard the doomed *Queen Elizabeth*. Neither man nor beast, it was between two worlds; and so was he.

He alone could travel unprotected on the lunar surface. The life-support system inside the metal cylinder that had replaced his fragile body functioned equally well in space or under water. Gravity fields ten times that of Earth were an inconvenience, but nothing more. And no gravity was best of all . . .

The human race was becoming more remote, the ties of kinship more tenuous. Perhaps these air-breathing, radiation-sensitive bundles of unstable carbon compounds had no right beyond the atmosphere; they should stick to their natural homes – Earth, Moon, Mars.

Some day the real masters of space would be machines, not men – and he was neither. Already conscious of his destiny, he took a somber pride in his unique loneliness – the first immortal midway between two orders of creation.

He would, after all, be an ambassador; between the old and the new – between the creatures of carbon and the creatures of metal who must one day supersede them.

Both would have need of him in the troubled centuries that lay ahead.

The Songs of Distant Earth

This is a little complicated, so we had better start at the beginning . . .

And that, incredibly, is in February 1957, half a year before Sputnik I heralded the dawn of the Space Age. I would have sworn it was a decade later, but the evidence in my notebooks is indisputable.

For some reason, at the beginning of that momentous year a phrase lodged in my mind and wouldn't go away; it echoed round and round my skull as persistently as the theme from the last movement of Sibelius' 2nd Symphony. It was obviously the title of a story, which I eventually had to write: you'll find it in The Other Side of the Sky.

Call that Mark I. What follows here is Mark II. The exorcism was incomplete, for in 1979, a mere twenty-two years later, the title started bugging me again.

And that was not the only thing bugging me. I had just seen two spectacular and highly successful space movies – Star Wars, Close Encounters of the Third Kind *– and* Star Trek *was still doing reruns all over the planet. They were well done and I greatly enjoyed them, but they all had one thing in common. They were not, in the strictest sense, science fiction, but* fantasy.

Now, I like fantasy every bit as much as science-fiction – its literary standards are usually higher, too – but I recognize the distinction between the genres. Critics have been trying for decades to define both categories, without much success. Here is my working definition: Fantasy is something that couldn't happen in the real world (though often you wish it would); Science Fiction is something that really could happen (though often you'd be sorry if it did).

Today, we are 99.99 percent certain that it will always be impossible to travel faster than light, which means that journeys to even the nearest star systems will take decades. This is no problem to the fantasy writer, who can happily cling to the 0.01 percent chance that there may be a loophole that Einstein didn't notice – and go racing round the galaxy, saving civilization once a week in prime time.

In September 1979, during one of my brief visits to England, I decided to accept the Universe as it really is. (As Dr Johnson once said: 'You'd better . . .') Was it possible, I asked myself, to write a completely realistic story using an interstellar – as opposed to a 'merely' interplanetary – background?

I also decided to kill two birds with one typewriter. Ever since 2001, Stanley Kubrick had been saying wistfully, 'What sort of movie should we have made?', or words to that effect. So I decided to write Mk II in the form of a movie outline.

This would have two advantages. The first, and most important, was the saving of time and energy. An outline compresses, in a few pages, all the basic elements of a complete novel – locale, characters, plot. Though the act of creation may take months, the actual typing can be done in a couple of hours; you can have all the fun and none of the drudgery. (Of course, you sacrifice emotion, atmosphere, 'fine writing.' But they can be added later, and perhaps on a firmer foundation.)

The second advantage was that it would keep Stanley quiet, at least for a while. In the event, he returned the outline with an unenthusiastic 'Interesting . . .' – which was exactly what I'd expected. (If he'd said, 'OK – when can we get started?', I would have been in a real dilemma. I *owe Stanley so much that I would have felt morally obliged to cooperate – even if it killed me. Which it probably would . . .)*

Breathing a sigh of relief, I sent Mk II off to my agent, who promptly sold it to Omni *Magazine. (Vol. III, No. 12). As soon as it appeared, wouldn't you know, a leading movie producer wanted to buy it – but only if I wrote the screenplay. This is a complicated, highly skilled yet essentially noncreative job I wouldn't touch with a bargepole, so the deal was off. (I am prepared to spend two or even three days – depending on the weather – going through other people's screenplays of my own novels. But that would be the maximum extent of my involvement.)*

So here is the final version of 'The Songs of Distant Earth' – which, incidentally, contains elements from another story, 'The Shining Ones' (published in the collection The Wind From the Sun). I still think it would make a damn good movie, even though it doesn't contain a single space-warp or black hole.

Perhaps more important is the fact that 'S.D.E.' acted as a stepping stone to something much bigger. It got me interested in writing again, and also focussed my attention on the fact that there was another unaccepted challenge still lying around. For years I'd said it would be impossible to write a sequel to 2001. But just suppose . . .

So in March 1980 I started to write an outline for 'Space Odyssey Two.' It wouldn't be too much work – just a few typed pages.

Nine, actually. But one thing led to another . . .

The locale is Oceana ('Shaana'), an Earth-type planet 50 light-years, and 500 years of voyage time, from the solar system, colonized 2,000 years earlier in the first wave of interstellar exploration. There is very little land; continents still lie 100 million years in the future, and there is still much tectonic activity. The largest island is about the size of Hawaii, and very similar to Hawaii in climate and culture.

Over the centuries the islanders – attractive, slightly feckless – have developed a stable, conservative society, largely based on intermediate technology. They still have access to all man's accumulated knowledge, but they have added little to it. Their boats, aircraft, and cars are built to last a lifetime, and they never throw anything away they can use again. Since there is no other habitable planet in the system, they have no spaceships, but they can still launch the (rather primitive) satellites essential for their scattered islands' communications and meteorological services.

Though they have had no physical contact with outsiders for centuries, they still inject their records and news, such as it is, into the local stellar network. The current update is long overdue, partly because of a mounting power crisis.

The Shaanans get most of their electrical power from OTEC (Ocean Thermal Energy Conversion), which employs the temperature difference between the warm surface water and the very cold water several kilometers down. (The first Earth-based OTEC factory began operating in Hawaii in 1979.) For some unknown reason, several of the factories have failed, apparently owing to damage at the deep end. Typically the Shaanans don't have the submersibles needed to investigate at such depths; they are still arguing about what to do next.

Our protagonists on Shaana are a young couple, Loren (a marine engineer; marine engineering on Shaana is one of the most important professions) and Marissa. Their placid lives are disrupted by the arrival of the first ship from Earth in many centuries – and the last one that will ever be.

Five hundred years earlier the sun went nova. There was just sufficient warning to seek out the population and evacuate the survivors in hyperships, each carrying one million sleepers, along with records of all mankind's treasures and knowledge, as well as gene banks of the main plants and animals.

Argo barely escaped in time. She left before preparations for the centuries-long journey were quite complete. She carries spectacular views of the destruction of the solar system, recorded by cameras on Earth and some other planets: Jupiter boiling, Saturn's rings collapsing, the sun finally devouring its children, but, most poignant of all, unbearably moving scenes of the last moments of beloved earthscapes and artifacts (*e.g.*, the Taj Mahal, St Peter's, the Pyramids, etc., melting down).

Because there is appreciable erosion from interstellar dust at one tenth the speed of light, *Argo* travels behind a huge ablation shield, formed of ice. This is now too thin for the voyage to continue; hence the stop at Oceana to build a new shield. About 100 of the ship's engineers have been revived for this task, among them Falcon.

During the decades of deceleration *Argo* has been

studying the Shaanans' radio transmissions and has a very good idea of the local culture. But so far there has been no attempt at contact, because of the long-established policy of noninterference. There is much debate aboard *Argo* about this, especially now that it is in orbit and the beauty of the planet below is clearly visible. Falcon spends hours scanning the islands through the ship's telescopes, vividly reminded of the world he has lost forever.

Contact is finally made, with the inevitable enthusiasms and frictions. The voyagers have power, knowledge, determination, but they are slowly seduced by the beauty of Oceana – such a contrast to *Argo*'s sterile corridors – and become appalled by the lonely centuries of travel that still lie ahead. The Shaanans are happy and perfectly adjusted (though getting worried about the power situation). Yet they become envious of *Argo*'s wonders and a little guilty about their past indolence.

Also, despite taking elaborate precautions, each group infects the other with nasty head colds.

It is agreed that *Argo* can siphon (by means of a space elevator at the equator) several million tons of water to build a new shield. It is frozen in the shadow of a giant sunshade; then it is assembled by robots in a slow-motion ice ballet, lit by the cold light of Oceana's three moons.

Meanwhile Falcon meets Loren and Marissa and falls in love with them both. Despite their cultural differences the two societies are equally civilized and sexual jealousy is (almost) extinct. But, ironically, another problem arises: Falcon is deeply attracted to Oceana, while Loren and Marissa feel the lure of the great, unknown universe beyond.

During the weeks of shield building, there is a catastrophic power failure in another OTEC grid. The Shaanans appeal to *Argo*. After some debate (they don't want to make the islanders even less self-reliant) the voyagers re-create a deep-diving submersible from the ship's information banks. Falcon plugs in temporarily to the recorded skills and personality of a long-dead deep-sea explorer and he dives with Loren. They discover that the installation had been damaged deliberately.

Diving deeper, they encounter the Shining Ones, giant squidlike creatures, which communicate in the total darkness of the abyss by beautiful displays of multicolored luminescence. They can even produce pictures the way giant TV screens do.

Falcon and Loren are also astonished to see that the squids are using tools fashioned from whalebone. They are on the verge of developing technology, and the OTEC conductors are their source of metal.

Falcon and Loren escape with difficulty. The Shaanans want to destroy the squids, but this horrifies the voyagers, who have already seen too much death.

With the help of special equipment and the ship's computers, they reach a limited understanding with the squids, which are bought off with a gift of metal. But one day the Shaanans may be faced with a more serious threat from these beautiful and magnificent beasts: the future of the planet will belong to the more energetic race. In this coming conflict *Argo* cannot, and should not, interfere. The threat from the deep may be exactly what is needed to revitalize the Shaanans.

Argo's shield is complete; the ship is ready to depart.

To help the Shaanans understand, Falcon takes Marissa (now bearing his child) and Loren up to orbit.

They enter the hibernaculum. At its portal stands one of the greatest works of art ever produced by mankind, the golden mask of the young Pharaoh Tutankhamun, one of the last treasures saved from Earth. Now it guards the sleeping as once it guarded the dead.

They pass thousands of men and women in their crystal cells until they find Falcon's wife, who is in the last stages of pregnancy. Falcon explains that they had intended the child to be born on Earth but time ran out. Soon he will join them both in their long sleep and will awaken in time to greet them when *Argo* reaches its goal 500 years later.

On the beach where they first met, beneath the light of the three moons, Marissa and Loren await the moment of departure. Thousands of kilometers overhead the plasma drive ignites brighter than 100 suns, as *Argo* draws away from Oceana and heads out to the stars.

Loren comforts Marissa and reminds her of the child they will cherish all their lives. Yet always there will be the phantom image of another child conceived 500 years before, to be born 500 years hence.

A child whose father will remember them when he awakens, centuries after they have turned to dust.

The Sentinel

Arthur C. Clarke was born in Somerset in 1917. He is a graduate of King's College, London (where he obtained a First Class Honours in Physics and Mathematics), a past Chairman of the British Interplanetary Society, and a member of the Academy of Astronautics, the Royal Astronomical Society, and many other scientific organizations. He served in the RAF during the Second World War and was in charge of the first radar talk-down equipment during its experimental trials. He wrote a monograph for *Wireless World* in 1945 predicting satellite communications, and did it so well that when the first commercial satellites were launched twenty years later they could not be patented.

He has written over sixty books, among them the science fiction classics *Childhood's End*, *The City and the Stars* and *Rendezvous with Rama* (which was unique in winning all three major science fiction trophies, the Hugo, Nebula and John W. Campbell Memorial Awards. In 1968 he shared an Oscar nomination with Stanley Kubrick for *2001 A Space Odyssey*. He became widely known for his non-fiction work with the television series *Arthur C. Clarke's Mysterious World*.

Arthur C. Clarke has for many years made his home in Sri Lanka. He is chancellor of a university there and founder of the Arthur C. Clarke Centre for Advanced Technology. He was awarded the CBE in 1989 and knighted in 1998.